"Introduce

The woman shot upright, the flowers in her hand flying every which way and the shears pointing dangerously near to Charles's chin. He gently lowered them but retained a hold on her wrist as she turned abruptly to face him.

"Good morning," he said, studying her features rather more intently than might be considered polite.

"Good heavens above! You startled me."

"Rutherford?" asked Charles, still staring down at her. Somehow he'd been caught in the magic of her eyes and could not look away.

"Miss Seldon, this reprobate is known to the world as Charles North. You will, of course, ignore his existence. Charles, do let the poor girl loose!"

Charles lifted the hand he held to his lips and then managed to release her. Speaking softly, he said, "Miss Seldon. It is a delight to meet you."

He was surprised to discover it was not merely a polite statement. He was delighted. The graceful woman he'd watched with the dogs was taller than he'd expected and he was pleased to note she did not attempt to make herself smaller by any of the idiotic tricks tall women used in an era when the tiny fairylike woman was the ideal. Too, there were wonderful reddish tints glinting in her overlong mahogany-colored hair, but her best feature was those eyes with their well-defined brows and dark lashes protecting deep blue orbs.

Charles, much against his will, was instantly aware of an attraction he should not be feeling. . . .

Books by Jeanne Savery

Published by Zebra Books

MISS SELDON'S SUITORS

Jeanne Savery

![Zebra logo]

ZEBRA BOOKS
KENSINGTON PUBLISHING CORP.

http://www.kensingtonbooks.com

Chapter One

"Now, my dear Miss Seldon, do not worry your head so. Lady Wilmingham is a good woman. She will see you right," soothed the vicar. He patted Miss Seldon's gloved hand, politely ignoring the small darn where a few weeks earlier a hole had appeared.

Matty held her reticule in both hands, gripping it tightly as if that would save what was lost. She looked around the formal drawing room and hoped her ladyship was warmer than her décor. "I feel exceedingly awkward . . ."

"No, no," huffed Vicar Baxter, "it could happen to anyone."

Matty blinked.

The vicar sported red spots high on his prominent cheekbones. "Oh, well, I didn't mean . . ."

The door was flung open by a bewigged footman, and her ladyship swept into the room. Matty, who had never met anyone she could not face with perfect equanimity, felt something inside cringe. This lady was not going to be helpful. She could feel it.

"Lady Wilmingham! You have grown younger

during my brief absence!" enthused Vicar Baxter, rushing to take her ladyship's hands in his.

For a moment Matty thought he meant to kiss them, but he merely squeezed gently and then, dropping one, turned and led the lady to where Matty waited.

"My lady, with your permission, I would present to your notice Miss Matilda Seldon. She has a tale of horror to tell."

"Then you just wait up a moment until I catch up," said a gravelly voice from just inside the door.

Vicar Baxter swung around. "Oh." His expression shifted to one of disapprobation. "Miss Abernathy." He bowed in an abrupt manner even as he glanced toward Lady Wilmingham. "I was not informed you entertained guests," he said repressively.

"Just Abigail, as you see," said her ladyship dismissively. "Now what is this all about?" She turned what appeared to be a permanently affixed glare on Matty.

The vicar frowned a moment longer, his eyes on Miss Abernathy. Then he shrugged his narrow shoulders ever so slightly and turned back to her ladyship. "My dear Lady Wilmingham, you will be horrified, I assure you. Now, Miss Seldon, do tell your tale. Just as you told it to me."

Matty bit her lip. She then drew in a deep breath. Finally she nodded. "As Reverend Baxter says, it is a tale of horror, my lady," she began in a soft but musical voice. "Complete with grief, a true villain, and myself in desperate need of aid."

Matty frowned when Miss Abernathy chuckled. It was a deep-throated laugh that drew smiles—or would have if the situation were not so dire. Miss Abernathy grinned, her eyes twinkling, and nodded encouragingly. "Go on, my dear," she said.

"And do make a really good story of it. We are all ears."

Matty glanced toward the vicar, who, noticing, stopped glaring at Miss Abernathy. He also nodded encouragingly to his protégée.

"I am the daughter of a vicar, my lady," she said. "My father died. A cousin I'd never met arrived in time for the funeral and offered me his family home as refuge since I was forced to vacate my old home quickly, the new vicar requiring the house. As well, my cousin offered to sell up my father's library for me, which was very nearly all poor Father had of value. My cousin took me into Hawkhurst . . ."

"From where, my dear?" interrupted Miss Abernathy whose features looked rather birdlike under her old-fashioned wig.

"Father's church was in Little Conghurst," said Matty politely. When Miss Abernathy nodded, Matty turned back to Lady Wilmingham, who still appeared less than friendly. Matty repressed a sigh and returned to her story. "He took me into Hawkhurst, bought my ticket, and put me on the coach. I fear I was tired, grieving, and not paying much attention, so we were hours on the road, actually through Arundel when—" Matty paused to fight back a sob. "—just for comfort, I felt in my reticule for my mother's wedding ring. I had put it and her short string of pearls and a broach into my bag when I packed my trunk, you see. I was feeling lonely and sad and wanted that little bit of contact with her."

"Your mother is dead, too?" asked Miss Abernathy.

There was no hint of sympathy, merely interest, in her tone, and Matty was glad of that. Sympathy would have let down the tears that threatened. "I was twelve when she died."

"Tut-tut. Not a good age for a girl to lose her mother," said Miss Abernathy under her breath.

"Get on with it, girl," snapped Lady Wilmingham, glowering at Miss Abernathy for the interruption.

"It wasn't there. The ring. Or the pearls. Or the broach, for that matter. I thought perhaps I had set my bag down somewhere and then I realized I had the strings tight around my wrist just as when my cousin handed it to me before we left my old home." A touch of horror lowered her voice. "I realized he was the only person who could have taken them."

"So?"

Matty sighed. "I will admit that in my grief I was negligent, but why should I not trust my own cousin?"

"Is this your whole story?" asked Lady Wilmingham, hiding a yawn behind her hand.

"No, no," inserted Vicar Baxter. "Go on, my dear. Tell her ladyship the rest."

Matty swallowed. "Now that I was no longer lost in my grief, it occurred to me that the sun was not coming in the left-hand windows as it should have been if we were traveling north, as we would be, if headed for the Sheffield area. My jewelry was gone and the stagecoach was not going in the right direction and I—well, I fear I panicked."

"You did not panic," said the vicar soothingly. "You merely asked where we were and where we were headed."

"Yes, but to speak to total strangers that way, so abruptly—" Matty drew in a deep breath and let it out slowly. Once again in control of herself, she nodded. "—but you kindly told me that Chichester was the end of the route, which I knew was quite the wrong place altogether."

"So," said the vicar, beaming, "I talked to her

and discovered the poor deceived young woman's story and decided I must bring her to you, my lady, for protection until she can write her relatives and discover what it is she must do."

"No money, of course," said her ladyship disparagingly.

"Not very much, my lady," said Matty, her head high. "Merely what was left of the housekeeping money which I placed in an inner pocket—" She touched her skirts. "—when packing."

"A remarkable story, Miss Seldon," said her ladyship in a cool, measured way that killed all hope. "I have not," she added, "been so well entertained in ever such a long while. Baxter, you have been hoodwinked finely and now you will return this chit to the village where she may, perhaps, find a cart headed into Chichester, where such as she may earn her living in the usual way." And, with that, Lady Wilmingham turned on her heel and swept from the room.

Matty, even though she had expected little else from the haughty woman, felt prickles under her skin and knew she was near fainting. She swallowed. Hard. And drew in a deep reviving breath.

"My dear woman!" Vicar Baxter cast her a horrified look. "Is it true? Have you tricked me in such a way?"

"I have not," said Matty stiffly.

"No, I do not think you have," said Miss Abernathy.

Both Miss Seldon and Vicar Baxter had forgotten her. Matty had not previously taken much notice of the woman, all her attention on Lady Wilmingham, hoping against hope that her ladyship would give her a roof over her head until she could sort out her life. This second woman was a little older, dressed richly in the height of fashion, but, incongruously, her head was topped by a powdered wig done up in the ornate style of her youth. A woman of uncertain age, but with a mischievous expression that gave her the appearance of youth. And, of course, that deep gravelly voice that sounded so odd coming from such a small woman.

"You believe me?" asked Matty.

"Of course." The elderly woman grinned. "Our Willy—her ladyship, I *should* say—must be very careful of her position. She rather fears being taken in, you see, by every stranger that approaches her. I, on the other hand—" Again that quick bright smile flashed and the twinkly look appeared that invited one to laugh. "—have no position to uphold and may do as I please and it pleases me to invite you to visit me while we see what may be done to set things right for you." Her brows arched. "Will you come?" When Matty hesitated, she added, "Please?"

"Miss—?" Matty realized she hadn't caught the lady's name and blushed.

"This is Miss Abigail Abernathy. She lives on an estate not far from Wilming Place." The vicar spoke somewhat repressively and Matty wondered why.

"Our good vicar," said Miss Abernathy, "would urge you to go elsewhere if he could only think of an elsewhere for you to go. He does not approve. Of me."

"If you would only be open with us," said the vicar, his fear for the young lady's future given release in expressing his exasperation with Miss Abernathy, "if you would tell us your antecedents, and why you, so obviously a lady, live alone as you do, and would explain . . ."

"But, Vicar," interrupted Miss Abernathy just a touch plaintively, "if I were to do so, you would die of boredom, the lot of you! I am your mystery lady. You are really rather proud of me, you know, and boast about me to visitors and when away as—"

She grinned when the red spots again appeared on his cheekbones. "—while on your visit home just now? No, no, it would never do to tell my secrets. Now, my dear," she said, turning back to Matty, "you will come, will you not? I am perfectly respectable, I assure you—"

But this was said with such a droll look Matty wondered if she should believe her.

"—and no harm will come to you in my house." That was uttered in quite another tone and was to be believed. "As the vicar said, I live alone in a great rambling house that needs young people to liven it up. Your presence will make me feel young again too. We may enjoy getting to know each other while we sort you out. Hopefully *not* in the blink of an eye as the saying is, because where is the entertainment in that? Oh, it will be such fun. *Do* come."

She beamed, an expectant look that made one believe you would be doing her a favor if only you would agree.

Matty glanced at the vicar, who was poker-faced and offered no advice. She sighed. "Miss Abernathy, thank you. I do not know what I would do if it were not for your kind invitation."

"Well. That is settled then. So—" Miss Abernathy offered her arm to Matty. "—shall we go?" Over her shoulder, she spoke to the vicar. "You'll see her trunk is brought to the Hall, will you not? Of course you will," she quickly added in her deep voice. "Now, my dear, I cannot be calling you Miss Seldon if you are to live with me for some little time. I am Abigail and you are . . . ?"

"Matilda, Miss Aber—"

"Tut tut!"

"Miss Abigail, then. But no one ever calls me Matilda. Just Matty," said Miss Seldon as the two left the drawing room, leaving the half-confused

and half-outraged vicar standing by himself in the
overgilded splendor of Lady Wilmingham's overly
decorated room.

"No good will come of this," he muttered. "No
good at all."

He shook his head and wandered out into the
hall where the young woman's trunk sat, looking
rather apologetic for its well-used existence and
looking even smaller than usual, sitting there on
the vast, highly polished floor of the Wilming Place
entry.

"You," said the vicar to the footman who stood
to attention near the stairs staring straight ahead.

The footman looked down his nose until he
could bring the vicar into view. "You spoke?" he
asked.

"I did. You will see that trunk—" The vicar
pointed one bony finger at the object. "—is sent
over to Abernathy Hall."

With that he picked up his hat and gloves and
walked smartly out the door where, sadly, he realized he'd a long walk into the village and his home.
"If the Good Samaritan had been treated thusly . . ."
he muttered.

But the Samaritan had had no expectation of
thank yous or remuneration and poor Vicar Baxter
was too honest not to admit it. His good deed had
not worked out as he'd planned, but Miss Seldon
did have a roof over her head this night and for
many nights to come and she did have the protection of a lady and he must be thankful for that.

Even if he didn't trust the lady one inch.

Chapter Two

Matty was at that stage of tiredness where, although her body craved sleep, her mind would not stop going in circles. She had turned down the lamp on the bedside table to the merest glow before she got into bed, afraid she would wake in the dark in a strange place and not remember where she was. So now she lay in the high fourposter bed and stared at the embroidered canopy stretched in an arch over the top. Fanciful birds fluttered among equally fanciful greenery. The colors had mellowed over the many decades of their existence and she attempted to put herself into a more restful state of mind by discovering the shier avians and those whose colors most agreed with the greens and yellows of the flora filling in all other space.

Unwilling to face her grief at her father's death just yet, she wondered about the woman who had had time and imagination to do such amazingly delicate stitchery. She counted fifteen birds in the area where light from her lamp allowed her search and then sighed, turning her eyes to her hands, which she held clasped together across her chest.

"You, my girl," she said to her index finger, "are nothing but a fool." The finger waggled and Matty sighed. "Yes, I know. Mitigating circumstances you would say. Still . . ." she began thoughtfully, then nodded, and continued, "one must agree, most definitely a fool. However did you come to trust a man you had never met simply because he told you he was your cousin? Very likely he was no such thing. Very likely, if you only knew, he goes about the country preying on innocent fools such as yourself, leaving the grief-stricken in worse case than they were. Thank the good Lord for Vicar Baxter—even if his plan to aid you was as useless as you suspected it might be!"

Still unwilling to think of the loss of her father, Matty considered her hostess, Miss Abernathy—Miss Abigail, rather. Or if she were to be as informal as her hostess suggested, Miss Abby. From things the woman had said about her twin brother running away from home and joining the rebels when the American colonies revolted, Matty guessed her hostess to be in her sixties. Or near that. And yet one had that odd feeling of youth, of life and living, and of a contagious, very nearly outrageous, *joie de vivre* when in the woman's presence. She was, decided Matty, a woman who gave generously not so much of her purse, although obviously she did not stint that, but of herself.

Matty mused a bit on the meaning of real charity, Miss Abernathy's sort of charity, and then allowed her thoughts to wander on to their arrival at Abernathy Hall. She smiled, recalling the odd assortment of pets that greeted them.

There had been the usual country dogs, one foreign creature, French, with only three legs, and another foreigner that was oddly shaped, its legs very short and its body very long. Miss Abigail told her it was a German dog, a dachshund. Two cats strolled along behind the dogs, one a disdainful old male with an ear bitten half off and a definite kink in its tail, the other a dainty white princess of a female cat dancing along on paws that barely touched the floor. There was a monkey, chattering and jumping up and down and not content until it was picked up and petted and cooed over. Oddest of all was a long-haired goat that pitter-patted up to her mistress, blatted once, butted her mistress gently, and then walked over to the door which a footman opened for her.

Matty was given a quick tour through the public rooms of the house, which were, Matty thought, quite as strange as Miss Aber—Miss Abigail's collection of pets. The house was full of odd furnishings, which, Miss Abigail explained, had mostly come from India. There were chests and low tables and cushion-covered benches with one end raised somewhat as would be a chaise longue but much wider than any chaise Matty had ever seen and the wood, wherever one could see it, deeply incised with high relief carving that looked to be exceedingly uncomfortable. There were magnificent carpets in jewel colors, both large and small, the smaller scattered here and there, sometimes one covering part of another. There was pagan statuary that made Matty blush, a tall brass vase full of even taller peacock feathers, and a multitude of other things she couldn't even remember.

But mixed among the exotic was the common everyday sort of furniture found in any English home, and although Matty could not conceive how, it all managed to coexist quite nicely with the alien pieces. Wing-backed chairs. Armoires that should have seemed out of place in salons but did not, although Matty had always thought of them as bedroom furniture. There were drop-leaf tables and half-round tables set against the walls, which could be pulled out, hooked together, and made into round tables. There were fanciful gilded frames around pictures or huge mirrors with matching ornate sconces on either side.

And finally, there was a magnificent pianoforte complete with a multitude of woods inlaid into rosewood that was polished until one could see one's face in it. Casually, Miss Abigail gestured toward it and said she hoped Matty played. Matty had nodded, adding, apologetically, that her playing was rather commonplace, and Miss Abernathy said that was far better than her own and they'd have the tuner in so they could enjoy the music—and, with a flick of her fingers, added, "See to it," to the footman trailing along in their wake.

Matty turned and saw the footman make a note with a stubby pencil in a tiny notebook held hidden in the palm of one hand.

The meal to which they'd been called soon after their tour of the Hall included the same sort of odd mixture of foreign and English food that the house did furniture. Matty had not been quite certain she liked the curries *or* the vegetables, which were cooked in the French fashion and still rather crisp. The sweets, however, had been out of this world and Matty, who rarely had the opportunity to indulge herself, feared she'd rather made a pig of herself. Miss Abigail had explained that she'd imported a French pastry chef for the purpose since she had, as was likely obvious from her plump figure, a sweet tooth.

Matty pushed her pillow into a more comfortable position and considered. She nodded. "Yes," she told her finger, "a strange woman altogether. It is not at all odd that her neighbors consider her something of a mystery." The finger nodded agreement.

Matty, under the necessity of maintaining silence on many subjects her father's parishioners would not care to have discussed with anyone but the vicar, had, when still very young, learned to tell things to her fingers. As might be expected, her fingers never betrayed her trust and it had become more than a habit, very nearly a necessity, this having something that would listen and consider, and, perhaps, agree—and then again, perhaps not. It was rather disconcerting, Matty had discovered, when her fingers made it clear she was quite in the wrong and must correct some fault or mistaken view—as had happened on more than one occasion.

"What am I to do?" she asked. "I am exceedingly lucky to have a roof over my head tonight, rather than finding myself a likely bridge from which to cast myself—are there, do you suppose, suitable bridges in Chichester? Yes, very lucky that Miss Abernathy took me in, but it cannot go on forever, of course. I must come to some decision concerning my future, find some way to make my living."

She considered.

A tentative suggestion that she might become a governess had her fingers laughing quite uncontrollably. Well, she'd known that was no solution, had she not, and only suggested it because it was a proper thing for a destitute lady to do? Matty considered further. She might, she thought, become companion to some elderly lady in need of such. Not Miss Abigail, of course—

Her finger drooped in reluctant agreement.

—since that sprightly lady would have no use for a downtrodden and overworked companion for many years to come. But someone like—oh, very likely someone like Lady Wilmingham. The finger drooped still more.

"Then what would *you* recommend?" she asked

it. "Perhaps that I could go as seamstress in some provincial shop?" she suggested doubtfully and shook her head in agreement with her finger. Matty would never be much of a seamstress. "I could, however, do rather well trimming hats. You know I have had quite sincere compliments when I've changed the trim on my bonnet . . . no? You think not? But why?"

Matty was forced to think. Very obviously there was some reason why she should not attempt to find work trimming hats. Ah. Perhaps it was because she'd no experience of *tonnish* hats? And it was well known that only a *tonnish* lady would actually go to the expense of buying a bonnet already trimmed? Anyone with any sense of the value of things trimmed her own. It could, after all, be done quite easily and, by and large, *far* more cheaply.

Matty sighed and lifted her eyes to the embroidery above her head. It was, she decided, quite obvious that she had no way at all of earning her living since she was too young to find work doing the one thing at which she was proven adept. *No* one would hire *her* to keep house for them. Housekeepers were like Mrs. Stone, Miss Abigail's housekeeper, to whom she'd been introduced during their perambulations through the house. One must be, if not actually gray-haired, then at least showing a few gray strands among the rest.

"Perhaps," she murmured and yawned, "looking for that useful bridge is the answer after all." And on that depressing thought, Matty fell deeply asleep and did not wake until the happy sound of a lusty wren singing just beyond her window brought her back to life.

* * *

In quite another part of the house, the evening was spent in quite another fashion. First Miss Abernathy had a long talk with her maid.

"Bitsy, you understand now?" she finished.

" 'Course I do, Miss Abby. You want me to discover if Miss Seldon is telling a tale to diddle the nobs or if there was actually a vicar by that name who recently died and if so was there a cousin settling up the estate."

"I don't know why I do not learn to trust you to know exactly what I wish of you," said Miss Abernathy, smiling. She handed over the sketch of Matty on which she'd worked as they talked.

"Nor anyone else," retorted the maid, who had been an impertinent chit and had matured into a brusque speak-your-mind sort of woman. She studied the portrait for a bit and then nodded. "A good likeness. If that's the vicar's daughter and she lived in Conghurst until recently, I'll have no difficulty finding someone to say it is she. So, I'll just be off to pack my bag, then." She accepted a small but well-filled purse from her mistress. "The mail goes through the village early so I'll not be here to help you dress," she added, warningly.

"Mary will do very well while you are gone. She cannot mend worth a pinch of salt, and I wouldn't trust her to wash my good silks, but I'll not have my stays on backward or my stocking mismatched."

Bitsy looked as if she wanted to disagree, but said nothing more about the girl. "Shouldn't take more than a few days," she said gruffly.

Once her maid was off, Miss Abernathy turned to her desk, where she wrote two letters. The first was to a Bow Street runner she'd once employed in a delicate matter and discovered to be trustworthy. As with most anyone interesting with whom Miss Abernathy had to deal, they had become friends—something else that would shock her neighbors if they were made aware of such egalitarian behavior on her part.

"Ned," she wrote, "I believe I've another task for you and would appreciate it if you could wind up whatever project in which you are just now involved, in order to make time for mine. I have sent Bitsy—you will remember Bitsy, I am sure—?"

Miss Abernathy wrote that bit with her tongue firmly in her cheek. She had never quite forgiven Bitsy for turning down Ned's offer of marriage. It was quite true that there would never be another Bitsy, but no one should give up all happiness because of a misplaced feeling of duty to another. It had quite put Miss Abernathy in her maid's debt and Abigail Abernathy was not one to remain in anyone's debt. Not if she had any choice in the matter. So, having Ned back underfoot might be just the thing to remind Bitsy she should get on with her life before it was too late.

"—and even if you do not, I must tell you I have sent her to discover if the essentials of the tale told by my newest protégée are true. She should return in only a few days with the necessary information and I would appreciate it if you could arrive no later than early next week?" Miss Abernathy reread her note, nodded, ended it, and folded and addressed it. She pressed melted wax with the signet ring she wore on the first finger of her left hand to seal it. A tiny but perfect figure of an elephant seated on its rear end and its front legs held up in the air appeared on the wax.

Miss Abernathy began the second letter. "Dear Charles . . ."

And then stopped. She frowned. Just what did she think Charles North could do? A barrister after all. He would not wish to involve himself with searching out relatives or discovering the terms of whatever will the Reverend Seldon might have left.

One needed a solicitor for that menial sort of work. Still, his name had popped into her head the instant she had wondered whom to consult. Moreover it stayed there. Miss Abernathy nodded, dipped her pen, and continued.

". . . I have had a small adventure which I believe you will find amusing . . ."

She related the tale of meeting Matty, described Vicar Baxter's face when it was decided Matty would stay with her, and then went on to explain why she had done anything so Quixotic.

". . . She reminds me a little of myself at that age, Charles. You are far too young to have any notion what I mean by that and I am not certain I can explain it, but there is something in her character that I believe will grow and become special if it may only be given the opportunity. Is that very immodest, my dear Charles? To first suggest the chit reminds me of myself and then to say there is something special about her? But, my dear boy, she needs the opportunity! I wish to see she has it. Since there is a villain involved in her current perilous situation, I am likely to need your advice and support. Is there a possibility you would find yourself free any time soon so that you could come for a much-to-be appreciated (by me) visit?"

Miss Abernathy reread her words, frowned, shook her head, sighed, and, deciding it was far too late at night to write another, she folded, addressed, and pressed her signet into a blob of ivory-colored wax, sealing the single page. The two letters were soon placed in the usual place in a big flat brass bowl in the hall where her butler would find them and see them on their way.

Miss Abernathy stared at them. Suddenly she grinned. Life had been a dead bore recently. With Miss Seldon's arrival, it promised to be something *less* than boring for an appreciable time to come.

Which was good. Miss Abernathy did not like to find herself bored. Life was too short and much too valuable to spend the least little bit of it in boredom!

Miss Abernathy took herself off to a bedchamber so exotic Matty would have blinked and blinked again. And there, waiting for her, was a gentleman dressed in old-fashioned clothes and wearing a powdered wig. He rose to his feet when she entered and held out a hand to her. Abigail went to him instantly and was enclosed in a warm embrace before, together, they lolled on a well-padded example of the overwide eastern-styled chaise longues. For half an hour she spoke to him of all that had happened that day and, as she did so, he played with the curl lying on her shoulder, winding it around his finger and smoothing it, letting it bounce in his palm, stroking it. . . .

Not long after the gentleman disappeared, Abigail, unlike Matty, fell instantly into a sound slumber and did not wake until a peacock raised its voice in a hugely loud and exceedingly ugly squawk. Once again Abigail Abernathy swore she would get rid of the stupid creature and never again be awakened in such a horribly unsettling way.

And just as quickly, the thought faded from her mind as she considered what she would do with her new guest on such a fine summer day.

Chapter Three

Matty twitched and then blushed, her eyes lifting to meet those of her hostess. "Oh!"

"My dear! I did not mean to startle you so. Of what were you thinking that you were in such a deep study?"

Matty bit her lip. "My father . . ."

Miss Abernathy sat on the far edge of the oriental lounge that Matty occupied. "Tell me," she said quietly.

Matty hesitated.

"I truly wish to hear. What, for instance, was it like, being the daughter of the village vicar? Were you kept close? Allowed no diversions?"

"Oh no, nothing like that," said Matty, horrified that anyone would think such a thing. "Why, I was invited to all the local parties and my father had nothing against dancing, you know. He said the ancient Greeks thought it a most perfect form of exercise and therefore good for one. He himself would on occasion join a country dance . . ."

Matty, once she'd begun talking, found she could not stop. She told her hostess a very great deal about her life in the vicarage, her duties and her small pleasures. ". . . but you must not believe my father was so selfish as to wish to keep me by him forever," she said after explaining how much her father had needed her to see he was fed and didn't forget everyday things such as getting out of wet clothes when he returned from a pastoral visit made in the rain or to be there to build up his fire when it was about to go out. "He was a rather otherworldly man, you know, but he was pleased for me when Jeremy courted me and we became engaged."

"Jeremy . . . ?"

"The son of the local squire. He was still up at Oxford, you see, and Father felt we should wait and Jeremy agreed. Jeremy thought *me* too young," said Matty, a mischievous look making her eyes sparkle, "not himself, of course." She sobered, her eyes losing focus. "Then he went on a walking tour with friends . . ."

"Something happened?" asked Miss Abernathy when Matty didn't continue.

Matty sighed. "They were in the Lake District . . ."

Miss Abernathy nodded. ". . . and decided to go fell climbing."

Matty nodded. "Yes. A sudden blinding mist rose, as they do in that region. His friend who came to tell me of the accident told me they couldn't see their hands before their faces it was so thick. There was a rocky slope, very steep . . ."

"He slipped and the rocks came down on him?"

Matty nodded and shook off her sadness. "It was a very long time ago and, oh, do look at the time! Why, I have talked on and on forever, it seems."

"And very interesting it was, too." The door opened and Miss Abernathy looked around. For a moment she looked disconcerted, glanced at Matty, and then back at her visitor. She glared very nearly as fiercely as Lady Wilmingham could.

"Rutherford," she said somewhat repressively. "Was I expecting you?"

"Have I done the unforgivable and arrived at an awkward moment?" he asked, smoothing a small dark mustache with one finger. He strode on into the room, straightening his yellow-spotted Belcher handkerchief, which he'd tied around his throat instead of a proper cravat, the capes on his long coachman's coat swinging. "You've company, Abby?"

"As you see," said Miss Abernathy. "Miss Seldon, allow me to present to you Rutherford Morton, a reprobate of a relative. Rutherford, Miss Seldon is the daughter of a vicar."

"Warning me off, Abby?" asked Rutherford, a slight smirk distorting his features. He approached and held out his hand for Matty.

Matty didn't like the way he appeared to tower over her and she rose to her feet. She did not offer her hand, but merely nodded. She was surprised to discover him not so tall as she'd thought, and decided it was his athletic presence and the way he held himself that presented him in a manner that was impressive.

"But she is a delight," enthused Rutherford. "Lovely. A pearl beyond price."

Somehow, without her permission, he managed to collect her hand between both of his. She let it lay there, limp and unresponsive, waiting to see what he'd do next.

"Such hair. Such eyes."

Matty's lips twitched.

"Such a delightfully rosy complexion."

"Such nonsense," murmured Matty. She turned to her hostess. "Does he have much success with this approach, Miss Abigail?"

"He claims he does," said that lady repressively.

"He needs practice," said Matty thoughtfully. "I

cannot believe any woman of sense would find such empty compliments the least intriguing.''

One dark heavy brow arched high. ''But she is wonderful,'' said Rutherford, grinning and holding her hand more tightly.

''*Just* like Billy Frensham in the village,'' said Matty thoughtfully eyeing the raised brow. ''I wonder . . .''

''Wonder?'' he asked, the smirk returning.

''Whether you, too, will come to a bad end.'' She attempted to pull her hand from his suddenly relaxed grip but it tightened before she managed the trick.

Rutherford chuckled but there was a strained note to his laughter. ''Where did you find her?'' he asked. He turned to Miss Abernathy, still not releasing Matty's hand.

''*I* found her,'' said Vicar Baxter in exceedingly disapproving tones.

They all turned to where the vicar stood in the doorway, scowling. ''Mr. Baxter, do join us,'' said Miss Abernathy, strolling toward him. ''I was about to ring for tea.''

''I merely came to see how Miss Seldon goes on.''

The vicar had no suspicion he told a lie. At least in part. He had never actually thought about his habit of arriving at the better houses just when some sort of meal might be available, but it happened far too often to be completely an accident.

''Such a terrible adventure!'' he continued. ''She must feel quite frail. Miss Abernathy, I do not understand how you could allow her to rise from her bed so soon after experiencing such desperation!''

''But I did not *allow* her. I came down this morning to discover she had already had a stroll in the gardens and cut flowers to replace those in the front hall, which were going off quite sadly, and that she was as ready for her breakfast as was I. And now I am ready for my elevenses. Do stop scolding and join us," she coaxed.

"I did not know Mr. Morton visited you," said Vicar Baxter, remaining right where he was.

"He arrived only moments before your good self," said Miss Abernathy.

"He does not, of course, mean to stay."

"Why not?" asked Rutherford, who had made the rather long detour to see Miss Abernathy, expecting to stay for no more than a few hours, overnight at most, before immediately reversing his direction and making his way to Brighton, where he would enjoy the summer months in the Prince Regent's favorite seaside town.

"Because," said Mr. Baxter in a tone that said that should be obvious, "Miss Seldon is visiting."

"I see no reason why that should interfere with my visiting Abby. I must see Davy at once. Excuse me, Abby, Miss Seldon . . ." He bowed to each and was gone from the room in half a moment.

Miss Abernathy sighed. "I do wish you would not," she said to Mr. Baxter.

"Would not?"

"Would not try to tell Rutherford what he must and must not do. By now, I'd have thought you understood that whatever it is you tell him to *do*, it is exactly the opposite which he *does*."

Poor Mr. Baxter looked bewildered. "How can a man his age possibly be so childish?"

"Not childish, Reverend. *Perverse.*"

"Childish," insisted the vicar. "Miss Seldon, I dislike saying evil of others or even thinking it, but I very much fear Miss Abernathy will not warn you of that man's character, which is not good. Especially it is not good where young women are concerned," finished the vicar in the most repressive of tones.

"I, sir, am more than seven and am not one who has more hair than wit," said Matty gently. "I am aware that Mr. Morton is a dangerous flirt. You may rest easy. I will not be taken in by him."

At her words, the vicar appeared to relax and, as Miss Abigail's butler wheeled in a tea tray loaded with good things to eat, he rubbed his hands. "In that case," he said, his eyes on the cakes and biscuits, "I may indulge myself in Miss Abernathy's excellent tea with a free heart."

He moved toward the table on which the footman was setting out plates and cups and saucers. He pulled out a chair and looked at Matty. "Will you join me, my dear?"

Matty looked at Miss Abernathy, who, she found, was trying very hard not to grin. Matty, however, found it something other than humorous that the vicar had named himself host and assumed he was free to arrange things as he willed. But since Miss Abernathy did not object, she docilely took the offered seat and soon found Miss Abernathy seated on her one side and the vicar on the other.

When Mr. Morton returned to the salon, he discovered that he must sit next Miss Abernathy if he was to join the party. Instead he had a word with the butler, who was just leaving the room and, a few moments later, was provided with a silver tankard filled with home brew. He carried it near and leaned against the wall just where he had the best view of Miss Seldon. He remained there, staring at her, the whole time the others sipped tea and ate and did their best to ignore his presence while carrying on something approaching a normal conversation.

Vicar Baxter was so unsettled by the experience, however, that, once he saw all his favorite biscuits had found a new home inside himself, he decided he must carry on with his parish visits. ". . . Mademoiselle Dubois is ailing again," he said to explain why he must make a rude departure.

"Our village seamstress? Her head this time or her heart?" asked Miss Abernathy, a trifle sardonically.

"Her head, I believe," said Vicar Baxter. He eyed his hostess with a disapproving eye. "You would suggest she pretends to suffer in order to make herself interesting?"

"Not at all. I am certain she truly suffers. It is just that she suffers so conveniently, becoming the most ill just when someone complains about how slow she is about delivering a promised gown. I happen to know Lady Wilmingham has been looking in vain for several items she wishes to take to Bath when she departs next week."

Vicar Baxter's mouth pursed. "As to that, I believe it is between her ladyship and Mademoiselle and not my business. I merely go to offer what comfort I may during her illness."

"And I am sure she will be pleased to see you," offered Matty, hoping to avoid a scene between her hostess and the man she was forced to feel a duty toward, thanks to his rescue of her. "Your prayers must be a comfort to the poor lady."

"Thank you," he said, bowing. He cast an enigmatic look toward Rutherford, said a curt goodbye to Miss Abernathy, and turned back to Matty. "Will you walk me to the door, Miss Seldon?"

She could do no less, but did not look forward to another lecture concerning Mr. Morton, which she could see the vicar wished to deliver. By asking tactful questions about Mademoiselle Dubois, she managed to bring Mr. Baxter to the door and out onto the wide top step of the flight that led down to the drive where the vicar's gig and horse stood. It was not a very good horse, she noted, obviously old and, she feared, suffering a bone spavin on its left rear hock.

Before Mr. Baxter could do more than take her hand and open his mouth to proceed with the lecture she had so far avoided, Miss Abernathy appeared. "If her head is truly aching, then I doubt she will be interested in food at just this moment, but do take this basket to Mademoiselle. Just a few delicacies to tempt her appetite. And tell her I hope she is soon better."

The vicar was forced to drop Matty's hand. He took the basket, said all that was proper, and stepped briskly down the steps. Miss Abernathy and Matty watched until he had slapped the reins against his horse's back, startling the poor creature from what had looked to be a comfortable doze so that it started slowly down the drive toward the lane.

"He is a prosy sort of man, but I believe his heart is in the right place," said Miss Abernathy thoughtfully.

"I am sure it is so but I must thank you for rescuing me. Again," said Matty.

"Rescuing you *again?*"

"First, of course, that you invited me to stay until I can receive word from my relatives, but just now I believe you helped me avoid a lecture if not a diatribe against your Mr. Morton."

"Hmm. Shall I give the lecture instead?"

"You do not trust Mr. Morton to behave properly toward a guest in your home?"

Miss Abernathy was silent for a moment. "Rutherford will do nothing obvious to harm you. He knows he'd have me to answer to if he were to attempt your seduction. You see I merely say 'attempt' since I have faith in your good sense." She studied Matty's rosy cheeks. "Have I been too blunt, my dear?"

Chapter Four

The following morning Rutherford had not yet risen when Miss Seldon finished her self-imposed duty of freshening the flowers on the main floor of the Hall. She was carrying the last of them through the entry on her way to the small salon when the double doors were thrust apart. The sun made the figure standing there nothing but a well-defined silhouette.

He was a willowy creature, his skintight trousers revealing overly thin legs. His coat, on which huge pearl-colored buttons reflected light, was so short it revealed equally narrow hips, the trousers rising somewhat above the waist and the front flap buttoned with two rows of smaller buttons. His hair was overly long and the light through the wind-tossed strands formed a sort of golden halo about his head, from which, the instant he perceived Miss Seldon, he swept a hat decorated with ribbons matching those forming a rosette at the top of the cane in his other hand.

"Mademoiselle!" he intoned. "Lady with flower-filled vase, standing in the sun, golden roses softly scented, no lovelier than she." He bowed.

"Steven," said Miss Abernathy from the stairway landing, "I was not expecting you. Or was I?"

Miss Abernathy sounded faintly exasperated and Matty wondered why.

"Am I de trope, good Miss Abigail? Should I go away?"

The young man moved forward and, as he passed Miss Seldon on his way to greet his hostess, pinched a part of her anatomy one was not expected to acknowledge. Matty jumped, turned, and, without thinking, tipped the vase in such a way that water ran out and down the back of the stranger's legs and into his boots.

It was his turn to jump and turn. "Here now!"

Miss Abernathy, who had not missed the little byplay, stifled a chuckle and descended to join the two, who glared at each other. "Miss Seldon, may I introduce to your attention, this pernicious scamp, Steven Howard. Steven, be pleased to meet my guest, Miss Matilda Seldon."

"Guest?" Steven, eyeing Matty's well-worn dress, turned bright red. "Guest! My dear Miss Seldon, do forgive my . . . my . . ."

"Impertinence?" asked Matty in a bright questioning tone.

"Er . . . yes. Impertinence. You *will* forgive me, of course."

He gave her such a hopeful puppyish look that Matty was forced to suppress a chuckle. "I will think about it," she said.

His expression fell into lines of abject remorse. Then he dropped to his knees, started to clasp his hands, discovered they were otherwise occupied, carefully set aside his hat and cane, and *then* clasped his hands. "Oh, please, forgive me? Miss Abernathy will never again allow me entrance into her home if you do not. I cannot bear to find myself exiled both from her entertaining self and your lovely self. Do say you will forgive me or I will follow you about on my knees—"

Matty backed up a few steps and he scrambled forward, his hands still clasped.

"—until you do."

"Miss Abigail, do you think the floors clean enough we may allow Mr. Howard to walk on his knees—or must I forgive him?"

"You must do as you please but you might take into consideration that he has learned a lesson."

Steven turned, still on his knees, and looked up at Miss Abernathy. "Lesson?"

"Yes. Never again will you attempt to pinch the maids until you are certain they *are* maids. *Especially* when they've a water-filled vase in their hands."

The blush, which had faded, returned, and Steven reached behind him to feel his damp trousers. "My delightful Miss Abernathy, surely you'll not be so cruel as to return me to my carriage before I've had an opportunity to make myself presentable?"

"Oh get up. Do," ordered Miss Abernathy. "Of course you must not leave in such a state. But I do not know why you have come."

Steven suddenly wore a slightly shuttered expression. "Er, because I like visiting you? Is that not reason enough?"

"Not when the Brighton Season is in full swing," said Miss Abernathy, crossing her arms and shaking her head.

Steven, sighing, rose to his feet. "Then if you will have the whole of it, I must see my cousin." A quick frown crossed his brow and he stared intently at his hostess. "He is here, is he not? Ruthie?"

"He is."

Tension, which one had not noticed the young man suffered, drained away. "Excellent. Very good.

In fact, quite perfect. You will excuse me while I go on up to my room and await the much-needed attentions of my valet?''

"We will see you at luncheon. I would not, however, awaken Rutherford even if you feel you are in the midst of an emergency.''

Steven, who had been attempting to engage Miss Seldon in an exchange of flirting looks, turned a startled glance toward his hostess. "Emergency? Oh, no. Nothing like! Of course not.'' Steven quickly bowed to each of the women in an attempt to cover his surprise his hostess had guessed the trend of his need to see his cousin.

"Rutherford was late returning from the village and might not appreciate interference with his beauty sleep," added Miss Abernathy.

"Thank you for your words of wisdom and kind advice, my dear Miss Abigail. I will be forever in your debt." He kissed his hostess's hand, bowed again to Miss Seldon, and took the stairs two at a time, disappearing to the left when he reached the top.

"I should perhaps warn you," said Miss Abernathy thoughtfully, "that my young friends have suites down that hallway. I rarely know in advance when they mean to appear on my doorstep, so their rooms are kept in readiness for them. Perhaps you should refrain from going that way in order to use the secondary stairs at that end of the house? Now that they have come?"

"I most definitely will not go that way again," agreed Matty. "He is very young, is he not?"

"He is not long down from Oxford. I wonder why he has come hunting Rutherford . . . ?" She frowned.

"Do you think he has found himself in a pickle and wishes his older cousin's advice?"

"A likely situation, think you not? He is that age . . ."

"He did not seem in desperate need, so perhaps it is nothing so very bad."

"As you say." Miss Abernathy turned slightly. "Ah, Forbes. There you are. We have had another arrival. Mr. Howard has come for a visit."

Forbes bowed and awaited orders.

"You will know what to do," said Miss Abernathy, knowing it was true. But then she took the vase from Matty and handed it to her flabbergasted butler, who looked as if he knew neither what it was nor what to do with it. Despite his expression, she added, "You will also know what to do with these. More water, I think." Then, drawing Matty's arm through her own, she walked her out the front door for a stroll in the gardens.

Charles North leaned back in his well-worn but exceedingly comfortable leather-covered chair and held up the short letter for a second perusal. "Seldon. Seldon . . ." He leaned to the side and craned his neck. "Ah, there you are, Timmy. Have you given over the old newspapers to the rag-and-bone man or might we find an obituary I seem to recall from some weeks ago?"

"Weeks, sir?"

"Perhaps no more than two? See if you can find one for a Reverend Seldon."

"Now, sir?" Timmy looked down at the boot he'd only half polished. Not that it needed polishing. The state of North's boots was Timmy's pride and joy and polishing them to a higher and still higher gloss the only job of work he really enjoyed.

"Since you are capable of working over that leather for hours on end, I think you'd best put them aside for now and return to them after you've discovered what I wish to know," said Charles and, once the lad was settled in the corner with a stack of newspapers, he read the letter from Abigail Abernathy for the third time.

It occurred to him it was months since he'd last visited Miss Abby. Luckily, the trial he'd successfully wound up just yesterday was the last item on his agenda for some time. It was his plan to take a run down to Brighton and impose on his sister-in-law for a bed. He'd meant to disport himself among his friends and have a quick look at the young women who had not caught themselves husbands during the Season—hoping against hope there was a jewel amongst them that had escaped the attention of more *tonnish* gentlemen. For several years he had, now and again, had the thought he might like a wife. But only if he could find one with whom he could live in contentment, a friend as well as a lover.

It seems, he thought wistfully, *that I ask too much.*

He took another look around the high back of the chair, saw that Timmy was occupied in the corner of the room, his grubby finger pointing to each word as he carefully sounded it out. Luckily the obituaries were placed in black-bounded boxes. The poor lad didn't have to attempt to read the whole of each paper looking for them!

A young lady, said Miss Abby. A vicar's daughter? Charles pursed his lips and his eyes narrowed. Was, perhaps, Lady Wilmingham correct for once? Was the chit putting one over on his old friend? Did Miss Abby need more advice and counsel than she knew?

Charles's face lightened with a sudden grin. Abigail Abernathy was unlikely to need either. She was one of the most astute women he'd ever met. Very likely the *most* astute!

Also the most interesting.

Half rueful, half in earnest, Charles wished Miss Abby might be correct that her Miss Seldon was a Miss-Abigail-Abernathy-in-embryo. It had just occurred to him that the reason he'd been dissatisfied with the recent crops of young ladies was that none of them were the least little bit like Miss Abby!

Charles decided that a jaunt into West Sussex might be far more interesting than an exceedingly predictable sojourn with his brother in Brighton. There was, after all, nothing the least predictable about a stay with Miss Abernathy!

"Timmy, have you not yet found it?"

"Give a man a minute here," growled the boy-verging-on-manhood. "Can't expect a fellow to go through stacks of papers instantly."

"Keep at it then," said Charles and, wishing he need not leave the comfort of his favorite chair, moved himself to his desk, where he wrote two notes.

The first to his brother and sister-in-law, regretting he was unable, after all, to join them in Brighton was easily written. He grinned as he penned those words. His brother's wife would not be unhappy with his nonarrival. It would mean another bed to offer one of *her* relatives.

The letter to Abigail was longer. Not only did it announce his imminent arrival, but asked one or two questions. First, did Abigail wish him to put forward inquiries concerning the young lady's possible relatives? Perhaps there was someone who would take the chit in and set her right. The other question was asked with more enthusiasm: Should he see if he could discover anything concerning the library the soi-disant cousin meant to sell?

Charles was a bit of a collector. Perhaps some or all of it could be retrieved and perhaps something of interest would be found among the more boring tomes. Royal Tunbridge Wells, for instance, had not only the healing baths, but an excellent bookstore, the owner of which might recently have bought up a decent library. Or perhaps farther away, in Canterbury ... or, as a last resort, the many, *many* possibilities right here in London. He would set men searching, if Miss Abigail so wished.

He laid to one side the letter to Miss Abigail. The other he added to a thin stack he'd written earlier, which Timmy would take to the central posting office, where it would, within hours, lie with many others in a mail sack on a Mail Coach bound for Brighton. His brother would receive it this evening or tomorrow morning at the latest. The one to Miss Abigail would go by a hired messenger who would await an answer. Depending on the answer, he and Timmy would be on their way either the following day or a day or so later.

Charles's private messenger arrived at very nearly the same time as Ned, Miss Abigail's Bow Street runner. The redbreast, as the runners were called in honor of the red waistcoat they all wore, waited patiently for her to finish reading it. She handed it over. Ned had already heard her tale of how she'd come to take Miss Seldon into her home and now, reading about Charles's suggestion for finding her father's library, he nodded. "I can set that search in motion as well as the finding of Ervine Pelling, assuming that was really the young man's name. Did Miss Seldon have no knowledge of relatives?"

"She remembered her mother mentioning there was a baron in her father's family and I checked *Debrett's*. A Baron Pelling exists and it appears the Seldons may be nearly related, the baron's aunt having married one, but then again, perhaps it is a different family, some other branch of the Seldon family. According to Miss Seldon, her mother never spoke at all about her own relations. It is not impossible, of course, that the woman was cast from her family for wedding a mere vicar. Such Gothic behavior still occurs.''

The runner shook his head. ''The things the nobs get up to! You can tell young Charles—'' The two had met during an earlier adventure in which Miss Abernathy had involved them. ''—he could do one thing before he gets on his horse and comes galloping to hold your hand. He could set someone to look into who *Mrs.* Seldon was and if any of her family survive her. I'll do the needful where young Pelling and the chit's library is concerned. I'll set others to checking the bookstores and my first job will be to see the baron and whether your villain is his son—and if he has gone to earth at home. Don't you worry your head—'' He eyed Miss Abernathy's old-fashioned powdered head. ''—in that respect.''

Miss Abernathy touched the powdered curl lying down over her shoulder, smoothing it. She grinned. ''Don't like my hair, Ned?''

''I do. I always did. Thing is, looks a little odd, what with modern cropped heads and all to compare it to.''

''One of the things I have always liked about you is your frank speech. One gets no Spanish coin from you, Ned.''

He nodded. ''And you never will. Well, if that is all, then I'll be on my way as soon as I've heard all Miss Bitsy has to say . . .''

Two spots of color appeared on his cheeks when Miss Abernathy's eyes twinkled at him.

''. . . which will be quite a lot I am sure, she being a wordy wench and not afraid to wag her tongue.'' He sighed and shook his head. ''The trail is already

colder than I like, but I'll sniff out the wheres and
whys of it all.''

"I'm sure you will," said Abigail, knowing of old
that Ned would know just how to go about it. She
was glad Bitsy had returned and she wouldn't say
a word if Bitsy and Ned disappeared for an hour
or two.

In fact she rather hoped they would disappear.
Ned needed time for a little proper wooing—as
he'd say himself.

Chapter Five

"Ah. Miss Matty," said Rutherford brightly.

Matty straightened from where she had been raiding Miss Abernathy's cutting garden of all its best blooms. "Mr. Morton," she said, glancing around. Matty relaxed when she saw two of the gardener's helpers working on a nearby flowerbed. Rutherford Morton would behave himself so long as there were witnesses nearby.

"Such a lovely rose," he said slyly.

"Miss Abernathy has several varieties of rose I've never before seen," offered Matty, hoping to divert him from any more trite compliments.

"But none so rare," he said, beaming, "as this example before me."

She grimaced. "Do you really find such nonsense helpful when talking to women?" she asked.

His left brow arced high.

She tipped her head. "I have always found that an irritating habit," she said.

His other brow rose to meet the first.

"Yes. That. Very likely because I cannot do it," she added and sighed.

He laughed. "You are a delight!"

"What may I do to change your mind?"

"There is nothing. It is too late. You have been revealed in all your glory. Allow me to carry your basket, Miss Matty, so you may have both hands free and may more easily continue your task."

Matty handed him the basket, but she did not lean to her task. Instead she frowned. "You," she suggested, "would be much more help if you would go around to the other side of the bed."

It was a narrow bed so he could not object that she could not reach the basket. The move would, however, put him in front of her. He frowned.

"Yes, I know," she said in a kindly tone, "but I assure you I will be far more comfortable even if you are less than happy." She smoothed her skirts over her derriere.

Rutherford shook his head. "You, my dear, are a spoilsport." But he obliged her and stepped across the bed. "Now you may continue. Tell me while you work, just where did Miss Abigail discover you?"

"I believe you were informed of my situation when Vicar Baxter arrived yesterday."

"No, only that he found you. Do tell," he coaxed.

Matty gave a brief rendition of her history.

"But your cousin is the veriest devil," said Rutherford and added in a mutter. "It seems there are a number of devils cluttering our fair countryside these days."

Matty glanced at him and found Mr. Morton staring at nothing at all, a faint frown drawing his heavy brows somewhat closer together than they normally grew. She leaned to cut still another bloom, wondering what had put the man into a pucker. Then, feeling thankful he was silent, she finished her work, straightened for the last time and, casually, reached for the basket. He released it into her hand, bowed in an absentminded sort of manner, and, still silent, wandered away, his hands clasped loosely behind his back.

"Well!" muttered Matty. "How strange," she added after a moment when she saw him kick a stone from his path. "I wonder . . ."

Then she shook her head, releasing the little scene from her mind, and went to the flower room at the back of the house, where she filled two new vases. The ability to form delightful bouquets from almost any flora available was her only ladylike talent, so Matty truly enjoyed the bounty of Miss Abigail's large garden from which to choose her blooms. Finished, she informed a maid where they were to be placed and went up to her room to change from her old gown, which she had not only managed to smudge with green but had also managed to dampen when filling one of the vases.

Changed and brushed, she had almost reached the hall when Steven Howard, who had been watching for her, appeared at the bottom of the stairs and held a hand to her. Reluctantly, Matty placed hers in his and allowed him to help her down the last few steps.

"I have had the gig harnessed," he said. "I thought perhaps, since the day is so lovely, you'd like a drive, like to see something of the area. We could go into Chichester if you wished. Or up onto the downs. Or to the shore. Or," he offered becoming somewhat desperate when Matty showed no interest in any treat so far mentioned, "I understand that the housekeeper at Arundel Castle gives tours. Oh, there are all sorts of things to see and do. Will you come?" he coaxed.

The open door darkened and Matty glanced that way. Vicar Baxter approached, frowning to see her hand resting in Mr. Howard's. Gently she released herself. "Vicar Baxter," she said. "You have, of course, met Miss Abernathy's young friend, Steven Howard?''

"Howard," said Baxter, making a half bow in the younger man's direction, but never looking away from Matty. "I am making a few visits and it occurred to me, Miss Seldon, that you might like to meet a few of Miss Abernathy's humbler neighbors. If you are free, of course. It is a delightful day and . . ."

"Here now! I already asked her to go driving," said Steven, rudely interrupting. "You can't ask her now."

"I *can,*" said the older man somewhat coldly, "and I *have*. Miss Seldon?"

Miss Abernathy, Ned Bright following after, arrived in the hall just then. She took one look at the glowering men and said, "Ah there you are, Miss Seldon. I need a bit of your time, my dear. Will you please join me in my study?" She continued on down the hall, Ned trailing after.

Steven glowered still more, this time casting his glowering look toward Miss Abernathy's back.

Vicar Baxter bowed and said, "You must of course go at once to attend Miss Abernathy. Perhaps another day, my dear Miss Seldon." He bowed again and, without a word to Steven, turned and walked out the doors and down the steps.

Matty cast Steven an apologetic glance. "A ride would have been most delightful, Mr. Howard, but as you see, I must say no."

She turned and Steven, not so easily put off, followed after. When she reached the hall into which Miss Abernathy had disappeared, Matty was glad he had. She hadn't a notion where to find her hostess. She asked.

"I will tell you if you agree to go driving with me as soon as Miss Abigail has finished with you."

"Mr. Howard," said Matty reprovingly, "my

father taught me that I was never ever to give in to blackmail of that nature, that anyone who offered such bargains would, forever more, expect me to ... to ... what is that expression? Knuckle under? Could that possibly be what he said?" When Steven nodded, she added, "Well then, to knuckle under to them forever more. So, no, Mr. Howard, I will not agree, but will find Forbes, who will direct me."

A door farther down the hall opened and Miss Abernathy looked out. "Ah there you are, my dear. Do come. Steven, go away. I will be busy for some time and you, I believe, meant to discuss something with Rutherford. Now would be an excellent ..."

"Oh well," interrupted Steven, "I did that last night. Not that he was much help," he muttered, scowling.

"He told you what you hoped you would not hear?" asked Miss Abernathy sweetly.

Steven blushed. "Oh well," he said and cast his eyes in every direction as if looking for a means to end the conversation. "Mustn't leave the horse standing," he said, his expression lightening at the thought. "Think I'll just toddle off for a little drive all by myself." He bowed to the two women and turned on his heel to disappear back into the entry.

"Now," mused Miss Abernathy, "what has our Steven been up to?" She huffed a soft huff of air. "I've no time for complications. He will just have to sort it out himself and perhaps he will learn a lesson in the doing. Come along, my dear. I wish you to meet Ned Bright, an exceedingly helpful gentleman who has, in the past, accomplished the necessary expeditiously and without raising a dust. Raising a dust?" she repeated brightly, when she saw Matty's shocked expression at the sight of Ned's red waistcoat. "Is that not the correct expression?"

"It is, of course, but perhaps not just in your

style?" asked Ned repressively. "Miss Seldon," he continued, turning toward the younger woman, "Miss Abernathy has told me of your cousin's black-hearted treatment of you. Before I set off to track the villain down and bring him to justice, I would ask you a few questions. First," he said, "can you describe your cousin? Perhaps draw me a picture—" His brows arched. "—or perhaps not," he added when she shook her head. "Miss Seldon?"

"I am no good with either pencil, charcoal, or watercolors, Mr. Bright, but I will do my best to describe in words the man who tricked me so." She did so, calling up every detail she could that might help the runner, who, for a moment when he'd first been introduced, she thought Miss Abernathy had brought in to arrest her for some unknown sin.

The runner asked several more questions, some of which Matty answered and some of which she could not.

"Well, then, I guess that is all I can do here. I will go immediately to Little Conghurst and attempt to pick up his trail from there. And I will see about making the rounds of bookstores to find the one where he sold your father's library. The list of books you have given me will help identify it. It is too bad there is not an inventory of the whole . . . ?"

"If there was, I assume my cousin found it when he cleaned out my father's study."

"Yes. Of course. There would be no reason for you to have packed it and brought it with you. I don't know what I was thinking."

"You were," said Matty, "thinking of anything and everything which would help in your endeavor. I don't know how I can ever thank you and Miss Abernathy for attempting this in my behalf. And, sir, if you find nothing else, I pray you find our family Bible.''

"I will try, but you are aware I am unlikely to return to you anything but the satisfaction of knowing the villain has had his comeuppance, are you not?''

"Yes and I hope for that too. I find myself rather small-mindedly longing for revenge. My father would not approve, but he did not find himself, as I did, in a position that, if it were not for Miss Abernathy's kindness, would have been utter disaster.''

Sometime later Mr. Baxter turned into the drive to Lady Wilingham's mansion. In only a few days she was to leave for her annual visit to her sister and he wished to pay his respects and wish her a good journey and a pleasant visit in Brighton. Or did she mean to go to Bath? He could, poor man, never remember.

"My dear Vicar," said her ladyship when he'd been announced to her, "Do join me in a small repast. I have been on the run constantly for days and days and am quite out of my mind with all the small worries and cares one suffers when one prepares to travel.''

The vicar ignored the fact it was not much over a hundred miles to Bath rather than the thousand her words and tone implied. "Tell me all about it," he suggested, once he'd seated himself and accepted not only a cup of rather weak tea but a plate with two biscuits of a type he did not really like. Lady Wilingham's taste in sweets was, unfortunately, of the plainer, cheaper, sort. As she talked, telling him her woes, he managed to snag one of the tiny fairy cakes, which were, by far, the best thing on offer, and he nodded and sipped, and ate. When it became obvious she was not going to pass the cake plate, he sighed softly and set aside his empty cup. "It sounds a great deal too complicated to contemplate. Perhaps you should not take the light of your features from us but should stay to brighten our days here at home."

She giggled much like a young girl at the compliment but shook her head. "No, although—" She stopped smiling and frowned mightily. "—perhaps I *should*. That chit Abigail took into her home . . . have you heard any more of her?"

"I visited to see how she went on, of course. She and Miss Abernathy were everything great, I thought. I dislike gossip, my dear Lady Wilmingham, but they are not alone. Both," he said in repressive tones, "that awful Rutherford Morton and that flibbertigibbet Steven Howard have come to visit."

"And we all know what that Morton man is like! Perhaps our Miss Abernathy is not so blind as I had thought. Perhaps she invited Morton so that he would take that chit away and install her in the sort of house in which she belongs."

Vicar Baxter's expression grew alarmed. "Lady Wilmingham, I protest. I am certain there is nothing of the sort in Miss Seldon's history. She is so obviously just what she says, the daughter of a vicar. I assure you, it is something a man of my calling could not mistake."

"You, my dear sir," said Lady Wilmingham complacently, "are, after all, merely a man. It is not unreasonable that she pull the wool over *your* eyes, but I find it quite humorous that she has managed to fool our very knowing Miss Abernathy!" And then her ladyship recalled that Rutherford Morgan was visiting Miss Abernathy. "Assuming she has."

The vicar nodded, knowing it did no good at all to argue with Lady Wilmingham when she had made up her mind. "I will continue to keep an eye on the situation while you are gone, my lady. We do not wish," he said with only a mild sort of sarcasm, "to find ourselves murdered in our beds or robbed by the young woman's cohorts."

Lady Wilmingham was not one to recognize sarcasm. Her brows rose. "I had not thought of such a thing. Do you believe it possible? I must remind my butler to check all the windows and all the doors several times a day. Perhaps I should have him post guards during the night hours?"

"I do not think you need concern yourself, Lady Wilmingham," said the vicar, wondering how to retrieve the situation. "I was not serious when I suggested such a thing."

"No of course you were not, but I do not doubt that you have noticed something about the wench you have not really understood and that is why you said it. I will have guards posted," she decided. "I wonder if I should also warn my neighbors . . ."

"I will say all that is necessary," said the vicar quickly.

"Very well. I have so much to do it is not possible to make a round of visits for the purpose. I will trust you to see to everything." She nodded regally and poured herself another cup of tea.

Very soon after, Vicar Baxter said all that was appropriate and, feeling something akin to relief that her ladyship meant to be away for a few weeks, took himself off.

Chapter Six

Charles North looked from the window of his hired post chaise. They were, he judged, within five miles of his goal. Finally. A broken axle, a cast shoe, and a small posting house that had no team available had put him hours and hours behind schedule.

One of these days, he thought, *I must buy my own carriage.*

He had had little use for one for many years, determined as he was to make a success of his chosen profession. His stubborn dedication to work and study had paid off, and now, when added to the allowance his father gave him and the quite satisfactory income from an inheritance from his godfather, he was more than just comfortable. In fact, he could, if he so desired, now afford some of the elegancies of life.

Including, he had decided some time previously, the luxury of a wife.

So, for the last two Seasons, he had indulged in a more active social life, accepting invitations to a few of the more interesting *ton* parties. He had even, twice, entered the sacred portals of Almack's.

Those visits had been sufficient. His notions of finding a wife differed, it seemed, from the usual practice, since he could not bring himself to look over the current offerings on the marriage mart, select one to pursue, and then, after a few awkward meetings, wed and bed her. He wanted more from marriage than his peers seemed to think necessary.

Which, he thought ruefully, *is one reason I am enduring this exceedingly uncomfortable journey at Miss Abernathy's request. If she had not made that intriguing comment concerning her newest protégée, I would very likely be sitting snug and warm in my favorite chair while Timmy yet again polished my boots. Or, since I had meant to go to my brother's, more likely I'd be enduring some insipid do in Brighton.* He shook his head, laughing softly. *Much better to visit Miss Abby despite the series of minor disasters we have had to overcome.*

But then he shivered. It might be late spring but the nights were still overly cool and he had not dressed for it, thinking to have arrived when the sun was still high in the sky.

"Want I get your flapper?" asked Timmy.

"My what?"

"That caped coat you just bought."

"Timmy, how often must I chide you for using cant."

"Didn't." The lad pouted.

"Then what is this word, 'flapper'?"

"Made it up."

Charles repressed a chuckle. The boy was irrepressible but it would not do to encourage him. "I suppose I must now chide you for calling a coat by a made-up word. Is it so very difficult, calling things by the names they are known by?"

"Makes me sound a prig," groused the lad.

"A prig? I sound a prig?" asked Charles politely.

Timmy's eyes opened wide. "No! Never said that.

Not you." His scowl returned. "Don't sound the same when I say 'em."

"I see." Charles thought about it. "No, I don't see. In what way is it different?"

"Don't feel right on my tongue, I guess," said Timmy, after thinking about it for a bit himself.

"Perhaps with practice . . . ?"

Timmy slouched, putting one foot on the seat beside Charles. He shoved his hands into his pockets.

"Timmy."

"Oh very well. I'll practice. Coat," he muttered. "Coat. Coat. Coat."

Charles, this time, laughed and noticed that Timmy glanced at him from under his lashes. He shook his head. "You, Timmy Gardener, deserve a smack."

Charles felt the coach slow for a turn and again glanced from his window. The bright moon and star-heavy sky gave enough light so that he recognized the gatehouse leading to Miss Abernathy's home.

"At last." He sighed. "What an abominable hour to arrive."

"Abommmminininable," repeated Timmy softly.

Charles hid another smile. The lad might find the *ton's* break-teeth words, as he called them, hard to use, but he was always alert to add new ones to his vocabulary.

" 'Tain't so late," the boy added once he'd assured himself he'd not forget the new word. "Not past eleven."

"Yes, but we are in the country, are we not? You know very well a country household takes to its beds far earlier than in town."

"Not an abommmininable hour in the city?"

"Not at all abominable," said Charles, tongue

in cheek. "In the Season, there are many entertainments which only get under way at eleven. Here people would be saying their good-byes and heading for their homes."

"Abomminnable," muttered Timmy.

Another few tries and he'll have it, thought Charles and watched impatiently for his carriage to arrive at the Hall's front door. When it did, he forbore waiting for the steps to be put down, but jumped to the ground and headed up the stairs to the massive front doors, where he lifted the iron dog's head and let it fall against the plate. He turned and smiled to see Timmy ordering the coachman and his outrider to be careful with the guv's boxes and bags, that there weren't to be any scratches when they'd finished unloading.

There was an exchange of personalities between Timmy and the coachman, but the luggage was being lifted down with care even so. Charles was known to tip well—when not displeased.

Charles turned back to the door and let the knocker hit the plate again and then again. Again he waited. This time he was rewarded with the sound of latches being unlatched, a chain dropping, and a heavy bar set to one side. Then the door opened.

"You," said a voice Charles frowned to hear. Rutherford stood in the open doorway, a nearly empty mug of ale in his hand.

"Morton?"

"What are *you* doing here?"

"I was invited." Charles didn't half like the notion that Miss Abigail might have filled her house with eligible men with an eye toward finding one for her protégée. Especially this one. "What of yourself?"

"Stopped by on my way to Brighton," said Rutherford, unknowingly relieving Charles's mind. He stepped back. "I suppose you brought along that jailbait valet person," he added, peering beyond Charles. "Always wonder if I'll be murdered in my bed whenever I find myself under the same roof as that one."

"He might pinch your ticker, but he won't put a sticker in your other ticker," said Charles with a deadpan look.

"Ticker . . ." Morton swilled down the last of his ale. "And *ticker?*"

"Watch and heart. One learns a great deal new vocabulary when one is with Timmy for any length of time."

"If he steals from me he'll find himself before the magistrate faster than he can say anything at all."

"If he steals from you, I'll have him before the magistrate, never fear, will I not, Timmy?"

"Don't steal."

"Anymore," said Charles, grinning.

Timmy eyed him. "Anymore," he agreed. He shrugged his new spring coat onto his shoulders. "Don't have to, do I?"

"And a very good thing, too," scolded Rutherford. "The ladies have gone up to bed. There is a cold collation set out in the game room if you feel peckish. Forbes is around somewhere and will set a couple of footmen to lugging your traps up . . . Ah there you are, Forbes. As you see, North has arrived." He turned on his heel and disappeared in the direction of the game room, his empty mug swinging between finger and thumb.

"Forbes? I'm to have my usual rooms?" Forbes bowed slightly, his eye on the two footmen who were bringing in Charles's trunks and bandboxes. "You, Timmy, may go up and see to the unpacking. If you need it, Forbes will find you a slice or two of meat and cheese once you are done. I'll just see what Morton is doing in the game room."

"Young Mr. Howard is also in the game room," said Forbes in repressive tones.

"Is he now? Miss Abernathy has her house very nearly overly full of guests, does she not?"

For half a moment Charles watched Forbes struggle against agreeing. Forbes had reached an age where he did not care for the extra work involved in having guests. "Miss Abernathy is enjoying herself a great deal," he said, finally.

"I am sure she is," said Charles and, thinking that nothing was likely to be truer, strolled off in Rutherford's wake.

The next morning Charles stood at his window and stared down at the south lawn, where a strange woman had assembled Miss Abby's pets. The goat munched on flowers from a nearby bush, the monkey sat on the woman's shoulder, his long arm clutching her around her forehead, and the two cats sat to one side, aloof but determined they'd not be left out. The dogs, except for the half-grown dachshund sat in a half circle, staring with obvious adoration up into the woman's face. Twice she sat the pup in place. Twice it followed her back to where she stood laughing down at it. She shook her finger at it and, for the third time, moved it back into place in the row. She put her hand on the three-legged poodle's head and turned it to look at the pup. She said something. The older dog nudged the pup back a bit with his nose. The pup, abashed, hunched down, its ears drooping. The older dogs waved their tails gently against the turf.

What, wondered Charles, *will happen next*? He lifted one arm and rested it against the window frame, leaning out the opening in his attempt to hear.

"Now, Beau," said the woman's soft and very pleasant voice.

The poodle limped forward. He sniffed whatever it was the woman held in her hand, looked up, wagged its tail, and waited. Even from so far away, Charles could see the animal tremble with excitement. Suddenly the woman threw whatever it was and the dog, bobbling along at a rapid pace, raced after it. The woman turned quickly, caught the young dog, and pressed it back into position in line.

One after another she threw the thing for a dog and had it returned and dropped at her feet. Finally, it was the dachshund's turn. It waddled happily up to the girl, sniffed the object, looked up at her, and turned back to sit in his place.

Hands on hips, she frowned down at him. "Come, Bundle."

Obediently the pup again approached. This time, once he'd sniffed, he turned his head and flopped onto his side.

"You are a lazy beast, Bundle. You need to exercise or you will grow so fat your tummy will drag along the floor."

The tail wagged in response.

"But it is quite true, I assure you." She again offered the object. Again the pup sniffed it. You could almost see a sigh of resignation as the animal climbed to its feet.

Charles smiled. The woman threw the thing only half so far as she'd done for the others. When the young dog brought it back to her she began the whole exercise all over again. At one point the tomcat approached. He looked up at the woman and meowed plaintively. She smiled and said,

"Patience, Ugly. You and Princess will have your share in a moment."

Charles, who had been about to leave his post to dress, waited.

Very soon she patted each dog, roughly or gently, as she perceived it preferred, and turned to the cats. The tom approached avidly, the white cat with great dignity. The tom meowed.

"Very well. But you are very greedy, you know." The woman dug a packet from her pocket and opened it. She gave a bit to each cat and then turned to where the dogs trembled in excited anticipation. She fed each one a bit and again patted them. "That's all," she said and watched the dogs race off toward the back of the house, the poodle straying behind to match the fat little dachshund's pace.

"You too," she said, when the tom meowed again. "You've had your share and you were not asked to work for it. Now go do your duty and chase down the mice Cook complained of only yesterday." The white cat licked its paw once or twice, wiped it over her face, and then turned and walked off in the direction taken by the dogs. The tom rubbed against the woman's ankles. She leaned down, tickled him behind his ears, and then straightened. "Enough is enough. I've the flowers to do, Ugly, and you've mice to catch."

The long-haired goat trotted up just then and butted Miss Seldon from behind. Catching herself she turned and, laughing, stood, hands on hips, looking down at the beast. The goat blatted.

"Ah! I see. You are missing your friend are you not?" She reached up and disentangled the monkey from where it grasped her head, lifted it down, and sat it on the goat's back. "There you go." She watched the goat, bearing the monkey, trot off and then picked up a long, shallow basket and shears

Charles had not previously noticed. Charles, suddenly realizing this was the woman about whom Miss Abigail had written, was pleased he'd shaved before going to the window. He would dress quickly, take the nearby secondary steps down, and be near a door leading to the cutting garden.

This, thought Charles, *is the perfect opportunity to get to know Miss Seldon.* He was wrong.

When he approached the garden he discovered Rutherford and Steven already there. They must have discovered Miss Seldon's schedule and decided to approach her while she worked. He came up behind her.

"Introduce me, Rutherford," he said.

The woman jerked upright, the flowers in her hand flying every which way and the shears pointing dangerously near to Charles's chin. He gently lowered them but retained a hold on her wrist as she turned abruptly to face him.

"Good morning," he said, studying her features rather more intently than might be considered polite.

"Good heavens above! You startled me."

"Rutherford?" asked Charles, still staring down at her. Somehow he'd been caught in the magic of her eyes and could not look away.

"Miss Seldon, this reprobate is known to the world as Charles North. You will, of course, ignore his existence. Charles, do let the poor girl loose!"

Charles winced as he realized how uncivilized was his behavior. He lifted the hand he held to his lips and then managed to release her. Speaking softly, he said, "Miss Seldon. It is a delight to meet you."

He was surprised to discover it was not a merely polite statement. He was delighted. The graceful woman he'd watched with the dogs was taller than he'd expected and he was pleased to note she did not attempt to make herself seem smaller by any of the idiotic tricks tall women used in an era when the tiny fairylike woman was the ideal. She neither bowed her shoulders, ducked her head, nor dipped her knees, a stance that made a tall woman waddle when she walked. Too, there were wonderful reddish tints glinting in her overlong mahogany-colored hair, but her best feature was those eyes with their well-defined brows and dark lashes protecting deep blue orbs. Not that she had perfect features. Her nose was perhaps a trifle too prominent and her chin decidedly too firm for current tastes in beauty, but the whole revealed a great deal of character and Charles, much against his will, was instantly aware of an attraction he should not be feeling.

Not, at least, until he ascertained that she was all she should be!

"Mr. North," said Steven, who had come around the bed and now jerked at Charles's sleeve. "Mr. North!"

"Hmm? Yes? Ah! Steven Howard. I had not noticed you." He had, actually, but Steven was very much like the puppy with which Miss Seldon had had to deal firmly. One dare not allow him free rein, or he would rapidly become irrepressible. Charles turned from Miss Seldon and, his hand on Steven's arm, walked off with him.

Miss Seldon stared after him. "Who is that?" she asked.

"I told you."

She turned to stare at Rutherford, her eyes wide and her face rather pale. "Who?"

"He is merely a solicitor who runs errands for Miss Abigail," said Rutherford dismissively. "Have you finished cutting flowers?" he asked.

He glanced toward where Steven was talking to
Charles. What was he saying to North? *Or,* thought
Rutherford, *how* much *is he saying?* Rutherford was
all too conscious of the exact topic of his cousin's
conversation and, since he had not decided what,
if anything, he'd do about it, was not pleased to
see Steven asking further advice, if not aid, of
another. For too long Steven had looked up to
him and, he ruefully discovered, he didn't like the
notion that admiration might go to another.

"You would like to join them," said Matty politely, seeing a way of ridding herself of his
unwanted presence. "Please do." She held out her
hand for her basket and, without a glance, Rutherford thrust it at her.

Matty, glad he was gone, nevertheless found herself cutting flowers pretty much at random. Saying
that Mr. North was a solicitor in that insulting fashion made him *more* interesting in Matty's eyes, not
less. A "mere" solicitor, after all, was not so far
above her unimportant self that she felt it impossible she might raise her eyes to him as someone
available, a man she'd felt drawn to in a way she
hadn't even felt for poor Jeremy, a man she
might . . .

. . . actually wed.

Matty gasped. She had put into words the
thought that had hovered in her mind from the
moment she'd looked into the square-chinned face
with its high forehead and generous nose. She liked
the medium dark hair that looked clean and
healthy, *alive,* and she approved of the conservative
style that she had been told by one of her father's
more modish parishioners was invented by Mr.
Brummell.

She found herself stealing glances toward where
the three men now conversed quietly.

How, she wondered, *did he get that gloss on his boots?*

And then, looking at the overblown bloom in her hand, the petals actually falling from it, she chided herself for a fool and concentrated on filling her basket with blossoms suitable to the bouquets she meant to put in the long drawing room.

Chapter Seven

"So you sent Bitsy to check up on her. You are quite certain this is the particular Miss Seldon who recently lost her father?"

"Charles, am I so lacking in forethought?"

"I'd not of thought so, but I must be certain."

Miss Abernathy allowed one brow to arch in much the fashion of Rutherford and, for the first time, Charles saw the relationship. With the arched brow one could see what was hidden from casual observation by their very different characters.

He smiled a rather rueful smile. "You are questioning why I am so adamant, are you not?"

"Yes."

"I first saw your protégée from my window." He described her behavior with the dogs. "When I joined her in the cutting garden . . ."

Charles's thoughts turned inward with the memory and he lost his train of thought. Miss Abernathy's chuckles brought him back to the present.

"Struck by a *coup de foudre* were you?" she asked, smiling.

Charles compressed his lips and then allowed them to relax. "Perhaps the French have that right," he admitted reluctantly. "Or perhaps not. I would not say it was lightning that struck me so much as that I felt as if I were drowning . . . Not the most beautiful woman I've ever met, of course."

"No, nor the most ugly," said Abigail.

"Definitely not," he said, and then realized she was teasing him. "You think me a fool."

"Certainly not. I have always thought your taste in women highly developed. After all—" A quick, slashing grin crossed Abigail's features and disappeared. "—you like *me*."

Charles chuckled. Then he sobered. "In your letter you said this young woman reminded you of yourself at that age."

"Exactly."

Charles stared at her, blinking, and after a moment in which he said nothing she added, "Never mind. Either you will or you won't and only time will tell. I would say, however, that everything is off to an excellent start." She came close to pouting. "I do wish Rutherford and Steven would go about their business."

"Surely you do not fear that Morton will seduce your ewe lamb under your very roof!"

"No . . . o . . . o . . ."

Charles felt a touch of shock. *"You do."*

"No, no. Definitely not. But he is capable of making a nuisance of himself. And Steven. Charles, you will laugh. When he thinks he has her quite alone he reads his poetry to her!"

"Poor girl."

"Yes. It would be kind if we do not allow them too much time alone. Especially you, Charles."

Charles grinned. "Abby," he said, forgetting proper forms, "is this you? Would you really turn your hand to matchmaking?"

Miss Abernathy tipped her head to the side. "I

might. Or is it not true you are in the market for a wife?"

"You know I am. Or rather that I have thought about looking about myself for such a one."

"Ah. Well then. That's settled, then. I'll do my best to forward the match."

Charles instantly frowned. "Abigail . . . about Miss Seldon . . ."

"Charles, you should trust me."

He merely stared.

"My dear boy, I sent a sketch with Bitsy. Miss Seldon is who she says she is. Did *you* set forward a search for relatives?"

Charles was once again fading into deep thought and had to force himself to think. "Search . . . ? I set my solicitor to work on it. A Baron Pelling exists and he'll start there. Finding her maternal relatives may be more difficult, assuming Pelling is *not* a relation and can tell us nothing of Reverend and Mrs. Seldon."

"Your man will do his best." Then Abigail grimaced in a fashion that did *not* cause disgust as the same expression might on another's face. "There are times, however, when I rather hope we will not discover the people who should be responsible for her. I am enjoying her company far too well to have her leave me any time soon."

"I doubt it will be long before we know something," warned Charles.

"Hmm. And when they admit the relationship and offer her shelter, then it will be necessary to discover how she'll be treated. I will not have her go to be a drudge in some hard-hearted relative's house."

"Did I hear a warning, my best of good friends?"

"Not to *you*. Only that I will hire her for a companion before I allow her relatives to turn her into a poor relation totally dependent on them. She deserves far better than to dwindle into an old maid serving my interests, but I know she'd be well treated under my roof."

"Do not allow yourself to get carried away until we know more."

"Advice you might take to heart yourself," she retorted and rang a hand bell. A footman entered. "Where is Miss Seldon hiding herself?" she asked.

"She is in the library, madam. Reading, I believe."

"*Alone?*"

"Yes, madam. As per your orders, we do not know Miss Seldon's whereabouts if Mr. Morton or Mr. Howard requests such information."

"And have they asked?"

"The both of them, madam."

"So . . . where are the gentlemen now?"

"I believe Mr. Morton rode into the village and Mr. Howard has closeted himself in the sitting room to his suite. He called for still more paper and fresh ink, madam."

"Oh dear," she said, her voice very slightly gruffer even than usual. "*More* poetry. Charles," she said, turning to him, "do go and retrieve our Miss Seldon so she may join us for a tea tray. Jasper," she added, turning back to the footman, "ask Cook to send up just the sort of tray I like at this time of day. She'll know."

Later that evening Charles stood near the door to the salon and observed its occupants. Miss Abernathy had involved Rutherford in conversation. Occasionally he glanced across the room to where Miss Seldon sat on a slipper chair, her ankles neatly crossed and her hands loosely clasped in her lap, but he was well enough amused by whatever it was Miss Abernathy discussed, that he made no effort to leave his hostess's side.

Miss Seldon, her head slightly bowed, listened

patiently to Steven's verses with only the occasional, barely noticeable, wince. For a moment he considered joining the two, but then the thought that he, too, might be forced to listen to Steven's very bad verse, sent him off toward the pianoforte, which, as he'd heard, had been visited by the piano tuner only that morning.

Charles had, on an earlier visit, attempted to play the instrument and discovered it so out of tune, his music was unrecognizable, but playing of an evening had become a habit. He not only enjoyed it, but had discovered his thoughts settled and decisions could be made while he played. His snug rooms were barely large enough to accommodate the necessary piece of furniture, but his playing was excellent and his neighbors did not complain. That is, they did not complain on those rare occasions when they happened to be at home at a time when he indulged himself. *And* assuming his own tuner had recently paid a visit—pianofortes, unfortunately, did not stay tuned for long and needed the services of a tuner far more often than one liked.

Because he was not alone, Charles played softly. His first choice was a variation on "Greensleeves," an old favorite of his father's. He followed that with a sonata composed for the pianoforte by Leopold Kotzeluch. He moved on to a currently popular ditty, which he had yet to perfect and soon abandoned. His thoughts turned to Miss Abernathy and her decision to marry him off to Miss Seldon and, while he debated just how cooperative he'd be in this effort, his hands moved on to yet another new piece, a composition by Herr Beethoven that had recently found its way to London and which his supplier had sent around to his rooms with the suggestion Charles would find it interesting.

Charles had. It was quite different from anything

he'd previously attempted and he'd found its powerful tones and difficult phrasing intriguing. He put aside all thought of his future and, deeply involved in his music and forgetting his audience, he played more loudly. Then more loudly still.

The music filled the room.

Forbes found an excuse to enter by pretending he must attend to a fire that did not require attending. He rearranged the tea tray, which Miss Abernathy had not yet touched. He picked up a newspaper the footman should have picked up much earlier . . .

It rustled . . .

. . . so he set it down again as quietly as he could. A footman moved a trifle from his place across the hall, coming nearer the salon. A maid who had been sent from the kitchen to see if everything was properly cleared from the dining room edged her way toward the footman and, as well as she was able, hid behind him.

Miss Abernathy's voice drifted away into silence.

Miss Seldon shushed Steven, who, when he heard Charles's music, flushed rosily, his jaw clenching at the thought that Miss Seldon found the music of more importance than poems written in her honor. But then he, too, found himself caught up in the soaring notes.

Only Rutherford sat back and, his eyes on Miss Seldon, found the whole a dead bore and wondered if there was the least possibility of getting the young woman alone that evening. Even for so little as fifteen minutes . . . His plotting kept him silent so the others had no difficulty enjoying the music.

"Excellent," said Miss Abernathy when Charles came to the end. She clapped loudly and was joined by the others.

Even, for half a moment, by Forbes, who knew

better than to pretend he existed, but was so enthralled by Charles's playing he forgot and clapped anyway. The footman, surreptitiously backing back to his place, bumped into the maid, who squeaked, blushed rosily, and then ran for the baize door to the servants' area. The footman, silently swearing at the chit for drawing attention to him, attained his usual position, determined that, if Old Forbes said one word to him for venturing from his place, he'd have a few to say right back at him about his own imprudence.

In the salon, Miss Seldon stared at Charles, surprised to discover he was such an excellent musician. "Please, Mr. North, what was that? I have never before heard it, I am sure."

Charles, rather embarrassed that he'd drawn everyone's attention his way, rose to his feet. "There is a shop in London I've patronized for years. The owner is kind enough to watch for music he thinks I'd like and he sends it to me. He found me this piece by the composer Herr Beethoven, a German I believe. My source tells me the poor man is going quite deaf. A terrible fate for a man who composes such magnificent music."

"A terrible fate indeed. For all of us as well as the poor gentleman himself."

"Why so?" asked Rutherford, who was tone deaf and had never understood anyone's interest in music.

"Because if he is deaf he'll compose no more. It is a shame."

"Do you enjoy music so much, Miss Seldon?" asked Charles when he saw Rutherford was about to make a sneering response. And then he wondered why he'd put himself out to save Ruthie from making a fool of himself.

"Yes," responded Matty a trifle shyly. "My father, occasionally, as a special treat, would take us into

Canterbury when the choir presented special performances. I can remember when I was only a child. Perhaps eight? He allowed me to stand between his legs and lean against him and I recall that I never took my eyes from the musicians. It was wonderful."

"Personally, I prefer poetry," said Steven, the faintest of sour notes in his tone.

"I enjoy good poetry—"

Charles wondered how she managed to say that with no special emphasis on the word "good" since she'd been listening to Steven's more than amateurish efforts.

"—but music! It is so very special."

Steven bowed and, without a word, left the room.

"Oh dear . . ."

"Do not look so conscience-stricken, my dear child," said Miss Abernathy with a smile that added a twinkle to her eyes. "Steven may have been ever so slightly insulted, but he will soon recover."

"But I did not mean to . . . I was not thinking of . . ."

"No of course you did not, were not." Miss Abernathy looked around, counting noses. She reached for the bell sitting on the tea tray and rang it. The footman entered. "The card table, Jasper. We will play whist."

"But I do not play," exclaimed Miss Seldon.

"We will teach you," said Miss Abernathy, her voice firm and it would have taken someone much stronger than Matty to tell the woman she had no wish to learn.

Chapter Eight

The next morning Matty yawned her way down the stairs and to the back of the house, where the dogs awaited her arrival. The dachshund yapped once and then gave the poodle an irritated look when the three-legged dog nipped him.

"Where are the cats?" asked Matty.

The white cat simply appeared, winding around Matty's skirts and looking up at her. Matty leaned down and petted her. "And your friend?" The cat meowed. "I hope he is all right," said Matty. The white cat licked her shoulder. "Ah. Well, that is good," said Matty, interpreting the animal's behavior as that of an unworried friend. "Shall we go?" she added, looking around. The monkey climbed down the vines winding up the side of the house and dropped onto her shoulder. "Hmm," said Matty, looking at the chittering beast. "*You,* you silly creature, were very nearly left behind."

They moved around the house to where Matty treated them each morning to their special run and, incidentally, a kind but firm hand used in training them. Princess was soon bored with watching the dogs run after the object Matty threw for them and wandered off. The monkey clambered up into a nearby tree and "criticized" the dogs' efforts. And, just as Matty was ready to quit and do flowers, Princess and the rakish tomcat appeared, ready for their treat.

Charles met her by the flowerbed. "You are very good with the creatures," he said, amused by her classroom technique.

"You watched?" she asked, her cheeks touched with the rose of embarrassment.

"From my window. I've an excellent view." He tipped his head toward the house.

"Oh dear." She glanced that way and the rose color deepened. "I did not think . . ."

"If you are worried that Ruthie or Steven have observed you, you will note they sleep with the curtains and windows tightly closed. I, however, have never been particularly impressed by the theory that night air is harmful."

She nodded. "If night air were harmful, then everyone would stay indoors from sunset to sunrise and we do not, do we?"

"My thinking exactly."

They stared at each other, smiling. Matty realized her expression must be particularly inane and, quickly, reached for her scissors and bent to her work. "I rather enjoyed my lesson in playing whist, but I fear it was dreadfully boring for the rest of you," she offered when the silence seemed to have stretched just a trifle too long.

"Hmm? Oh no. You are never boring, Miss Seldon."

She cast him a disbelieving look.

He chuckled. "That did sound rather trite and *boring*, did it not?"

"Very Stevenish," she agreed and then blushed red. "Oh dear. That was not well said of me!"

"I have marveled at your patience," offered

Charles and held out the basket so she could lay the bloom she held onto the long shallow bed.

"Poor boy. The pangs of young love and being in love with love can be so tiresome for others, but, I think, a necessary part of growing up." After a moment Matty glanced at Charles and then away. "He is worried about something," she said in an offhanded manner.

Charles nodded. "Yes. Like many cubs when first on the Town he fell into the hands of a Captain Sharp. He owes the man money he cannot pay and is afraid to go to his father. On the other hand, he thinks the man cheated and doesn't think he ought to have to pay. He has, I think, asked Ruthie to help him prove the man a slippery customer who, er, diddled the pasteboards. Ruthie, for reasons I've yet to ascertain, pooh-poohs Steven's belief but is himself unhappy about something to do with the man, whoever he may be."

"Is Mr. Morgan also under an obligation to Steven's Captain Sharp?"

"Hmm." Again he held out the basket and again Matty laid a long stemmed bloom into it. "I had not thought of that. You are a sagacious woman, Miss Seldon."

"Nonsense. I have simply had a great deal of experience dealing with the problems of a village in which many different types of people reside. My father was . . . was . . . well, I sometimes thought him a saint. He was otherworldly, if you know what I mean."

"Which meant that you must deal with his congregation's problems?"

"Many people came to me. Oh, not with big things, not when their faith was involved, but with their little everyday sort of problems. They loved my father and were proud to have him as their vicar, but they knew he wasn't of much use when it came to practical matters."

"So you learned to understand people and the clues they give one, often without knowing they are doing so." He nodded. "I have learned much the same thing by dealing with the men and women I defend before the bar."

"Defend . . . ?"

"I'm a barrister. Did Miss Abernathy not explain . . . ?"

"Mr. Morgan said you were a solicitor," she said, a trifle more on her stiffs than she'd previously behaved when she'd thought him more her social equal.

"Hmm. Did he do so? I wonder why."

"Perhaps," she said, still a trifle withdrawn, "he thought to do me a service."

"Or do me a disservice."

She glanced up and then, quickly, back down at the flowers she was sorting, finding the stems she wished to cut.

"Miss Seldon, I am no different from how I was five minutes ago. Do not change toward me as you are doing."

She stilled. "I am, am I not?" She straightened and looked at him straightly. "It is bred into us, is it not? This knowledge of our place in the world which eases our way, telling us with whom we may relax and to whom we must show deference?"

He chuckled but then sobered. "I wonder," he mused.

"Wonder?" Again she dared to raise her eyes to meet his steady gaze.

"Wonder if such knowledge is not more a barrier to life than a way of easing one's life by teaching us how to behave on all occasions."

She tipped her head. "You would say we are too rigidly confined and miss a great deal because we

dare not go beyond our own tightly drawn boundaries?"

"I will be very unhappy, Miss Seldon," he said
softly, "if you draw boundaries which exclude me."

Again she dared look at him and a certain
warmth in his gaze drew her. Color came and went
in her cheeks and, quickly, she returned to her
work. Very soon, she laid the final flower into the
basket and straightened. "I must put these in water
at once," she said, reaching for the basket.

"Yes. It is rather heavy and I will carry it for you."

It would be undignified to struggle for possession
of the flowers so she let go. And, since there was
no getting rid of him, as she wished to do so that she
might attempt to sort out what had just happened
between them, she'd no alternative but to allow
him to stroll beside her to the back of the house
and into the stone-floored room set aside for the
making of bouquets.

Nor did he leave her while she worked. "You do
that very well, you know," he said. "I do not believe
that I have ever before seen such lovely bouquets
here at Miss Abernathy's."

"It is," admitted Matty, "my one talent. The
sort of talent a young lady should exhibit, I mean.
Although I should not, perhaps, say that. Particularly not here where the blooms are so profuse that
one has choice beyond need and anyone might
form a bouquet worthy of the King."

"Ah! There you are," said Miss Abernathy, coming into the workroom just then. "Forbes was right.
As he usually is. And you, too, Charles? I sent the
footmen searching for you. I have planned a picnic.
We will drive up on the Downs to a place I know
where we may set up the telescope and look out
over the Channel. I love watching the ships and
attempting to identify them. Come along. Jenny
will finish that, will you not, Jenny?" she asked of

the maid who had been hovering nearby, watching intently to see how the flowers were placed so as to make such wonderful displays.

Jenny blushed. "I'll try, ma'am, but I can't do the job Miss Seldon does. She's a great hand at flowers, Miss Abernathy, ma'am."

Matty's cheeks matched the maid's.

"Look, Charles. They are *both* blushing." Miss Abernathy laughed.

An hour later Matty turned away from where Rutherford helped Miss Abernathy set up her telescope on a rise of ground not far from where footmen set up tables and chairs for their picnic. The view out over the flat lowlands and on to the channel was incredible. Matty had never before seen the coast or the huge expanse of water beyond and she had stared at it for a long, long moment.

To see it for the first time from such a distance is surely more intriguing, she thought, *than if one were standing on the shore near it.*

"What are you thinking?" asked Charles softly, bemused by the awed look on her face.

"What? Oh." She told him.

He, too, looked at the distant prospect. "I think I understand what you mean," he said slowly. "It is like a story laid out before one, a good one that makes one wish to read on, to learn more."

She turned to stare at him. "That is exactly what it is like. Thank you."

"Why do you thank me? It was you who put the thought into my head."

"But I would never have had the words to express it so neatly."

"Words," said Steven, approaching in time to hear this last, "are very important." He tugged his coat around so as to be able to pull a small roll of paper from the pocket in the tail of his coat. Very slowly, his eyes holding Matty's, he pulled on the ribbon bound around it. Still holding her gaze, he unrolled the sheets and held them up. Only then did he turn his eyes from her.

"Steven . . ." began Charles.

"Mr. Howard," said Matty at the same moment. And then each fell silent, deferring to the other and it was too late.

"The sea less blue, the rose more pale, one look at you, that tells the tale," said Steven and looked expectantly at Matty.

"But, Mr. Howard," said Matty, pretending bemusement, "if that is to me, then I feel I must inform you I am not at all sad. Not at all."

He reread his words and frowned. "The color refers to your lovely blue eyes," he said with a touch of accusation. "I did not mean that you were blue-deviled!"

"Or that she was an intellectual woman?" asked Charles, smiling.

"Oh." She realized more was required of her. "Well . . . the thought is very pretty."

"And your lovely complexion sets the rose in the shade," added Steven.

"What sort of rose?" asked Charles. "Some are white, some a deep red, and one finds every shade in between. One must know exactly . . ."

"You are," interrupted Steven, "deliberately making difficulties." He scowled at Charles. "I am certain Miss Seldon knows I would use only the most flattering of comparisons when writing poetry in her honor."

"Of course I do, Mr. Howard," said Matty, wishing she knew how to depress his pretensions. "But occasionally one wishes to converse in . . . in . . ."

"Prose?" suggested Charles.

"Well, I don't suppose I'd have used that word,

but yes, that is what I mean. Poetry is wonderful but it has its place, don't you know?" After days of politely listening to Steven read his less than adequate verses, she was growing a trifle desperate.

"But I thought you liked my reading to you," he said a trifle plaintively.

"I think Miss Seldon means that she does but doesn't wish it all the time. That there are other things she wishes to do, perhaps."

"Like . . . like . . . ?" Steven gave it up and stared at Miss Seldon. Then he drew a deep breath and said, rather plaintively, "But there are no shops. One cannot go shopping. And there is no music. One cannot dance." He stared around. Suddenly his features lightened. "Ah! You would like a glass of lemonade." And off he rushed to ask a footman to pour one for her.

"I believe," said Charles just a trifle pensively, "that the lemonade is still on the cart. Perhaps if we were to stroll that way—" He pointed toward an outcropping of rock. "—we could be out of the way before he returns?"

"A stroll is *just* the sort of entertainment I was wanting," said Matty firmly. *Especially* if their walk took her away from Steven's seemingly vacuous mind, which, so far as he'd revealed, was filled with nothing but conventional manners and uninteresting thoughts.

By waiting until Steven was preoccupied with haranguing the footmen to greater efforts, they managed their escape. Charles, knowing it was quite wrong to take Matty off so that they were alone together, chose a route which curved around the high point on which Miss Abernathy directed Rutherford where and how to place her telescope. Matty caught her hostess's eye and waved at her. Miss Abernathy nodded and turned back to seeing that the tripod was settled firmly and did not wobble.

"I have not seen her use a telescope before," said Matty, saying the only thing running through her mind she felt suitable for speech with the man walking at her side. Most of her thoughts were, she felt, totally unsuitable. In fact, they were things she should not even be *thinking*.

"Hmm? The telescope? It is a hobby of long standing. She once mentioned the instrument belonged to an old friend of hers and that when he died he left it to her."

"Does she study the stars, then?"

"Yes. She searches for comets, I believe. Yes, that is it. She said she wishes to be first to discover a new one so that she may name it in honor of the man to whom the telescope once belonged."

"An interesting way in which to honor his memory, is it not?" asked Matty.

Charles grinned down at her. "Yes, but an ambition unlikely to be achieved. Miss Abernathy spends too little time at it. Others, more persistent, are likelier to discover her comet before *she* finds it."

"But still, a nice thought. Such a monument to a man's memory would be forever, would it not?"

"Certainly far longer than anything man is likely to construct here on earth. Hunt recently published one of his friend's poems on that very subject. Did you see it?"

She shook her head.

"Shelley wrote about an ancient tyrant and, after describing a ruined, broken, statue lying in miles of barren sand, he penned, 'And on the pedestal these words appear: My name is Ozymandias, king of kings; Look on my works, ye Mighty, and despair! Nothing beside remains, Round the decay of that colossal wreck' and so on, but I am boring you with more poetry when you admit you've suffered enough of that sort of thing."

"This is different from tributes to one's eyebrows or the dimple in one's chin. Can you," she asked diffidently, "recite the whole?"

Charles was happy to have something so innocuous to do when the things he wished to say to this woman would *not* do. Not at all. At least not so soon after meeting her. He had just finished quoting the whole of the rather short poem when Rutherford's voice called their attention to the top of the hill.

"Yes?" responded Charles.

"Our picnic is ready for us," yelled Rutherford, frowning down at them. "Miss Abernathy says I am to tell you that you will reach the table soonest by continuing on around the hill."

"Very well." Charles offered his arm and he and Matty set out at a brisker pace than they'd used to reach this point. "I believe," said Charles, "that our walk was just the thing. My appetite appears to have improved and I am now ready for a luncheon. And you?"

"To eat. But . . ." She paused and then, subdued, she added, "Yes, of course."

Charles glanced down at her. "Of what were you thinking Miss Seldon?" When she didn't respond, he continued. "I would be your friend. Friends wish to help each other, you know."

Matty's lips pressed together as she realized that friendship was not what she wished from this man she'd known so briefly. "I was thinking," she began slowly, wondering how to phrase it so he'd not be embarrassed, but without lying, "that with the weather so perfect, the day so lovely, the company so right—well, that perhaps I am wrong to feel so happy?"

"Because your father is not long dead?"

"Yes."

"Would not he have wished you to be happy?"

"He was not so selfish as to wish me misery."
She sighed. "Still, I miss him terribly and it feels
wrong to delight in so much when he will never
again enjoy such treats."

"But, my dear," said Charles, a trifle surprised,
"I thought you said he was rather otherworldly. I
assumed his head was so much in the clouds that
he would not have noticed the day or the company
or . . ." He stopped. "You shake your head."

"He loved music, beauty, and good conversation.
He was happy at parties watching the young enjoy
their dancing, even joining the occasional set himself. He was . . . naïve and bemused," she finally
said, "only when dealing with problems normal to
everyday living, the spats between husband and
wife, the minor depravities of a young girl experi-
menting with life, that sort of thing. His own experience was on such a higher plane he simply could
not understand that not everyone knew the joy of
such a life."

"And he had no help for them. So you did it
for him."

"When I could," she said. "But enough of such
nonsense. Miss Abernathy's cook has outdone herself, has she not? It would be more a sin if we do
not enjoy such delightful victuals than if we do."

Charles laughed. "You are a delight, Miss
Seldon."

"Nonsense," she said, blushing.

Rutherford, watching them approach, was not
pleased. Somehow everything seemed to interfere
with his plans so that his campaign for Miss Seldon's favor was proving inadequate. The artful little Miss Seldon, or whatever her name might truly
be, was destined for great things. Things which did
not include a sober settled existence as some man's
wife. Rutherford was determined to show her the

way, which meant he must find the means of thwarting Miss Abernathy, who was, it seemed, determined to put a spoke in his wheel!

Neither was Steven pleased to see Miss Seldon and Charles on such excellent terms. At long last, when he had finally found himself holding the much-to-be desired glass of lemonade, there was no Miss Seldon in sight. Nor was Charles North. Steven was not mature enough to take such setbacks in stride. One dislikes admitting it, but there was no other word for it. He *pouted* throughout the meal and was only brought out of the sullens when Miss Abernathy suggested, very much in the manner of offering a treat to a child, that he might like to be the first to look through her telescope and see what he could see.

Chapter Nine

The next morning, thinking back over the preceding afternoon, Matty tried to understand why she was less than pleased to find herself surrounded by three eligible suitors. Or perhaps merely two? Poor Steven so obviously suffered from something similar to calf love, merely reveling in the state of being in love rather than truly loving, that she could not count him as a real suitor even though his behavior was more nearly what romantics told one to expect.

Still, she should be enjoying herself a great deal, having three men pursuing her—and . . . she was *not*.

"Why?" she muttered to her fingers. She lay in bed trying to make herself get up and begin her day but her thoughts would not allow her that freedom. Her first finger stuck up into the air, almost quivering. "You think you know?" she asked. The finger waggled a trifle wildly. Matty sighed. "Yes, I fear I also know. The truth of it is that I've no suitors at all, have I? Charles is enjoying a mild flirtation to while away the hours of his visit here with Miss Abernathy."

Matty suffered a brief sensation of deep regret, but then sighed and continued with her thoughts. "Mr. Rutherford, I daresay, is seriously pursuing me—but *not* with the most honorable of intentions." She sighed again.

"And of course one cannot consider Steven, poor boy. It would be despicable to trick him into asking for my hand and accepting it when, very soon now, something will occur to turn his mind from me on to other things. Such as," she continued more slowly, "whatever it is that brought him here, running hotfoot after his cousin, and obviously needing advice and counsel." She stared at her fingers, recalling Charles's revelations. "Gambling debts . . . Should I interfere?" Her fingers did not appear to be in agreement on that topic, interfering with each other in such a way Matty could catch no sense from them. "You are no help," she muttered and giving up her rather one-sided discussion, flipped the covers back, and crawled from her bed. The maid scratched at her door.

"Yes?" asked Matty, who had begun locking her door since she'd seen Rutherford watching, with a speculative expression, her passage toward her bedroom.

"Warm water, miss, and perhaps I could see to your fire?"

Matty turned the key and told the child to come in. She turned to put on her wrapper, turning back at a faint noise to see Rutherford standing in doorway.

"Out," she said.

The maid turned so quickly she slopped water all over the carpet.

"Get out!"

The maid, seeing that Matty spoke to someone else turned to see who it was. Her eyes widened.

She backed into the corner formed by the massive armoire and the small table, on which rested the washbowl and soap dish.

"But, my dear, I wish a few words with you and it is impossible to find you alone during the day," he purred.

"Ellen," said Matty, not looking at the girl, "I want you to come over near me . . . Now," she added when the maid only cowered more deeply into her hiding place.

The child skittered from her corner and ran to Matty's side.

"As you see, Mr. Morton, I am not alone. And I have no desire to speak with any man who has the mistaken thought that I might be willing to see him in my bedroom," she said coldly.

"My dear girl," purred Rutherford, frowning at the maid, "if you've any notions of bringing North up to scratch, let me disabuse you. And, if you were so stupid as to trick Steven into a proposal, I assure you our family would take the matter in hand instantly and you would find yourself in serious difficulty. Far better than you come to an arrangement with me, don't you see?"

"I don't understand any of that. Nor do I *wish* to understand whatever it is you would ask of me, so you need not explain more fully. Ellen, Mr. Morton is leaving now and I want you to close the door and turn the key."

Rutherford scowled more deeply. "You insist on making this difficult, do you? We'll see. Miss Abernathy is no fool and I am certain that very soon now she will discover the truth and be more than happy to see the last of you. When that occurs, my dear, you'll find my offer far less generous than if you were to come to terms now and be done with it. When we meet at teatime, you may give me the nod and I will come to you in the small arbor when we've finished and can disperse." He bowed and backed from the room, closing the door behind him.

"That . . . that . . . !" Matty, who was never at a loss for words, found herself quite unable to express her feelings.

"You tell Miss Abernathy, miss," said the maid firmly. "*She'll* not allow him to give you a slip on the shoulder. *She'll* sort him out."

Matty drew in a deep breath. "That is very good advice, Ellen." She moved toward the armoire. "I doubt very much he'll return, but do turn that key for me!"

Her thoughts whirled. She found it is one thing to suspect that a man had designs on one's person and quite another to have him come as near as possible to speaking the words. Angry words ran through her mind. Words she'd not have used about any man, words she was unaware she even knew, rattled each other as she denigrated Rutherford's morals, his person, his family, and finally, his mother—

—at which point Matty drew herself up short. She had no reason to suspect the woman was a bitch, nor did she have any right to call a wellborn man a bastard!

But what could she *do?* As she dressed, Matty considered. Informing Miss Abernathy of the problem would very likely get Rutherford cast from the house. He would shrug and take himself off to Brighton, where he would disport himself in the manner he obviously enjoyed, but without the problems of seducing a troublesome young lady.

After a moment she shook her head. Too easy. Far too easy.

Matty, who never in her life had felt more than mere irritation for anyone, discovered a desire for revenge had lodged in her heart. And somehow she meant to plot a way of achieving it.

"Just not right now," she muttered, fastening the last of the buttons gracing the front of her work gown. "The dogs are awaiting me," she added by way of clinching the matter.

Matty had finished the flowers and followed the maid into the front hall, where one of the bouquets was needed, so she was there to greet Vicar Baxter when he arrived.

Reverend Baxter beamed. "Miss Seldon. I had hoped to find you lacking diversion and in need of occupation. Will you join me in my rounds?" The vicar sobered and, more quietly, added, "There are two women who might be happier to discuss their problems with a woman. I do what I can, but of course I've no wife to deal with such things. You, your father's daughter, will know what is needed and it would be a boon to me."

"Of course I'll come," said Matty. She turned to the maid. "Please find Ellen and ask her to bring down my cloak and bonnet. Reverend Baxter, I must find Miss Abernathy and inform her where I'm going."

"The footman can take her a message." The vicar turned to the tall young man and barked an order.

The footman looked to Miss Seldon, who sighed and nodded. "Please, George, pass on the word, if you will be so kind."

Reverend Baxter frowned ever so slightly but said nothing. He waited, silent and slightly severe. Matty was very glad when her maid scurried down the stairs with the garments necessary for such a jaunt.

"Thank you, Ellen. That will be all."

When the girl disappeared through the green baize-covered door at the back of the hall the vicar gently scolded Matty's behavior. ". . . because they are merely servants, you know, and you must not encourage them. You will do better in future," he added.

"I am to be impolite to them because they do me a service?"

The reverend blinked. "Put that way it sounds rather absurd, but that is not the way of it, is it? They are paid to do, as you say, the service. One need not be rude, of course, but excessive kindness will lead to the creatures taking advantage of you. If you think about it, you will understand. Come along now. I must not be late."

"Late?"

His high cheekbones sported spots of red. "I am invited to a luncheon with Miss Crachet but must see three of my parishioners before I may allow myself that indulgence."

Matty nodded. She had been reared to do her duty before all else and approved.

"You will like Miss Crachet."

Matty cast him a startled look and, about to climb into his gig, stepped back. "But I am not invited. I do not know the lady."

"You will meet her when we arrive. She lives alone now her mother is dead and will like to know another lady."

"But it is not the thing to simply arrive with no warning."

"I am the lady's vicar. What I do cannot be wrong."

Matty blinked. Did he mean the normal conventions did not apply to him? He had made the statement with a touch of arrogance she could not like, but she did not know how to object.

"Come now. We will be late."

Their first stop was to condole with a father concerning a son with a broken arm. The vicar was somewhat disconcerted to find the man so lacking in sensitivity as to call the boy ". . . a damn fool, pardon your presence, Vicar, but he should not have been climbing around in the apple tree that way. The lad's got no more sense than his baby sister!"

"I am sure you are correct," said Matty soothingly, "but perhaps the lesson will be well learned and the boy more careful in future?"

"He will if I've anything to say about it!" groused the farmer.

Matty turned to the boy's mother and determined that the woman knew how to care for the arm and didn't need counseling on ways and means. Then she asked about the baby.

"A good child," said the proud mother, drawing Matty to where the infant lay in its cradle in the warm inglenook kicking her heels and gurgling. "Never a peep out of her from her evening feeding to daylight! That imp of Satan—" She nodded toward where her son sat on a bench below the high window, nursing a cat. "—got us up twice every night for months. I swear I was so tired I didn't know if I was coming or going."

"She will be a help to you, too, as she gets older."

Vicar Baxter cleared his throat and Matty looked his way. He pointed discreetly toward the door, indicating it was time to leave. Matty made her good-byes and followed him to the gig, wondering that when he said he wished her help with the women he gave her no time to ascertain if help was needed.

"Our next stop is a widow lady who is giving concern to her neighbors."

"What sort of concern?" asked Matty.

"She is convinced someone is stealing her food."

Matty frowned. "You think she makes it up?"

"She is lonely. I think she wishes to make herself

interesting. I am hoping you may explain to her that such behavior only engenders disgust."

"But what if someone *is* stealing from her?"

He looked startled. "Nonsense," he said sharply, but was silent as they continued on their way—and shocked when, upon approaching the widow's cottage, they discovered her chasing a laughing boy from her tiny garden, the lad holding high a meat pie he had obviously obtained from the woman's kitchen.

Matty hopped down from the gig before it fully stopped and ran after the boy, catching him by his shirttail and drawing him to a stop. The lad was well dressed and she did not believe him in need of extra food. Besides, the extra weight he carried around his middle indicated he loved to eat and was allowed to do so. She marched him back to where the vicar waited, his mouth agape.

"Now you return that pie to this lady instantly and promise you will never do such a thing again. You, who obviously have never gone hungry a day in your life, to take the food from the mouth of a lady who very likely has difficulty putting that food on her table! You are a poor excuse of a boy and must be the despair of your mother and make your father exceedingly sad to think he has failed to raise you to be a proper son."

The boy scowled. "Vicar, tell her who I am."

"He's the magistrate's son, Miss Seldon," said the vicar in hushed tones. "You are out of line to scold him so."

It was Matty's turn to gape. "You would say that it is right for him to steal this woman's food?"

The vicar looked confused. "But the magistrate . . ."

"The magistrate, if the widow so desires, must prosecute his son as he would any thief. He should sentence him as he would any lad. Is your father a hanging judge?" she asked the boy, who turned pale and looked at the pie in his hand for a moment and then shoved it toward the widow, who took it from him and held it close. "Well?"

"I . . . I . . ."

"Surely you do not believe that because your father is magistrate you may do anything you please in any way you please? To the contrary," she continued, "you are obliged to present a *better* face to the world than the average child simply *because* of who your father is!"

"But . . . but . . ."

"I don't know your name, Missus—" continued Matty, turning to the widow.

"Widow Button, if it please you."

"—but if you wish transport to the magistrate so that you may complain to the boy's father we will take you there at once."

"Miss Seldon!" hissed the vicar. "I am certain young Martin will do just as he ought in future."

"Will you?" asked Matty, glaring at the boy. The lad pushed his toe into the dirt of the road. "Answer me."

He lad looked up, scowling. "Who are you to tell me what to do?" He flicked a glance toward the vicar.

The vicar sighed. "Martin," he said, obviously reluctantly, "that was excessively rude of you. Now tell Miss Seldon that you will never steal from Mrs. Button again and we will all go about out business."

"You perhaps suggest it is all right if he steals from someone else?" asked Matty before the lad could do more than open his mouth.

"Of course not. Stealing is wrong."

The boy looked confused.

"And you do not mean to tell his father of his behavior? That he *laughed* when Mrs. Button chased him and her dinner from her garden?"

It was the vicar's turn to look confused. "Er, Miss Seldon," Reverend Baxter whispered, "you do not appear to understand. He is the *magistrate's* son."

"So?"

"But do you not see . . ."

"I only see that a terrible wrong has been done and you feel nothing need be done about it," said Miss Seldon accusingly.

He stiffened. "Miss Seldon, I am the vicar. You will cease chiding me."

"Then you mean to do your duty?"

Mrs. Button and the boy stared from one to the other. Mrs. Button's eyes twinkled, but the boy looked frightened.

Vicar Baxter looked from one to the other and sighed. "Yes I will do my duty. After lunch," he added, after a glance at the hunter-style watch he pulled from his fob pocket.

They returned to the gig after a few more words with the widow and drove on. Not far down the road, Matty looked across a meadow and glimpsed the roofs of Miss Abernathy's house. She laid her hands on the reins held in Reverend Baxter's rather inadequate grasp.

"I believe," she said, "that I should leave you now, since I feel very uncomfortable appearing at a lady's table when uninvited. It is quite likely she'll not have enough food for an extra mouth and be embarrassed by my presence. Also, I have need of exercise so I will follow that path home." She pointed and the vicar pulled up with more alacrity than might have been expected so that Matty could climb down. "You will," she said sternly, "go directly to the magistrate once you've finished your luncheon?"

"I will be so embarrassed," he said in a complaining tone.

"You are the vicar and have a duty to Widow

Button. She has been badly maligned. You yourself
went so far as to imply she lied and, instead, you
discover she has had the food stolen from her very
table, which cannot be so very well provisioned
that she can afford such loss.''

"I suggested she lied?''

"You said you thought she was telling stories to
make herself interesting. It will not do, Vicar!
Surely the magistrate is a Christian man and will
see she is compensated.''

The vicar gulped and red spots appeared on his
cheeks. "You are right to remind me that the least
of these shall inherit the earth and that it is as
difficult for a rich man to enter heaven as a camel
to thread the eye of a needle,'' he said, much
subdued. "I will see the magistrate.''

"Thank you. I know it takes courage to do such
a thing, but you will find it when you need it.''

"Yes,'' he said a trifle doubtfully.

"Of course you will,'' she said bracingly.

He straightened his shoulders and nodded.

"Now I will be off and you shall continue with
your parish visits,'' she said encouragingly.

"You are an excellent woman, Miss Seldon,'' he
said before he flicked the reins and set his poor
horse to a gentle trot.

Matty shook her head at the reluctance in his
tone, fearing he'd find some excuse to avoid
explaining the whole to the magistrate. When the
vicar's gig was out of sight, she turned and began
the half mile walk to Miss Abernathy's across the
fields. She had not gone far before she wished she
had her pattens or at least that she had worn her
heavier shoes. She would, she feared, ruin the slip-
pers she'd not changed before joining the vicar
for the most ridiculous morning she'd spent in a
very long time. The vicar, she feared, lacked good

sense and was, it seemed, overly impressed by titles and riches.

She had not gone far when a "haloo" had her turning toward a spinney not far from the path. "Steven," she said, feeling a morning of folly was now to be capped by still more.

"I have been finding my muse here near a tiny pond surrounded by bracken. There are tiny wild violets hidden in the grasses and a dry old log to make a fine seat. Will you join me?"

Matty studied his retreat as well as she could at such a distance and decided it was far too isolated a spot for any sensible woman to find herself in. Especially when she knew the man's feelings were more than a trifle warm. She shook her head. "No, I believe I must stroll on."

"I will join you. I am having difficulty with my newest poem and perhaps you can find me a rhyme. The word is 'oranges.' "

He walked toward her, his eyes straying over her form, and then, suddenly turning fiery red, he shook his head.

"Then again perhaps not," he said more firmly than Matty had ever heard him say anything, which surprised her until it occurred to her to wonder to what he was comparing his oranges.

He turned the conversation to innocuous subjects and, for the first time ever, Matty actually enjoyed talking to him. He brought up the Season, which had just ended, and Matty asked him to describe a *tonnish* ball. "You did say your sister had her come-out this year, did you not? How did your mother decorate for it?"

He brightened. "It was my notion and, amazingly, my sister thought it a good one. Usually, she doesn't think very much of me at all, you see," he added, half amused and more than half chagrinned.

"I believe it is the way of siblings," said Matty. "I'd not know since I've none, but it is the impression I have gained by watching other brothers and sisters. What was your notion?" she asked.

"An ice maiden's bower!"

"You decorated all in white?"

He nodded. "Well, and black, of course. Branches painted to look as if the frost had touched them, and other tricks of that sort. We used lots of mirrors and white tissue and starched lace and silver net and all the flowers, of course, were white. It was different from anything that had been done in years and was talked about forever. My sister was so pleased."

"And your mother?"

"Oh, Mother is always proud of me," he said in a dismissive sort of way. "The only other fete to come close to ours . . ." He described another in very slightly deprecating tones and then spoke of other entertainments, each party an excuse to tell of some social success on his own part.

Matty was very glad to reach the house and to be able to honestly say she must run up to her room and change from her damp shoes.

She met Charles at the top of the stairs and he tipped his head at her. "You have been gone for hours. Did you enjoy your morning with Vicar Baxter?"

Reprehensibly, she giggled.

"Now," asked Charles, "does that mean it was very good . . . or very bad?"

"The vicar is a man of little sense, I fear, and I could not stop myself from putting my oar in. If you are interested, I will tell you later but I *must* change my shoes!" And, with that, she turned toward her room in the east wing.

* * *

The runner, Ned Bright, returned the next day and was closeted with Miss Abernathy for some time before she sent for Charles . . . and almost as an afterthought, for Miss Seldon.

"Tell them what you told me," ordered Miss Abernathy.

Charles and Ned were shaking hands but Ned turned and nodded. "Miss Seldon, I have found your father's library. It is still packed in crates, the owner of the bookstore in Royal Tunbridge Wells not having got around to sorting and shelving them. He was appalled to learn the books had been stolen and has agreed to hold them as they are until we catch up with Pelling." Ned tugged at his chin and looked a trifle embarrassed. "Now that last, well, that may be something of a problem, I fear."

"Go on, Ned," encouraged Miss Abernathy.

"Why a problem, Ned?" asked Charles. "He can't have gone far, surely?"

"That right there *is* the problem. He may have."

"Have gone far?" asked Matty, speaking for the first time.

"Exactly. I traveled north to visit his home—just in case the fox had gone to earth, you see."

"And?" asked Charles, impatient to learn the whole.

"Talked to his eldest brother." He turned to Matty. "You've a whole regiment of Pelling cousins, miss, a nice family I thought, but not, perhaps, so wealthy as it might be."

"It is nice to know I am not alone in the world," said Matty. "Please tell us what you discovered."

"Seems there's one bad apple in the barrel," said Ned and sighed. "Almost always is when you've a family that big. George—that's the eldest's name—didn't know much about *your* family except that it existed. He did know where your father lived and, learning he was dead, sent condolences, by the way.''

Matty nodded and bit her lip to keep back a rude request that Ned tell them about Ervine Pelling.

Charles was not so reticent. "Get on with it, Ned. You are dragging it out until we shall wish to scream. Or perhaps,'' he added thoughtfully, ''give you a punch in the nose.''

Ned chuckled. "Very well. One way or another, your cousin Ervine has been in trouble almost since he left the cradle. A few years ago Baron Pelling cast him from the family home and told him to never come back. He has, according to George, who has kept track of his brother, lived by his wits. And, again according to cousin George, Ervine's wits resemble a corkscrew, which makes it difficult to guess what he might do next.''

"A coxcomb and a gull catcher, is that it?''

Ned nodded. "He preys on females and, when he finds a naive young man, parts his gull from any ready the lad may have. Occasionally he has managed to bring some young fool around his thumb and dip the corkbrained idiot into deep doings indeed.''

"Then he is a man like the one who has upset Steven so,'' said Matty. "I do not understand why someone has not guided Steven in the way to go on, watched out for his interests.''

"His interests? As *I* understand it,'' said Charles with only a touch of acid, ''it was Ruthie who introduced Steven to gambling in the first place.''

"Then it is because he feels guilty that Rutherford has been so subdued?'' asked Miss Abernathy.

Matty blinked. *"Subdued?"* she asked, disbelieving.

Charles laughed. "When he is not preoccupied in some mental dilemma, he is quite different."

Miss Abernathy smiled. "Yes. Loud and boisterous and, very often, a great deal of fun."

"For you."

Miss Abernathy had the grace to look a trifle chagrined. "Well, yes, I suppose if anyone reared in this namby-pamby era looked at his behavior from a modern point of view, then they would be very likely to disapprove, but I was *not.*"

"You *approve* of his wildness?" asked Matty, suddenly wondering if the vicar had not had reason for distrusting the woman as a protector for an unmarried female.

She waved a hand, airily. "Oh, there are rules, of course, that must be followed."

"But," asked Charles, his eyes on the fingernails of his right hand, "does Ruthie *know* your rules?"

Miss Abernathy opened her mouth to respond and closed it. She glanced at Matty who, despite her best efforts, was blushing rosily. "He hasn't done more than *flirt* with you, has he?" she asked Matty.

Matty didn't know where to look and the blush now felt painfully hot.

"He has," Miss Abernathy answered her own question. "Drat the boy! Now I will have to have an exceedingly uncomfortable talk with him. I do so hate playing the spoilsport, but there *are* rules." She leaned forward and patted Matty's hand. "I don't know exactly what he's done, but I'll see he doesn't do it again. You may feel comfortable again, Miss Seldon."

"Assuming Rutherford agrees to follow the rules," said Charles softly. Miss Abernathy glared at him and he added, "But we are embarrassing Miss Seldon. Ned, what do you mean to do next?"

"I've sent to the ports to have Pelling stopped

if he attempts to leave the country, but I doubt he will. Not, at least, until he collects what he is owed by the various pigeons he's plucked. Or what he can get of those debts."

"Ah! Steven is such a pigeon for someone. I now understand why Steven has stayed here so patiently," said Miss Abernathy, chuckling. It seemed she'd recovered from the vexation of discovering Rutherford was importuning her guest. "I had thought it Matty's charms, but I see he is really hiding from his creditors."

"Miss Seldon's charms undoubtedly have a great deal to do with his deciding this is a good place to hide," said Charles bitingly, "but I suppose something must be done about Steven's problems as well as Miss Seldon's. But first of all, Pelling must be removed from proper society for everyone's sake. Ned, you have not said what you yourself mean to do next."

"I doubt Pelling has any notion he's hunted. Very likely he'll appear in his old haunts eventually. There is the problem, of course, that I don't yet know those haunts, but most likely all the worst dens of iniquity. Given the time of year, that would be in Brighton where the prey he likes to hunt is currently pastured and where it now grazes."

"Very poetic, Ned," said Miss Abernathy. "Perhaps you would like to meet Steven."

Ned looked confused.

"Steven," explained Charles, "is our resident poet. That is, he is if you can call the stuff he writes poetry. I do not think Miss Seldon, for instance, would do so."

Miss Abernathy chuckled and Matty smiled, but, since it was very true she found Steven's verses less then appealing, she said nothing in response to Charles's teasing.

Chapter Ten

Soon after that Charles walked off with Miss Seldon, leaving Ned with their hostess, the two of them discussing in more detail exactly what he meant to do. Miss Abernathy had suggested the young people leave them and had, at the same time, asked that Bitsy be sent in with a tea tray.

"Why Bitsy?" asked Matty, once Charles had passed the order on to Forbes. "Bitsy is Miss Abigail's personal maid, not a parlor maid."

"Miss Abby is matchmaking."

"Bitsy . . . and Mr. Bright?"

"Hmm. She will regret it if Bitsy ever says yes, but firmly believes that is what her woman *should* do."

"Mr. Bright has asked Bitsy to wed him?"

"Some years ago now. Why did you not tell Miss Abby Ruthie is harassing you?"

"He is her relation. I am a mere charity case. It didn't seem right that I complain to her when I am capable of seeing he does not harm me."

"My dear naive woman! Have you never heard of abduction? Ruthie is not beyond such behavior."

Matty blanched but rallied. "That makes no difference now. Miss Abigail will speak to him and he will desist." She looked into the far distance. "You seem to know them all very well," she said in a rather small voice.

"Is that a question?" he asked, smiling down at her.

She looked up, met his eyes, and felt herself blush. "I suppose it is."

"I'm what is known as a younger son, you know? My family allows me to show my face now and again at *tonnish* dos so I have met Steven Howard once or twice since he's come down from University. Ruthie and I attended the same school, Winchester, where we were thrown together. We rather lost touch when I went on to University and he did not, but again, London is a small place, really. We have met occasionally at clubs and race meets."

"You go often into society?" she asked a trifle diffidently. It seemed to Matty that everything she learned about Charles North sent him drifting further and further away from any possibility they might share more than a temporary friendship.

Not, she scolded herself, *that I believed anything would come of that . . . that odd feeling of connection. Of course I didn't.*

Unfortunately, the scolding did not convince her of the truth of that and she bit her lip. "You enjoy the Season?" she asked, asking the same question in a different way.

"There were a fair number of years when I avoided everything but those occasions where my mother insisted I put in an appearance. Family weddings and funerals, or a cousin's come-out ball. You know the sort of thing."

She didn't, of course, but could guess.

"Recently I have come to believe that, having worked very hard at it, I've established myself in my profession to the degree that I may return to some of the pastimes I once enjoyed." He shrugged. "The thing is, I find them less enjoyable than I once did. I now prefer to go only where there will be good music, or to an occasional play, or where the company has some special attraction—like coming to visit our delightful Miss Abby. At my age I suppose it is ridiculous, but more and more I find I am attracted to my own fireside." He chuckled. "An old and surly curmudgeon before I reach my thirty-fifth birthday, that is what I've become!"

Matty laughed but something inside her curled up into a very tight coil and she knew that once she was alone, it would straighten out and hurt and perhaps she would cry a little before she took herself in hand and became, again, the sensible woman she knew herself to be.

"You do not contradict me," he said, pretending chagrin. "You think it true!"

"I have no notion whether you've become a miserly sort, but you are not old and I have yet to see you show the least sign of surliness, so you must not expect me to tell you you are talking bibble-babble when you know it yourself!"

"Ah. That puts me firmly in my place."

"And what, dear Charles, do you perceive to be your place?" asked Rutherford, coming up behind them. And then he changed the subject before Charles could respond. "Is it true our Abby has a Bow Street runner closeted in her private study?"

"Which question do you wish answered?" asked Charles dryly, turning himself and Matty so that they faced the angry-looking man.

"Is he a runner?"

Charles nodded. "Ned Bright. He helped Miss Abigail with a little problem some years ago and you know Abigail! She chooses her friends where she will. She liked Ned. When he's in the area he stops by to see her. And Bitsy." Charles added the last with a quirk to his eyebrows that was suggestive.

"Oh." After a moment Rutherford added, "I see." But he cast Matty a speculative look before he turned away and walked off, his hands clasped loosely behind him.

"Now what has our Ruthie got on his conscience?" muttered Charles. He shook himself lightly. "Not that we really wish to know. So, let me see, what did I mean to ask you? Ah! I must drive into Chichester this afternoon. Would you care to come with me? Miss Abby will arrange for a maid to accompany us," he added before Matty could open her mouth either to accept or to deny him.

Matty *had* been about to say it wouldn't do, but the suggestion that a maid would accompany them changed her mind and allowed her to accept the offered treat. At her advanced age, it was perfectly acceptable for her to go about chaperoned only by a maid. And, besides, there were a few things she needed. Personal things one did not wish to ask one's hostess to supply. Tooth powder, for instance.

So it was that Lady Wilmingham, whose trip to Bath had been delayed, looked out her coach window and saw Miss Seldon and Mr. North strolling down the pavement and about to enter the chemist's door. She grimaced. "Just what I expected of the chit. I wonder. Does Abigail know that young person goes off with Abigail's young men? Or is Abigail so lost to proper behavior she encourages the hoyden to do so?"

Lady Wilmingham's downtrodden maid did not point out that Bitsy, Miss Abernathy's personal maid, followed in the duo's footsteps. She had long ago discovered that her ladyship, once she'd made up her mind about a thing, had no desire whatsoever to have it changed for her.

Her ladyship went happily off for her holiday with a widowed sister who lived in Bath with the delightful knowledge that Abigail would, one way or another, soon get her comeuppance. Lady Wilmingham had never, once, in all the years she'd known Abigail, been able to find the woman in the wrong, so she was delighted to know that, *this* time, she herself had the right of a situation.

Lady Wilmingham enjoyed the sensation of looking forward to gloating—in a genteel manner, of course—over her friend once it became clear to all that Miss Seldon was *just* the sort of female her ladyship had predicted the chit would be.

Matty lay in her bed that evening and stared at her forefinger which, if one were as familiar with her fingers as Matty had become, was telling her she must take hold of herself, must make decisions, must do something, *anything*, before it was too late.

"*Anything*," she muttered. The finger wiggled rather wildly. "That was rather melodramatic, was it not?" she asked. And then she sighed a gusty sigh. "On the other hand, you are correct. Listening to Charl . . . *Mr. North* speak of his family in that easy way told me as nothing else could do that it will not *do*. They will have plans for him so I must not fall in love with him. There is no future in it. Only pain." The finger wiggled again. "Thank you. I am fully aware it is too late, but I must go on as if it were not." She lifted her eyes to the embroidery on the tester covering her bed and blinked rapidly. "He is just the sort of man I always hoped to meet. He is—" For a moment she bit her lip and then nodded. "—even more the man I could love than was poor, dear Jeremy." She gave fleeting thought

to her dead betrothed and tucked fond memories
of those days of her youth back where they
belonged. "So," she asked, staring hard at her
finger, "tell me what to do."

For a very long moment she lay there perfectly
still. And then, suddenly, her finger bent ever so
slightly and she relaxed. "Yes. *Of course*. Why did
I not think of that long ago?"

Elsewhere in the Hall, Miss Abernathy lay cud-
dled in the embrace of her lover and spoke softly
of all that had gone on that day. ". . . so you see,
dearest, things are progressing just as I'd hoped."
A moment later she pushed away, far enough so
that she could stare at the man. "You cannot think
her such a dolt!"

Half a moment later, Miss Abernathy fell against
the cushions, alone again. She pouted, looking
around the room, but it did no good and, finally,
she sighed gustily.

"If I apologize will you come back?" she asked
softly.

There was no response and she sighed again—
but much more softly—snuggled in among the
cushions all by herself and frowned lightly. *Could
Matty Seldon think Charles too good for her?* Miss Abernathy thought about it, the frown deepening.

"Pish," she said aloud and pushed herself to her
feet. "Now what can I possibly do about such a
thing as that?"

Still elsewhere, Rutherford tossed and turned,
wondering if the runner was truly visiting Abby
only because he was enamored of Bitsy. "Or," he
murmured, "is he looking for my stupid cousin?
Thank God Steven took himself off to that race
meeting yesterday!"

But did runners look for someone merely for
the collection of a bad debt? Especially when the

debt holder was a man who was more than a little bent and not that fond of the law?

And then another possibility snuck under Rutherford's guard. Was Abby not so complacent as he'd thought? Was she having Miss Seldon investigated? Would she have the chit taken up for running a rig once she could prove there was a rig?

The thought of Miss Seldon languishing in the local magistrate's unpleasant cell sent a shudder up Rutherford's spine. It must not be. If that was what the man was up to, then there would be no question of waiting for the plum to drop in his hand.

He must pick it!

"Tomorrow?" he asked himself softly. He shook his head against the crisp linen covering his pillow. He much preferred the chit to come to him willingly. He would save her from herself if he must and she would not object when she understood what it was he'd saved her from, but *only* if he must. He did not want her acceptance of her place in his life merely for reasons of indebtedness.

The decision made, Rutherford pulled the covers higher, turned on his side, and went to sleep.

Steven, unaware of anything but the fact he'd managed to lose still more money he did not have to lose, finished the last of the bottle of brandy he'd asked Forbes to place in his room, and weaving more than a little, managed to make it from fireplace chair to bed—and was sound asleep almost before his body fell onto the mattress.

The only occupant of the bedrooms on the family floor to take himself to his night's rest in the usual fashion was Charles. He readied himself, had a last word with Timmy concerning the need to press a coat *before* spending any more time on boots, settled into the bed warmed by the warming pan the young man took off with him, and fell into pleasant dreams in which Miss Matty strolled by his side around the lake on his family estate and, rather vaguely, two small children, a young maid running after them, laughed and played somewhere in the distance.

It is, he thought, half waking at one point, *a very nice dream.*

Matty awoke early. Even before going out for her morning romp with the animals, she went to the library, where she knew she'd find pen, paper, and the other necessities for writing a letter. She dipped the pen into the ink and wrote, "The most Reverend and Right Honorable, the Lord Archbishop of Canterbury . . ." and then stopped for so long the ink dried.

Finally she decided that a simple request for help with finding a position, most happily with some elderly lady who needed young limbs to fetch and carry for her, would be better than a long and involved explanation of why she no longer resided in Little Conghurst, merely stating that she was with a friend who could not keep her forever.

My Lord Archbishop John Ross, she began . . .

The letter was folded, sealed with a neat white wafer, and placed in the large brass bowl where mail was put for Forbes to collect and send off to Chichester, where it would be put on the Royal Mail Coach. She wondered briefly how long it would take for a response to reach her, but, the request made, there was nothing more she could do, and Matty, sensible woman that she was, put it from her mind and went off for her playtime with the dogs.

Charles, standing in his window as had become his habit, enjoyed watching her, the dogs, and the other animals almost as much as the participants below enjoyed themselves.

"You say it was in the bowl?" asked Miss Abernathy, staring at the letter Forbes had just put into her hands.

"Yes, madam. I thought you would wish to know."

"Quite right, of course. Why do you suppose she is writing her father's archbishop?"

"I believe the usual reason in such cases is to beg for aid or assistance."

"Drat the girl." Miss Abernathy brushed the letter back and forth against her hand. Finally she nodded. "You will, of course, deliver this along with the rest of the post—but, Forbes . . ."

"Yes, madam?"

"Forbes, I've a letter to write and I wish it, too, to go out in today's post, so do not rush to send her missive into Chichester. In fact—" She put the letter into her reticule. "—I believe I must retain it for a bit. Thank you, Forbes."

"You are welcome, madam," he responded with a regal nod of his head.

Miss Abernathy half closed her eyes and stared at nothing in particular, deep in thought. Then she nodded and moved to the small writing table set before the window at the side of her study. It was a north-facing window with a pleasant view of the South Downs, but today she paid the constantly changing scene no attention, merely setting out paper and pens and uncapping her ink bottle.

And then, very much like Matty earlier that morning, she did no more than head the letter, "Dear Archbishop Ross . . ." before stopping and thinking yet again.

When she did plunge into the body of her letter,

she wrote fast and furiously and went into great
detail on all the things Matty had decided the good
bishop would find uninteresting and unnecessary.
Miss Abernathy finished her story and then, at the
end, told the bishop she had high hopes a very
good marriage would be arranged for Miss Seldon
before the month was out and that, if by chance,
that did not occur, then she had every intention
of offering Miss Seldon a position here at Abernathy Hall as her secretary and companion. She then
included several names and addresses the bishop
could contact in order to establish that Miss Abernathy was, indeed, a gentlewoman and respectable—people who had known her, of course, only
since she arrived in West Sussex to live in the house
provided for her there.

Miss Abernathy reread her letter, grinning here
and there as she did so. The good bishop would
very likely find her epistolary style of letter writing
rather full of adjectives and perhaps a trifle too
full of exclamation points, but she was quite certain
he would understand that Miss Seldon had found
herself in difficulties but was now in the hands
of a generous and good-hearted woman with the
young woman's best interests at heart.

She looked at Matty's letter, back at her own,
and then nodded. She enclosed Matty's within hers
and sealed the whole into a plump and rather heavy
packet.

The good bishop, she thought, *will be forced to pay
out quite a few pennies in order to receive this news of
one of his flock!*

Chapter Eleven

The monkey sat on the goat's back and, when Matty finally appeared that morning, scolded her wildly, chattering away at a great pace and flinging its thin little arms about wildly.

"Yes I know I'm late. I apologize," she said, trying to keep the dogs from jumping all over her.

"Sit! Now!"

They sat and Matty turned to see who it was they obeyed with such promptness. "Oh. Mr. Morgan," she murmured. "Thank you," she added a trifle belatedly.

"Shall I find someone to take all these creatures away so they will not bother you?" he asked.

"Good heavens no! They have been waiting for me. Come along," she said to the dogs.

But Rutherford took it to himself. "Come along where?" he asked, falling into step beside her.

Matty sighed. "Every morning I spend a few minutes playing with them all," she said. "Assuredly, you would find it quite boring."

"I never find you boring. You are the most amazing woman I have ever met."

She glanced at him. It was very much like the

sort of thing Steven would say, but, coming from
Mr. Morton, it sounded quite different. "I am nothing special."

"You haven't a notion how special," he said, and
this time there was the teasing note with which she
was familiar and which she disliked heartily. "You
do not wish to know in what ways you are special?"
he asked.

"No. Ah. Now then," she said, turning to the
dogs. They instantly formed a half circle—even the
little dachshund—and looked at her expectantly.
She pointed to one of the larger dogs. He came
up and sniffed the "bird" she had made from a
branch, some rags, and some old pheasant feathers. She threw it as far and as hard as she could.
The dog ran off.

"You do this every morning?" asked Rutherford.
She nodded, watching the animal return in great
loping bounds. When the dog gave her the bird,
she threw it again. "Why?" he asked.

She glanced toward him and back to the dog.
"Because I enjoy it," she responded.

"You enjoy playing with these great stupid
beasts?"

"Yes." She threw the bird a third time and, when
it was returned to her, patted the dog and pointed
to his place. She did the same with the next dog
and the next.

The monkey dropped from the goat's back and
came to climb up onto her shoulders and she heard
Mr. Rutherford mutter, "Here now!" but merely
settled the creature more comfortably before toss-
ing the bird still again.

It was the poodle's turn next. Rutherford backed
away. "How can you bear to have that disfigured
cur anywhere near you?"

"Disfigured?" She stared at Rutherford, at the
dog, and back at Rutherford. "You mean the loss

of the leg? What nonsense. Do you, then, demand perfection in everything around you?"

"I feel ill when near the maimed," admitted Rutherford with a faint shudder.

"That is too bad. If you lived in my old village, you would have had to forego the company of the most interesting man there. He was with Wellington in India and followed him to the Peninsula, where he took a ball to the thigh. He lost his leg, but he did not allow it to make him bitter. He returned to live with his brother, where he taught himself all sorts of skills to make himself useful. And he is much desired at parties, where he is a great raconteur."

"It something of the sort were to happen to me I'd kill myself," said Rutherford.

"Nonsense. You are not such a coward."

"*I* think it cowardly to impose such on others."

"How did you ever come to believe such a thing?" asked Matty, shocked. "Believe that those who love you would feel imposed upon, I mean."

He looked into the distance, his mouth a firm hard line. "I couldn't avoid it. I saw how my father's condition ate into my mother. He was a burden not only to himself but to all of us."

"Hmm."

He turned a hard stare her way. "You think me hard and unfeeling."

"I hope," she said gently, "that it is merely that you misinterpreted what you saw when you were a child and too young to understand."

"I was nineteen when he died."

For a moment Matty remained silent, just looking at him. "Then I pity you," she said.

For a long moment he stared at her, meeting her level gaze. Then, uncomfortable, he shrugged and, with a curt good-bye, stalked off, his shoulders hunched.

Charles approached as soon as Rutherford was out of sight. "What was that all about?"

Instead of answering his question, she asked, "Do you know anything about Mr. Morton's father?"

"He was crushed in a riding accident, his hip destroyed. I have heard the pain made him a bitter man who made life difficult for those around him."

"Yes, so I understood, from what Mr. Morton said, but . . ."

"But?"

"But why is *he* so bitter?"

"Rutherford? He allowed you to see it?"

"He commented on Beau's problem." She gestured at the poodle. "Our conversation went on from there."

"You have been honored, I think," said Charles, slowly.

"I have?" The dachshund, losing patience, trundled over and yapped at her. She tossed the bird and looked back at Charles.

"He never talks about his family or his growing up in that household." Charles smiled. "I wonder what it is about you that draws out a man's true nature even when we would hide if from you?"

Matty felt a blush. "Nonsense. I am just me."

"Aha! That *is* the reason."

Matty tipped her head, blinking. "I don't understand."

"Far too many people try very hard to be what they are not. It is special that you do not. And do not ask why they do such a thing, as I see you are about to do, because I do not know."

Matty tossed the bird again and, when she turned back, discovered the cats sitting tall and alert, one on either side of Charles. She smiled down at them. "You are becoming adept at knowing just when I am ready to hand out treats, are you not?" she asked.

"I am?" asked Charles, startled.

"Not *you,*" she said, laughing. She drew the packet of food scraps she'd begged from Cook from her pocket, gave the cats theirs, the dogs theirs, allowed the monkey to pick out its bit of fruit and, when the goat trotted up, held her arm so that the one could climb onto the back of the other before giving the goat the last of her scraps. "A goat will eat anything," she said.

"Yes. And I am becoming very nearly hungry enough to do likewise. Will you join me at the breakfast table?"

She shook her head. "I must do the flowers first. If I wait too long, the day is so far gone the flowers will not stay fresh as they do if cut while the dew is still upon them."

"Is that the secret?"

"Secret?"

"Of your lovely bouquets."

She blushed at the compliment. "Certainly it was no secret where I lived. Everyone knows that flowers should be cut very early in the day."

"Perhaps then it is just that you understand them as you do those animals and they obey your wishes, forming themselves into the delightful designs we all enjoy so much."

"You are speaking arrant nonsense," she scolded.

He laughed. "No, I am attempting to flirt with you, but you do not cooperate."

"I do not know how," she said and drew in a deep breath, wishing he would *not* for the simple reason she wished so much that he was not playing that sort of game but was seriously interested in her. But that could never be and she tucked the yearnings well back into a dark and hidden corner of her mind. "You said you were hungry," she added suggestively, wishing he would go before she revealed more of her emotions than was proper.

"I will wait. I will allow myself to fade away to nothing," he said in dramatic tones, "while you cut your flowers and do your bouquets. And I will hold your basket for you," he added, picking it up from where it awaited her near the cutting bed."

He handed her the shears. She took them with some reluctance. "You are, I fear, in a teasing mood this morning."

"I will cease teasing and become serious, then. Did you know that Miss Abby has had a letter from the runner? He has found your cousin's trail and is following it. If he catches up with the man, he will bring him here and you may decide what to do with him. Perhaps you should think about that?"

"About what to do?" Matty frowned. "What *can* I do?"

"You can accuse him before a magistrate of at least two crimes. Theft of your father's possessions, which was your inheritance, and of deliberately sending you into danger by putting you on the first coach to come through the village rather than on one which would take you to his father's home."

"And what would happen to him?"

"Each crime is serious, but very likely he'd not hang. I think he would be transported to our penal colony in the antipodes."

Matty winced.

"Surely you believe he deserves to be punished."

Matty bit her lip, staring at the flower in her hand. "He did evil, but is it my place to judge him? Or to send him to be judged by others?"

"It is, perhaps," asked Charles gently, "the duty of the next person he harms? Or perhaps not? The next person may not be so lucky as you were and will find herself without the protection of someone as generous and good as Miss Abby."

Matty looked down. After a moment she raised her eyes and met his steady gaze. "You are correct. I am a coward. When he is brought here you must tell me what to do to see justice is upheld, to see he can no longer harm the innocent."

"I will support you through the difficulties you foresee." Still gentle, he took the flower from her hand and laid it in the basket. "But you must not allow my news to worry you. It is possible he will *not* be caught, you know."

"He is my cousin," she said. "Is it very bad of me to hope he is not?"

"Because then you will not have to face the magistrate and accuse him of villainy?"

"You read me so easily."

"You are honest and have a soft heart. You would like to believe everyone as good as you yourself, but you are too wise to accept it as true. You . . ."

"*You,*" she interrupted, "make me blush at such nonsense."

Later that day when Matty was reading in the library, she happened to raise her eyes and glance out the window, where she saw Steven slinking along as if he feared he'd be seen. She frowned. When he ducked behind a rather large bush and peered around it, she rose to her feet. When he ran to the next one and, again peered around it, she cocked her head.

"Now what is the matter with our Steven?" she asked herself softly. The fingers on her right hand twitched. She looked down at them. "Do you think so?" They curled into a fist and uncurled. Matty nodded. "Very well. Now which door is he likely to come through?" she asked herself.

She left the library, her feet moving so quickly and lightly it seemed to Charles, who watched her,

that they very nearly did not touch the floor. He
followed when she turned down the hall to a side
door and was not so far behind that he did not
hear her say, "Well, Steven? You are in a fine dither,
are you not?"

"Oh!" Steven jumped, turned, and backed away
as if he'd return to the outdoors.

"Enough of that, now," said Matty firmly.
"There is a small sitting room just along here. You
come in, sit yourself down, and tell me what has
frightened you so badly."

"Not scared," said Steven—a comment belied
by his teeth, which rattled against each other when
he unclenched them enough to speak.

"No, of course not," she said soothingly and
took his arm, leading him into the room. "I should
never have suggested such a thing. What I meant,
of course, is that you are bothered by something
and have been ever since you arrived." While she
spoke, she almost forced him into a chair before
seating herself. "You have not been happy and,
are, I think, worried about something. You will feel
ever so much better after you tell me all about it."

Charles eased the door open a crack just in time
to hear her last words. He nodded to himself. The
boy needed help of a different sort from what he'd
needed when he first arrived . . . assuming that
expression he'd noted when Steven turned from
quietly shutting the door and saw Matty standing
behind him had been one of utter panic as he'd
thought.

"Come, Steven, do tell me." When he shook his
head vigorously, she suggested, "You are in over
your head and someone is threatening you. Is that
what has happened?"

His eyes widened painfully. "You are a witch!"

"Not at all. Merely I have had a great deal of
experience with the people living in my village and

people are pretty much the same everywhere. Now what is it?"

Again he merely closed his mouth and shook his head.

"Gambling debts perhaps?"

He groaned.

"Is it so very bad?"

He nodded, a look of defeat on his young features.

"I suppose your family allowed you to come to Town with no one to guide you and teach you the way of things," she said sorrowfully.

"M'parents didn't want me to go on to Brighton for the summer. M'mother said I was too young and my father said if I got myself into trouble I'd have to get myself out."

"I see." Silently Matty berated Steven's parents for their lack of understanding and for giving him no aid in setting his feet on the right path. "So you fell into the hands of a card shark? Do I have that right?"

Steven almost smiled. "Sharp. Card sharp."

"Thank you. I will remember."

"But—" He frowned. "—in a way you are right. They *are* sharks just waiting to gobble up little fish like me."

"I don't see how he, whoever he is, can have thought you wealthy enough to be able to pay excessive debts of honor."

"My family . . ."

"Ah. Yes. Of course."

The two remained silent for a bit. Steven sighed. Matty hid a smile. "Well, Steven, are you going to tell me how much?"

"You cannot help me. I don't know why I've allowed you to know so much as you do. It isn't the thing, talking to females about one's problems."

"You told me because I am your friend," she said patiently.

And, thought Charles, *because you have a fine way of forcing halflings such as Steven to do your bidding!*

"Friends help each other," she added softly.

"Nobody can help."

"That's a ridiculous exaggeration," she said a trifle sharply and Steven, without thinking, straightened his spine. "I presume your sharp has tracked you down and is demanding his money?"

The momentary resolve faded. Steven nodded, his whole body expressing the bleak hopelessness he experienced. "I didn't think he'd find me here. When Ruthie couldn't . . . I mean, I thought that, come quarter day when I get my allowance, I would pay him as much as I could and he'd wait for the rest." He heaved a huge sigh. "He says he has to have it all and right away."

"Is that usual?"

"Well, in honorable circles, you pay your gambling debts as quickly as you can, but if you cannot do so immediately, then *usually* the other man will give you time to make arrangements."

"Steven, how old are you?"

"Nineteen."

Even younger than I thought! thought Matty. "I seem to remember . . ." She paused, thinking. Finally, in a musing tone, she said, "Steven, I wonder if you can be held responsible for debts incurred at your age. Do you know what I think?"

He shook his head.

"I think we should ask Charles."

"Already asked if I could borrow . . ."

"No, no. Ask him about the *legalities.* It may be that since you are not of age, that you cannot be forced to pay."

He looked at her, utterly shocked. "But it's a gambling debt."

She blinked.

"A debt of honor!"

She grimaced. "I have never understood how it is honorable to cheat someone out of money needed by their family for food and a roof over their heads."

"What?"

Matty shook herself. "I apologize. I was thinking of something that happened near our village. The man was so deeply in debt he committed suicide and his family ended up in the workhouse. And this, because it was gambling debts, was considered honorable behavior on the gentleman's part!"

"I may end up in a debtors' prison, but I don't think my family will be harmed," he said rather tentatively. "In fact," he said, standing, "that is what I should do. I will go instantly," he said, straightening his shoulders and flinging back his head in that overly dramatic way of the romantically inclined youth, "to the local magistrate. I will ask him how I go about pronouncing myself a bankrupt and unable to pay my debts."

"Can we not ask Charles about this first?" she asked, concerned by his sudden decision.

"There is nothing he can do."

"That," said Charles, opening the door, "is not quite accurate. I would not loan you money, Steven, to pay a gambling debt, particularly not when you think you were cheated, but, in law, I may be able to help you. Given your age—or lack thereof. Or, there are, perhaps, other ways it might be done, assuming . . ." He looked at Matty. "My dear, I think we will do far better if you go away. We've things to discuss."

"You will . . . ?"

"I will see to everything," he said gently.

The man and Steven, who had revealed himself as the mere youth he was, stood shoulder to shoulder, silently waiting. Matty looked from the one to the other and back to Charles.

Charles smiled slightly. "I know," he said softly. "You have done the work and now I waltz in and tell you to run along and play."

She grimaced and he nodded. And waited. She sighed as she moved toward the door. Once there, she paused, her hand on the handle. "Do allow me to know how it all comes out so I will not worry," she said and quietly shut the door behind her.

The two were closeted for some time before going to find Rutherford, who was in the stable checking what he feared might be a spavin forming on one of his team's ankles. At first, he said no to Charles's plan in stern tones.

"Most definitely not! I am a lot of things, but I am not a cheat. How can you ask such a thing of me?" he groused.

"Because, if the money was lost to a cheater, then, surely, getting it back by cheating cannot be thought wrong," explained Steven earnestly.

Rutherford sighed, glanced at Steven, and then off into the distance, and, after a moment, nodded. Reluctantly. "Charles, I'd like a word with you before we settle our plans. Steven, you go into the house and tell Forbes to tell anyone looking for you that you are not at home. And then you stay inside and away from windows, do you hear me?"

Steven nodded and, suddenly lighthearted, completely certain his big cousin and kindhearted Mr. North would make everything right again, ran back into the house.

Charles watched him go and then turned back to Rutherford. "All right, Ruthie, what *is* the problem, since I don't believe a word of your high-minded claim that you won't cheat? Oh—" He held up a hand when Rutherford bristled. "—I do not mean that you *are* a cheat, but I've trouble accepting that that is the real reason you did not wish to help."

"I'm under a . . . an obligation to that peep-o-day boy myself."

"You, too, owe him?"

"Not money. I still haven't quite figured out how it happened, but he saved me from a harpy who got her claws into me before I knew what she was doing." His weathered skin actually paled. "Charles, I think I might actually have had to marry the woman!"

Charles frowned. "I don't suppose it is possible our pigeon knew your harpy before she extended her claws?"

Rutherford stilled. And then, very softly, he swore long and volubly. "I was set up!"

"And you've been doing his bidding ever since?" Charles was surprised to see color appear in Rutherford's cheeks. "I see you have. Supplying unplucked pigeons for his banqueting?"

"Something like that," muttered Rutherford, looking everywhere but at Charles.

"Steven?"

Rutherford shook his head. "No, that was already too far along for me to get Steven out of it before I knew it was going on. In fact, I didn't know about it until Steven showed up here, demanding I help him."

"But you didn't."

Again color showed, this time in Rutherford's ears. "How could I? I believed myself between Scylla and Charybdis!"

"But you think I may be correct in thinking your evil genius had a hand in your becoming entrapped by the harpy?"

"Yes. I even saw them together a year or so later and never thought anything about it."

"Who is this particular evil gent?"

"Hmm? Oh. Ervine Pelling."

"Pelling! Ervine Pelling?"

"Yes."

"But you know we've been looking for the man. That he cheated Miss Seldon of her inheritance."

"I do? Did he?" Rutherford first looked startled, and then after a moment his eyes narrowed. "Or perhaps he is playing another game, a deep game, and your Miss Seldom is not the angel you think her."

"Nonsense."

"Perhaps."

"Ruthie, believe me. Miss Seldon is exactly who she says she is."

"Of course," said Rutherford, agreeably—but not agreeing.

He hadn't a notion what game was afoot, but he knew Pelling and, knowing Pelling, was certain that, before long, Miss Abby's runner would prove him right. Abby was no fool, after all, and if she had a runner checking on the chit, then the young person was no better than she should be and would be very happy to find herself *not* clapped up behind bars. And she would be generous with her favors when she realized he'd saved her from disaster, either prison or the long dangerous journey to the antipodes!

But there was time before he need do anything about that and there was still the chance she would come to him voluntarily when she realized she'd no hope of Charles. And if that did not happen, he had his valet primed to watch for the runner's arrival. *That* would be the time to abduct Miss Seldon—or whatever her name might be.

Once she knew the game was up, she'd be more than content with what he could offer—rooms and a maid and enough money for her food and a bit for a trinket now and then. The decision made, he nodded, then realized Charles was looking at him oddly, and, once again, felt heat under his skin—this time up his throat.

"Sorry. Was thinking of something else. What did you say?"

"I asked when you think we should begin our raid on Pelling's resources? I'd like to wait a bit if possible, but cannot think how we might delay him. Steven seemed to think him in something of a hurry."

"That's easily done. We send Steven to tell him he's revealed all to Miss Abby, who means to frank him, but can't raise the money all at once, and it will be a few days. A few days are enough?"

"I would think so." Charles wondered exactly where Miss Abby's runner might be at this moment. He wanted the man available to take Pelling prisoner once they had skinned him of enough to cover Steven's debt, Pelling's gambling "losses" canceling Steven's.

And a bit, just enough extra, he thought, *to cover what the man owed Miss Seldon?*

Rutherford cleared his throat. "Shall you tell Steven what he is to do or shall I?"

"Hmm? Oh you do it," said Charles. "I've something else to which I must attend."

"If you mean to look for Miss Seldon, I believe you'll find her with those blasted dogs again," said Rutherford nastily. "I swear, it is as if they understand every word she says."

Charles chuckled. "But, Ruthie! They do! Ask her if you do not believe me. Or better, ask *them.*"

The sally drew a reluctant smile from Rutherford before he walked off, wondering where in the great house he would find Steven in order to give him his orders for putting Pelling off.

Chapter Twelve

A few evenings later Miss Abernathy looked into the salon, saw Matty sitting at the pianoforte, and entered. "I have just been informed that we are to be deserted. Why, I wonder, did all our men decide to go out at the same time?" she asked a trifle fretfully. The tone was out of character, and she knew it. She smiled a wry smile. "Matty, dear, as you see I am a trifle concerned. There was something about the way Steven smiled or perhaps it was Rutherford's overly nonchalant air . . . And Charles does *not* enjoy the sort of evening Ruthie enjoys so . . . well . . . Anyway, *something* was not quite—" She pressed her lips tightly together and then sighed. "—not quite *right* you see."

When Matty opened her mouth to reply, Abby added, "This is nonsense. What could possibly be wrong? I am very sorry to bother you with my megrims. Would you mind very much playing for me? I know you do not feel you are very good, especially when compared to Charles, but you will admit, I'm sure, that *no* one is particularly good when compared to Charles. I am in the mood to enjoy the simple sort of songs you play."

Matty had been about to explain to Miss Abby what Charles had told her—not that he'd wanted to, but she'd insisted—but when Miss Abernathy asked for music, she decided to leave the poor woman in ignorance. If Charles had wished her to know, he'd have told her.

"Of course I will play for you," she said.

She was still playing when Vicar Baxter was announced. Then Miss Abernathy, in only a faintly exasperated tone, greeted him with the words, "Well, Vicar, you have arrived just in time for tea and biscuits, have you not?"

"Oh dear," he said, his tone slightly false. "I had not realized it was so late. I will go away at once."

"No, no, you are very welcome to share our little repast. Matty, do tell Forbes to tell Cook to be particularly generous with the sweets."

Matty, glad to escape the room while she overcame her irritation with the vicar's presence, greeted him rather shortly as she passed him. She delivered her message and then went on down the hall toward the library, where she hoped she would be able to bring herself to a proper frame of mind. It was really too bad of Reverend Baxter to arrive just when she wished to spend all her time worrying about the men. What if the plan did not work? What if the villain, whoever he might be, managed to turn the tables and take their money instead of losing as they meant him to do?

Matty sighed. Worrying would do no one any good at all, and as it had been obvious that Miss Abby, too, was not happy with the visit, she had better return to the salon and support her hostess as best she could.

"Such a lovely picture she makes, does she not?" said the vicar, beaming at her as she entered the room. "So bright and cheery and with just that touch of liveliness that gives those about her a happy glow."

"We are all pleased to have Miss Seldon visiting," said Miss Abby. "Did Forbes say . . . ?"

"He'll have the tray up in no more then ten minutes," she said. "Would you like me to play some more?" she added, thinking that if she were playing perhaps no one would need to make conversation.

"No, no," said Vicar Baxter before Miss Abby could do more than begin to nod her head. "You come over here and tell us what you have been doing since last I visited." Again the vicar beamed at her.

Hiding a sigh, Matty obeyed, although she did *not* take the chair the vicar patted, the one beside his own, but joined Miss Abby on the sofa. "I have done nothing out of the way, Vicar."

"Is that not wonderful?" he asked. "She is content with the drift of her days and the small womanly tasks every woman knows how to do so well, making man's life a joy."

"Small tasks?" asked Miss Abby.

"I refer, of course, to the seeing to the management of your home, the cooking, the cleaning, the mending, and perhaps, if there is time, a little gardening so that the outside is as lovely as the inside."

Matty stared. "But, Reverend," she said, "I do none of that."

Spots of color appeared high on his sharp cheekbones. "No, of course not. You are a guest after all. Although I am certain you do your own mending, some fine work, and those personal chores—" He paused when the women glanced at each other, their amusement obvious. "—chores which—" A look of bewilderment contorted his features. "—you shake your head."

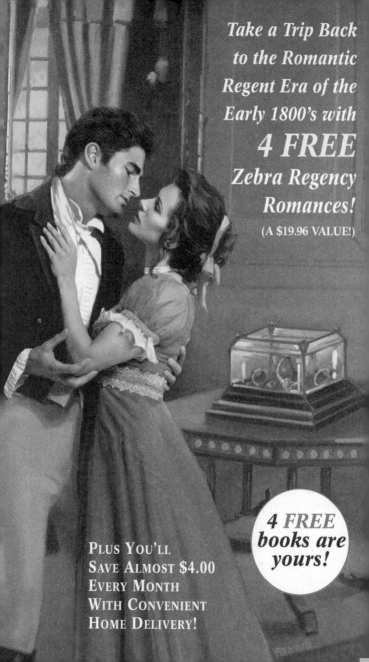

We'd Like to Invite You to Subscribe to Zebra's Regency Romance Book Club and Give You a Gift of 4 Free Books as Your Introduction! (Worth $19.96!)

If you're a Regency lover, imagine the joy of getting **4 FREE Zebra Regency Romances** and then the chance to have these lovely stories delivered to your home each month at the lowest price available! Well, that's our offer to you and here's how you benefit by becoming a Regency Romance subscriber:

4 FREE Introductory Regency Romances are delivered to your doorstep (you only pay for shipping and handling)

4 BRAND NEW Regencies are then delivered each month (usually before they're available in bookstores)

Subscribers save almost $4.00 every month

You also receive a **FREE** monthly newsletter, which features author profiles, discounts, subscriber benefits, book previews and more

No risks or obligations...in other words, you can cancel whenever you wish with no questions asked

Join the thousands of readers who enjoy the savings and convenience offered to Regency Romance subscribers. After your initial introductory shipment, you receive 4 brand-new Zebra Regency Romances each month to examine for 10 days. Then, if you decide to keep the books, you'll pay the preferred subscriber's price, plus shipping and handling.

It's a no-lose proposition, so return the FREE BOOK CERTIFICATE today!

Say Yes to 4 Free Books!
Complete and return the order card to receive this $19.96 value, ABSOLUTELY FREE!

If the certificate is missing below, write to:
Regency Romance Book Club
P.O. Box 5214, Clifton, New Jersey 07015-5214
or call TOLL-FREE 1-800-770-1963

Visit our website at www.kensingtonbooks.com.

FREE BOOK CERTIFICATE

YES! Please rush me 4 Zebra Regency Romances (I only pay for shipping and handling). I understand that each month thereafter I will be able to preview 4 brand-new Regency Romances FREE for 10 days. Then, if I should decide to keep them, I will pay the money-saving preferred subscriber's price for all 4...that's a savings of 20% off the publisher's price. I may return any shipment within 10 days and owe nothing, and I may cancel this subscription at any time. My 4 FREE books will be mine to keep in any case.

Name _____

Address _____ Apt. _____

City _____ State _____ Zip _____

Telephone ( ) _____

Signature _____
(If under 18, parent or guardian must sign.)

RN112A

Terms and prices subject to change. Orders subject to acceptance by Regency Romance Book Club.
Offer valid in U.S. only.

PLACE
STAMP
HERE

REGENCY ROMANCE BOOK CLUB
Zebra Home Subscription Service, Inc.
P.O. Box 5214
Clifton NJ 07015-5214

"I have never learned to sew properly. My nurse, my mother, a neighbor—all tried to teach me the way of it, but my fingers simply would not cooperate. They all gave up on me," said Matty sadly and glanced at Miss Abernathy from the corners of her eyes.

Abby's eyes twinkled. "I know exactly what you mean, child. I think everyone who had a hand in raising me, including my *father* tried to teach me fine needlework. It is beyond me. I enjoy looking at it, but the notion I must set needle to cloth—" She threw up her hands. "—No! Never."

The vicar, his back straight as a poker, looked still more bewildered. "But cannot every woman sew? Is it not the womanly thing to do?"

Matty looked at Miss Abernathy, who looked back. Matty shook her head ever so slightly. Miss Abernathy drew in a shallow breath and let it out in a faintly huffy sort of manner. And then she gave Matty a look that said, *Oh very well I'll do it,* and turned back to the vicar.

"Mr. Baxter," she asked politely, "can every man ride and shoot?"

He blinked. "Ride and shoot? But what has this to do . . . ?"

"But, Mr. Baxter," said Miss Abernathy softly, "is it not the manly thing to do? To ride and shoot?" She knew very well that Mr. Baxter did neither and, with difficulty, kept all expression from her features.

"Harrumph. We were discussing women and womanly ways."

"But you were suggesting, Vicar, that all women are the same, that they all have the same talents and can all do all things womanly. Why should it be any more true that all women do all womanly things than that all men do all manly things?"

The red reappeared in the vicar's cheeks. "I am

quite certain I never said that all women were the same. It is obvious that not all women are the same. You and Miss Seldon are not at all like Lady Wilmingham. You are not ladies, after all.''

Miss Abernathy turned to Matty and, very solemnly, said, "We have been insulted, my dear. And by a vicar, no less.''

"It is too bad when I have always tried very hard to be a lady,'' said Matty, sadly.

The vicar stood, scowling from one woman to the other and then, when Miss Abernathy chuckled, slowly sank back into his chair—neither right on the edge as would a servant nor relaxing completely into it, but, as was his habit, a nicely judged halfway point that was neither subservient nor pretending to equality.

"Mr. Baxter, we are teasing you,'' said his hostess. "Do have another biscuit. They are the lemon ones you like so well,'' she added, coaxingly, realizing she had, perhaps, allowed her sense of humor to carry her a little too far when her prey was so very solemn and unbending.

"As you know,'' he said sternly, "I merely meant that you were not . . . not . . .''

"Born into the aristocracy?'' asked Matty and, when he nodded, smiling approvingly at her, she decided they had had quite enough of that topic. She said, "It has been a while since I last saw you. I have wanted to ask how your discussion with the magistrate went?''

"Magistrate . . . ?'' Vicar Baxter shifted uneasily in his chair, moving an inch nearer the front edge.

"About his son?'' said Matty encouragingly.

"Oh. Oh, well . . .''

"You have talked to the magistrate, have you not?''

"Oh, yes.'' The vicar brightened, sitting still more upright. "I had a very nice chat with him just the other day. He was walking through the village and was so very obliging as to stop and speak with me." The vicar preened himself slightly.

"And you told him of his son's misdeeds, did you not?"

A smug look of self-satisfaction appeared. "As it turned out, it was unnecessary. The boy was hiding nearby and every so often I would look his way. The lad, of course, thought I was telling tales about him to his father and will, from now on be exceedingly discreet in his behavior. And I managed it without upsetting Lord Whitsome. Was that not wise of me?"

Matty ignored his question. "And when the lad realizes his father has no knowledge of his recent behavior he will continue to be cautious and restrained?"

"I don't understand." The vicar pokered up.

"I am certain you do."

"What is this?" asked Miss Abernathy. "What do you discuss? Are you speaking about that young Whitsome bully? The brat who terrorizes the village lads?"

"Does he? I am not at all surprised," said Matty. She adopted a look of sorrow. "With no one to set his feet on the proper path, the lad will go from worse to worse. Very likely, when he is not yet thirty, he will find himself in prison. Debtors' prison if nothing worse."

"What are you saying?" asked the vicar, who was not a truly stupid man and only needed a hint or two or three to bring him to a proper way of thinking—although his character was such that he tended to forget such hints as quickly as he could. "You think he will do *worse* as he grows older?"

"If he is not firmly stopped now? Yes I do. Since he is stealing at age twelve, or whatever he is, what do you think he will do at twenty when he wants something and can get it no way but by force?"

"Oh dear," said the vicar, feeling exceedingly unhappy. "Oh dear me. You would say I *must* speak of this terrible thing to his father?"

"To the *father*," said Matty gently, "rather than to the magistrate?"

"Yes. I see," said the vicar, no less sadly. "I am now forced to see why you urged me to this course of action once before. I apologize, Miss Seldon, for not understanding the difference between the man and his position. A father would not like it that his son was behaving badly and would, however angry it made him, wish to have it pointed out to him, would he not?"

"No man wishes to hear that his son is less than perfect, but the man has a duty to the boy, must see that the child is taught what is right and what is wrong."

"Yes. I will put it just that way, Miss Seldon. You are the daughter of a vicar and you have learned your lessons well. I admire you for it." He rose to his feet, said all that was proper, bowed to Miss Abernathy and then to Miss Seldon, and his feet not exactly dragging, took himself off, wondering when he could do that which he had very much hoped he could avoid—although, in his heart, he had known he could not. . . .

But surely it was too late tonight and could be put off until morning . . . ? His pace quickened.

"Now he is gone," said Miss Abernathy a minute or two later, "do tell me the whole."

Matty described the scene with the old woman in the village and the boy who had stolen her dinner. ". . . so you see, although I did not like ruffling his feathers as I did, I had to encourage the vicar to do right by the lady. And, although he may not agree, of course, right by the lad and his father."

"Of course you did. The vicar is a bit of a weakling when it comes to those he perceives as his superiors. He finds it very difficult to show them disapproval and wishes to be thought well of by them. The fact is, he is a bit of a toady. I cannot like that in him. You, my dear, appear to have the knack of shaming him into doing the right thing."

"It is not my place . . ."

"But someone must do it. I am glad you insisted he speak to Lord Whitsome. Come now, do have another of Cook's very fine lemon biscuits since Vicar Baxter was too upset to finish them." Taking up another biscuit herself, she repeated her earlier desire to know what her guests were up to, to go off as they had with no word of why or where.

Again Matty was tempted to explain, but again she decided it was not her place. If Charles had thought Miss Abby should be apprised of the situation, then he would have told her. She turned the subject to Lady Portentmere's evening party, to which Miss Abernathy and her guests were invited less than a week hence.

"Lady Willy will be sorry she misses it," said Miss Abby, smiling with just a touch of glee. "Lady P. and Lady Willy are rivals in the local social scene and I am a trifle surprised at Lady P.'s holding a party while Lady Willy is not here to be chagrined at how finely it is done. Perhaps Lady P. has company she wishes to entertain?"

"She did not say in her invitation that she had someone she wished everyone to meet?"

"No." Miss Abernathy frowned. "But her ladyship is just the sort to wish to spring a surprise on her neighbors." Miss Abernathy frowned a sudden sharp frown. "Oh dear. I hope it is not that utterly poisonous niece. Her ladyship knows Charles is visiting and it would be just like her to try to snatch him for Violet."

"Violet?"

"Miss Tenton. She has been leading apes for years, but Lady P. will not give up hope of snagging a good party for her."

"Surely her parents . . ."

"Oh," interrupted Miss Abernathy, "they take her to London each year, where she insists on designing her own gowns. She would look very well, actually, if she did not insist on covering herself in lace and ruffles and silk flowers and beads and every other form of decoration she can find. I once saw her wearing a gown *completely* covered with ruffles. You cannot imagine what it was like. But that is not the worst. She will not put up her hair. It is very fine, very long, pale blond hair that flies every which way, getting into people's food or catching on other people's clothes or on things. And when it does she stops absolutely still until someone, anyone, untangles her." She shook her head. "I fear she is growing more and more eccentric as she ages. Someday she will have a certain cachet among the *ton*, but she is, as yet, too young to be more than a byword."

"But has no one tried to . . ."

"Explain to her? Of course. But a more stubborn woman you have yet to meet. She can be *told* nothing. I think perhaps I should warn Charles—but then perhaps he will decide to remain at home that evening. I do not wish him to do that, but—" The frown returned. "—warning him is what I *should* do."

"Surely Mr. North has had years of avoiding matchmakers?"

"There is that, of course—" Miss Abernathy shifted in her seat, then shook her head. "—but no. I do not trust Lady Portentmere. Not where her niece is concerned."

"She would attempt to compromise him?"

"She would."

"Is he so very much a catch, as they call it?"

"Charles? Oh, not such a *very* great catch, I suppose. A very good family and his fortune is not contemptible—although, assuming Violet actually managed to snare him, her ladyship would consider it paltry."

"But then why would her ladyship *wish* her niece to . . . to snare him?"

"But I have said! She is desperate to see her niece wed!"

Matty nodded. She managed to hide it pretty well, but inside where it did not show, her mood grew exceedingly morose. *I knew Charles was above my touch, so why,* she berated herself, *did I allow myself to fall in love with him? And when? And how?*

Such thoughts whirling in her head, she didn't notice that Miss Abby fell silent, watching her young guest. Miss Abby was not unhappy with what she saw. Now if she could convince Charles he was in love with Matty, they could get on with the reading of the banns and, once his parents arrived, hold a very pleasant country wedding.

I will choose a bouquet of roses for her from my favorites. And I will give the girl a trousseau as my wedding gift to her, thought Abby. *Then I will deed Charles that little property just outside Chelsea. It will do nicely for a quiet retreat for him and his little family when London becomes unbearable.*

She frowned very slightly. "When they have a family, that is," she muttered.

"What?" asked Matty, pulled from her meandering thoughts.

"Did I speak aloud? Do disregard it."

And both fell back into a reverie of what might be or would be or could be or would never be or whatever permutation fit whichever head one was in at the moment.

* * *

Miss Abby only pretended to go to bed that evening. She went up to her rooms when Matty went up, but after a long comfortable coze with her paramour, she returned to the downstairs, where, after telling Forbes he could lock up all but the door nearest the stables and take himself off to bed, she sat alone in a small sitting room, the door open, along the hall through which the men must come.

"She knew what was in the wind. I should have insisted she tell me," Abby muttered more than once. Twice she added coals to the unneeded but comforting fire. Thrice she refilled her wineglass with the exceedingly heavy burgundy Forbes had found hidden away in a back corner of the wine cellar. A very good burgundy, but rather wasted on Miss Abby, given her mood of the moment.

It was very nearly three in the morning when a rather boisterous trio saw the light and burst in upon her.

"Miss Abby, you waited up for us," caroled Steven gaily. He was, obviously, a trifle up in the world. "How very nice of you. You can be the first to congratulate me on escaping a very close call indeed." He fairly danced around the room.

Rutherford stalked to a position before the fireplace and stood there, arms akimbo, sourly watching his young cousin.

Charles came to Miss Abby, took her hand between his, and looked into her eyes. "You guessed something was up, did you not? I am sorry we worried you. I should have explained before we left, but I thought it better if I *not* set you fretting."

"Twice I asked Matty what you were doing, but both times, for some reason or another, we were interrupted. I cannot think why. Not that it is important, of course, since you are all returned in good health and Steven is, once again, in high spirits and as he was used to be. But now it is over, can you not tell me?"

Rutherford grunted. "Not a pretty story, Miss Abby. Steven got himself in way over his head and, tonight, we used the sharp's own methods to get him back above water. Not honorable, but he is not an honorable man."

"Why did you not come to me?" asked Miss Abby, frowning at Steven.

"No, no. Couldn't ask help of a *lady*," said Steven, a look of horror widening his eyes.

"He is very young," murmured Charles near Miss Abernathy's ear.

"Yes, but not so young he has not learned a lesson, I hope," she said in clear tones.

Steven sobered. "Oh I have learned my lesson very well indeed. I never *ever* want to go through anything like that. Never again!"

"Was it difficult?" asked Abby. "Rescuing him?"

"The man hadn't a notion we'd combined to see he went down to the tune he did. And then, once we had his wager in hand, we turned it over to Steven, who waltzed in and handed it back to him."

"At that point I believe he suspected us of collusion, but since he'd cheated Steven, he could hardly call us on our machinations," said Charles. "I very much dislike behaving in such a way, but this is one case where I think the means do justify the ends. A defense based on an eye for an eye," he added in thoughtful tones, "might be the best approach if one were to go before the bench."

Steven, who had imbibed enough to make him a trifle more than merely merry, began humming a tune that both Charles and Ruthie knew was *not* suitable to a lady's drawing room. They looked at each other, nodded, and one on either side, led Steven from the room. At the door, Charles turned, mouthed, "I'll return," and continued on his way.

"Is Steven in bed?" asked Miss Abernathy some little time later.

"Ruthie is doing his best to get him there, but the boy is so relieved to be out from under that atrocious load of debt, it may be a bit before he actually falls asleep. Miss Abby, the villain involved is our old acquaintance Pelling. I very much fear he is on his way out of the country right this very minute and only waited this long to see if he might collect what Steven, hmm, *owed* him. He had poor Steven frightened half out of his wits with threats of taking him to law and making a scandal of him. But the problem is that I don't know where to put my hands on your runner so that Pelling may be taken in charge."

Abby frowned. "I cannot help you. Ned only contacts me when he has something to report. In the meantime, have you done nothing about keeping an eye on Mr. Pelling?"

Charles grinned. "Oh yes. I've set Timmy to following him and sending word to me where he moves. If we are lucky, we may yet take him, but that depends on when we next connect with Bright."

"You will recall he has sent notice to the ports that Mr. Pelling is not to be allowed to leave. Ned knows how anxious we are and I have heard nothing for some time now, so perhaps it will not be long."

"Good." Charles yawned a jaw-cracking yawn. "I'm getting too old for these wild nights. I never was a gambler, so this evening's affair was particularly stressful. Ruthie took charge and I followed his lead. He did it very well, by the way."

"Ruthie would see it as the sort of challenge in which he revels." Miss Abernathy frowned. "Charles, have you noticed that our Ruthie is acting a trifle strangely?"

"He is? In what way?"

"I cannot quite put my finger on it, but do you ever have the ... the ... *feeling* he ... that he—" She clenched her fists and shook them. "I cannot put it into words. Just something about the way he occasionally looks at Matty. Something . . . hungry? I sometimes suspect he doesn't believe she is an innocent."

It was Charles's turn to frown. "I do not see how he can have gotten such a bacon-brained notion. He knows, surely, that we are trying to take Pelling up for his blackguard behavior toward her, does he not?"

Miss Abernathy said, "How can he not? We have made no attempt to make a particular secret of it. Have we?"

"*I* haven't discussed the details with him. I have not felt it my place to talk about your business, but he has been here for some time and I do not see how he can have failed to hear the truth of the business."

"No, nor anyone else either." It was Abby's turn to yawn. "Very likely I am tired and seeing boggles where there are none. It has been a long night and I am for bed." She moved to snuff the candles and Charles saw to the fire before, together, they left the room. They were picking up their bed candles when Abby recalled that she had to tell Charles that she feared Lady Portentmere might attempt some matchmaking at the party to which they were all invited.

"Not Miss Tenton," guessed Charles, giving her a look of amused outrage.

"I very much fear it, Charles. It has been years

since she first tried to marry off the widgeon. I should warn you she very nearly had Lord Denton trapped. If he had not gone out the window, he'd have been marched down the aisle faster than fast.''

"The window?''

"She got him very slightly drunk before she herself walked him upstairs to bed. She led him to his bedroom door—except it wasn't his. It was Violet's. According to the story, she turned the key on him once he was in the room.''

"I'm trying to recall the Portentmere mansion. Doesn't that mean they were on the second floor?''

"Yes. He was lucky in that there is an rather ancient wisteria running up that side of the house.''

Charles whooped with laughter and then looked around, embarrassed. "Sorry. I hope I didn't wake anyone, but can you not see poor willowy Denton, all dressed up in his foppish best, clambering down a vine? And of course he would find he was locked out of the house. I wonder what he did?''

Miss Abby smiled. "It is said he spent the night in the barn, awakening when the grooms began working with the horses, and, since that meant the house was open, he went in, had his valet called, and left with only half his possessions. He was so fearful that someone of importance—''

"Lady Portentmere, you mean.''

"—would awaken and somehow manage to trap him all over again.''

"I wonder why that bit of gossip never made the rounds of London? It is such a juicy bit!''

"I don't know, but—'' She sobered and lay her hand on Charles's arm. "—I want you to be on your guard.''

"Me?''

"You.''

"How flattering,'' he said dryly. "I will, of course, make it quite impossible for Lady Potentmere to nab me. I've plans for my future which do not include Miss Tenton," he finished on what *would* have been an obscure note if Abby had been unaware of his feelings for Matty.

They said good night and each went into the proper hall and to the proper room.

Chapter Thirteen

Letters arrived the next day for Charles. They were from his solicitor and included not only Baron Pelling's address, but that of Lady Southend, who it turned out, was Matty's maternal aunt.

"Lady Southend?" Abby's eyes widened. "But I have read about her in the papers, have I not? Is she not that tilt-nosed Tory hostess who does her best to show up the great Whig hostesses?"

"She is. From what little I've seen of her a more supercilious, a more prideful woman does not exist."

"That is harsh, Charles."

"But would appear to be true."

Abby frowned. "There is something I'm forgetting. Something I know . . ." She shook her head. "It will come to me. In the meantime I suppose I am expected to inform her of her niece's plight."

"Both her ladyship and the baron have a right to know they've a near relative in need. Then it will be their decision to do as they will with the information."

"You are talking like a lawyer, Charles," said Abby, an edge to her voice.

"Am I? I apologize."

She chuckled. "Nevertheless, you are correct. But, Charles, I will not allow that child to go where she'll be bullied or used or . . . or . . ."

"Or is unloved."

Abby's eyes twinkled. "How well you know me, Charles. And it is true. I have learned to love her."

"I do not find that particularly surprising," he said.

She waited but he said no more and she sighed. *Will he never admit he has fallen in love with the chit?* she asked herself.

Charles, aware of Abby's thoughts, repressed a smile. It was not yet time for him to make his move. Little Miss Seldon must first know exactly what her position was so that she would rid herself of her insecurities. He would not have her come to him feeling as if she were a petitioner. Nor, for that matter, did he wish to play the part of the bountiful doler-out of rescues and protector from life's ills. He wanted her love and her acceptance of his love, and *companionship* as well as the delights of the marriage bed.

"I," said Miss Abby with dignity when she realized he'd say no more, "must write my letters. I wonder why I bother. Why do I not merely tell the child I have become used to having her around and do not wish to lose her?"

"Because you wish her to have a choice."

"Well, yes," said Abby doubtfully, "but perhaps she will choose the road of duty, believing I offer only out of pity. Or something equally ridiculous."

"You will convince her of the honesty of your offer," he said, nodded, and took himself off with a final comment that he must not interfere when she had work to do.

"Work!" Abby blinked at the closed door. "Oh. The letters. Blast the man. Why does he not merely say that Matty's future is assured and I need not worry my head about her?" And then she recalled his comment that the child should have a choice. She nodded her understanding. "Idiotic to be so chivalrous," she complained. "He will lose her yet."

Later, when finally alone in her bedroom, she related the scene to her love, who set her away so he could stare into her face. She immediately became defensive. "Yes, I know I was rather terse in my letters. I do not *wish* her relatives to come to her rescue!"

He simply stared.

Abby snuggled closer. "Do not scold me. She would be perfect for Charles and how could he do better? Unless, of course, she had a fortune to offer him—but if she did he would not look her way, feeling *he* was not worthy. Why—" She pushed up until she could stare at her companion. "—are men so stupid?"

She pummeled him. "Do not laugh at me!"

Their tussle led to more amusing behavior, and soon after, Miss Abby was alone.

"Nevertheless," she said to the empty room, "she *will* wed him, whatever sort of mess the two of them make of things! I will see all ends as it should."

It occurred to her she was acting very much like Lady Portentmere, pushing, as she was, for a match between the two.

But, she insisted to herself, *there is a difference. I know these two are right for each other. Lady P. would wed Violet to a man with one leg and that one in the gout, just to see her wed!*

The next day Abby suffered through another visit from the vicar, who arrived just in time for lunch. "I have come because I have had word from Lady Wilmingham, which I was certain you would wish to hear," he said, beaming. "She will return from her visit to her sister far more quickly than she was expected to do."

"Oh?" asked Miss Abby, realizing the vicar wished to be prodded into giving all his news.

"Yes," he said in his usual portentous news-giving manner. "She received an invitation to Lady Portentmere's party and decided it would be rude if she were not to attend."

"Hmm." Abby couldn't think of a proper comment for that, so she said nothing more on the subject. "I assume her sister is well and that Bath society is much the same as usual?"

"She has, she said, had a very nice visit except that the weather has been terrible, the waters taste more vile than usual, her sister is not quite up to snuff and, therefore, not very good company and, for reasons she did not go into, Bath society is *not* so amusing as in earlier years."

Again Abby could think of nothing to say that the vicar would not find insulting. "She will be glad to be home again, then," she offered when the silence went on just a trifle too long.

"Yes. I see Miss Seldon is not sitting down to lunch," said the vicar, looking around with a frown.

"I sent her with Charles into Chichester to do an errand for me."

"Well chaperoned, I presume?" asked the vicar, looking horrified at the notion Miss Seldon had gone off with Charles North.

Abby widened her eyes. "Of course. Bitsy is with them. I defy any man to get around Bitsy."

The vicar struggled with his feelings about the impertinent Bitsy. It was very true Miss Abernathy's maid would allow no hanky-panky, but only because she was not properly demure and self-effacing. The conflict kept him silent for long enough Abby was able to finish her sweet in peace.

"And your other guests?" he finally asked.

"Hmm? Oh, Steven has run off to Brighton. The lure of the Regent's summer capital is too much for him when compared to the sedate pace here. Ruthie is around and about somewhere. He is not an eater of luncheons but I presume he has not gone far."

In fact the door opened just then and Rutherford looked in. "Oh. Vicar Baxter. You here?"

It was such an inane comment from someone as quick as Rutherford that Abby instantly sat up and took notice. "Is something wrong? In the kitchens perhaps?" she asked.

Ruthie grinned. "Quick as a whip, Miss Abby. That's you. Better go see to it."

"If you will play host to the vicar, I will go at once," she said, folding her napkin and laying it near her plate. "I apologize," she said to the vicar, but in such an absentminded way he was insulted. She was gone before he could comment, however.

Abby knew very well there was no problem in the kitchen. Forbes would have whispered the information into her ear if that had been the case. Instead, her butler stood in the hall awaiting her.

"It's that runner, madam," he said. "I have put him in your study."

"Very well. Thank you very much." She started toward the hall that led to her snuggery but turned at the last moment. "If you can possibly do so tactfully, will you ease our other guest on his way?"

Forbes very nearly smiled, hiding it with a bow. "I will do my best."

"You may laugh if you wish," said Abby, hurrying on toward her meeting with Ned and not waiting to see how Forbes reacted to her awareness that he'd found humor in her request.

"Ned. What have you discovered?"

"Pelling is in the area."

"Perhaps he was," she said, giving him a teasing look, "but it is not unlikely he has gone."

Ned straightened. "What do you know that I do not?"

"Charles and Rutherford made a may game of him." She explained about Steven's debt and the solution. "Charles's man is keeping an eye on him."

"Excellent. And where is Charles?"

"I sent him off with Miss Seldon. They are in Chichester," she explained. She eyed him. "Perhaps you should go after them? If anyone knows where that Timmy has gotten to, Charles will."

Ned frowned. "Well, if you think there is that great a hurry . . . I was rather hoping . . ."

"Where is your head, Ned? Bitsy is *with* them, of course."

"Oh. Oh! In that case . . ." He grinned. "I'm off." And he was.

Miss Abby, hoping that the vicar, too, was "off," returned to the hall. She was disappointed. "He's still here?"

"I believe he asked for a second sweet, madam."

"Oh dear, he will eat them all," she said in a worried manner.

"It is just a thought, madam, but perhaps Cook has not sent the whole of her baking up to the breakfast room?"

"Ah! Of course. There are no flies on Cook!"

"Ahem. Yes. Of course."

Abby cocked her head at her disapproving butler. "Flies?"

He nodded regally.

"Forbes, has it ever occurred to you it is not your place to correct me?"

"I would never dare to correct you, madam," he said, horrified.

"Would you not?" She tapped her foot. "I stand

corrected," she added, her features totally controlled and utterly sober. And then, her eyes twinkling when Forbes had a great deal of difficulty maintaining a properly sober expression, she deemed him well punished and went off to join her guest in the breakfast room.

"Ah! And where is Rutherford?"

The vicar half rose from his seat but settled back when Miss Abby seated herself, nodding to the footman to fix her a plate with another sweet.

"I believe I may have said something to upset Mr. Morton," said the vicar pensively.

"Surely not," said Miss Abby, and then, mentally, kicked herself for the sarcastic tone of that.

"You mean it would be very difficult to upset Mr. Morton, of course," said the vicar, blind to his own tactlessness. "I merely felt it my place to explain to him that he and Mr. North were quite wrong to . . . to . . ." The vicar could think of no polite word for cheating.

". . . get the money for Steven from Mr. Pelling, who cheated Steven by cheating him in return? Charles pointed out that the Bible calls for an eye for an eye. Cheating a cheat seemed appropriate to all of us."

"The ends do not justify the means," said the vicar pontifically, his nose in the air.

"Yes. In general I would agree with you. In this particular case I wonder." She caught the vicar's eye and held her gaze steady. "You, then, would expect Steven to pay the man what he lost even though Pelling had cheated in order to make Steven lose to him?"

The vicar looked confused.

"Yes, well, it is a moral dilemma of the worst sort, is it not?" asked Miss Abby a trifle sternly. "We could see no other way to solve it and did our best."

"You had a hand it this?" asked Vicar Baxter, his eyes wide.

"Only in the sense that I approve what they did. They saved Steven, who is very young and, thanks to his cousin and Mr. North, is no longer such an innocent that he will fall into the hands of another plausible rogue. Steven is worth saving. The villain is not and needs to suffer for his behavior."

"Ah well, as to that, we are told to leave vengeance to God."

"I am not speaking of vengeance, but of suffering. The villain will suffer for his sins."

"Yes, but . . ."

Abby waved him to silence. "We will not agree. I am not certain I agree with myself. And yet, as I said, there was no other way. Steven . . ."

"Ah yes. The young err and learn from their errors. You would say he suffered enough, but did he?" asked the vicar rhetorically. "Should he not have . . . ?"

Abby interrupted, naming the amount Steven had owed.

"Oh dear," said Baxter in a small voice. "Oh yes. I see."

"We will discuss it no more."

"No." The vicar straightened his shoulders. He glanced toward the buffet, noticed there was still another tart, and nodded to the footman that he'd have it.

Abby watched it disappear with a touch of sadness. Cook's tarts were her favorite dessert. She hoped Forbes was correct and Cook had not sent up all of them to grace the luncheon board.

It seemed forever before the vicar left. He had to detail all the parish business he'd been about that day and comment, again, on Lady Wilmingham's imminent arrival, and say a few words about Lady Portentmere's upcoming entertainment and then a few more words about Lady Wilmingham and add one more comment on the evils of taking justice into one's own hands and then finally remembered that he had to return home in order to work on Sunday's sermon.

In fact, he had overstayed his welcome far longer than he should in the hopes he'd gain a glimpse of Miss Seldon. Unfortunately for him, he was unable to think of one single other thing about which he might speak and left a mere fifteen minutes before Matty and Charles returned.

"Was it a pleasant jaunt?" asked Abby of Matty.

"Very pleasant," was all she said before excusing herself and leaving the room.

"Pleasant?" asked Abby of Charles, who grimaced. "Tell me," insisted Abby.

Charles sighed. "Very pleasant and very bland. Our Miss Seldon was the absolutely perfectly behaved young lady, utterly polite, utterly correct, utterly boring."

"Why?"

"I don't know. I was hoping you could tell me."

"I will see what I can discover."

Upstairs, alone, Matty allowed her tears to fall without check. Once or twice she glanced at the little ormolu clock, which lived on her mantel. At the end of five minutes she wiped her eyes, washed her face, and turned to stand at her window. "He is so very wonderful," she said sadly, softly, and turned at the tap on her door.

"Yes," she called.

The door opened and she berated herself for forgetting to lock it. Especially since Rutherford stood in the opening.

"You must come at once."

"Come . . . ?"

"Please do not argue with me, Miss Seldon. It is imperative that we hurry."

She studied his grave face, his faintly agitated manner. "Miss Abby . . ."

"You must come," he interrupted, looking down the hall and back toward her. "At once."

"I do not trust you."

He ran his fingers through what had been a perfect example of the windswept, completely ruining his valet's work. One curl slipped down to form a question mark in the center of his forehead. "Miss Seldon, will you not believe that I have your best interests at heart and come with me? Before it is too late?"

She hesitated. His voice and manner convinced her he was sincere, that he believed what he said, but what, exactly, was it that he believed.

He held out his hand. "Come. I will not touch you or hurt you. I promise."

Still she hesitated.

"My promises are to be believed, Miss Seldon," he said and said it so simply that she was forced to believe him. "You may need your pelisse," he added, gesturing to where it lay across the arm of her chair.

He was as good as his word and didn't even touch her to help her into his curricle. As soon as she was settled, they were away. Once they were on the road and his horses well under control, she asked him to explain himself. "This is not the way to the village so where is Miss Abby? Where are you taking me? I thought something was the matter."

"It is. Terribly the matter. You did not believe, surely, that Miss Abby was such a fool as to take your quite ridiculous story seriously, did you? The vicar, perhaps, but not our Miss Abby. Miss Seldon, or whoever you are, she called in a runner to check on you."

"Ned Bright? The Bow Street runner?"

In his surprise, Rutherford dropped his hands, his horses—not chosen for placid natures—picked up speed. He had his hands full for several minutes, bringing them back to a trot. "You knew?" he said when he could speak.

"Ned is attempting to track down my despicable cousin and, if he can, return a bit of my small inheritance which Ervine stole from me. I would be happy if he discovered nothing more than the family Bible or my mother's bits of jewelry."

"Miss Seldon, enough of this pretense," he said, irritably. "You and I both know you are not the innocent you pretend to be. You need not continue your act. I have you safe and you will not be taken up for the little twister you are, will not find yourself in gaol or transported to Botany Bay, so let us be done with this. I am *saving* you from all that, do you not see?"

"Mr. Morton," said Matty, sitting up straight and clenching her hands in her lap, "I haven't a notion what you have in your head, but I have not lied about my circumstance. I quite agree with you that Miss Abby would not accept my mere word about this, and she did not. She admitted to me that she sketched my face and sent it and her maid to Little Conghurst to see if I am who I say I am. The sketch was a good one and Bitsy verified my every word. So, if you would truly save me, as you call it, you will turn this curricle around and return, at once, to Miss Abby's."

Rutherford drove on, frowning mightily. He did not wish to give up his own interpretation of what he considered the facts of the case. He wanted Miss Seldon and he wanted her on his own terms. But if she were, truly, the daughter of a recently deceased vicar, if she had been tricked by some wicked cousin, sent off to nowhere with nothing to sustain her, then his behavior in stealing off with her was very nearly as despicable as the cousin's.

Was as despicable and would ruin her just as surely.

"Mr. Morton?"

Rutherford pulled his horses to a standstill. "You know the redbreast? The runner?"

"Yes."

"You believe he has been set to track down this cousin you say ruined you?"

"Well, he would not have done it if it were not for Miss Abby," responded Matty, a wiggle of hope edging its way into her heart.

"Who would do such a thing? What sort of man would . . ." He glanced at Matty, who was covering a grin. "Well, yes," he blustered, "but I thought I was rescuing you, not making things worse."

"Shall we return to Miss Abby's?" asked Matty carefully. "You may ask her if I am in danger of finding myself taken up as a slippery customer. Do I have that right?"

"You do." Rutherford cast another suspicious glance her way.

"It is a term the runner used and I thought it particularly descriptive," she said.

Rutherford sighed. "Very well, Miss Seldon. We will do as you ask. But I hope you are not deceiving yourself as well as Miss Abby."

Matty looked at him in wonder. "You truly believe I am an opportunist, using Miss Abby in some devious manner for my own advantage!"

"But of course. How can it be otherwise? Such an obviously stupid tale of evil cousins and mistaken coaches."

"Ervine Pelling is an evil man! He did exactly as I said he did, you . . . you thatch-gallow!" said Matty.

It was the worst she could think of and, finally

roused to outrage, she used it. Matty was not used
to having her word disbelieved. It had been bad
enough when Lady Wilmingham did so, but to
have Miss Abby's relative call her a liar was just too
much.

"Pelling!"

"Yes. Much to my regret, I am forced to call him
'cousin.' "

"One cannot," said Rutherford absently, "choose
one's relatives, only one's friends."

"That is so trite it is hoary with age," said Matty
as scathingly as she could.

Rutherford had turned his team and was headed
back to Abernathy Hall still more quickly than he'd
left it. He hoped to return while the servants were
still at their dinner, hoped they would not be
caught returning. It was too bad of Abby not to
have let him into her counsels, not to have told
him what was in the wind. What was he supposed
to have thought about such a thin tale as the chit
had spouted? Utter nonsense. No man would have
believed it.

And then more than usually honest with himself,
Rutherford added the thought, *Especially when I
didn't want to believe it.*

He was not in luck. Forbes opened the door
to Miss Seldon and looked beyond her to where
Rutherford waited to see her in before driving his
horses on around the house to the stables. Even
that might have been all right if only Miss Seldon
had *not* looked a thundercloud.

Rutherford heaved a massive sigh and began to
compose the words to the necessary proposal in
his mind. She had been compromised. It was not
what he wanted—but wedding her would not be
totally bad. He had, after all, wanted her in his
bed. He still did.

Rutherford ran Miss Seldon down in the

library—of all places. She was sitting near the windows, a book in one hand, a finger marking her place, and Miss Abby's huge old war-torn tomcat in her lap, rumbling and grumbling with an overly loud purr.

For a moment Rutherford watched them. Miss Seldon, he thought, looked sad. He wondered if it were a result of his unnecessary attempt at rescue. She stopped the petting motion and the cat touched the back of her hand with his paw, batting it when she did not immediately return to caressing him. The tom was obviously a self-centered sort of creature, wanting what he wanted right now, since, whenever Miss Seldon ceased her gentle running of her hand over his back and down his sides, he lifted a paw and patted her hand or her cheek until she returned to the work he had set her.

Another odd instant of self-awareness lit a light in Rutherford's mind. He was like that. Especially where women were concerned. When he wanted a woman's attention, he wanted her full attention and would not be above demanding it—as did that ragged-eared, crook-tailed tomcat.

Am I to be as scorned as I felt scorn for the cat? he asked himself. The reluctant answer was yes.

It was a humbled Rutherford who crossed the room and knelt before a startled Miss Seldon. "I have compromised you. I have come to ask your forgiveness and to make amends."

"What?"

The tomcat sat up on her lap and glared at Rutherford, looking for all the world like a guard on duty.

"I don't understand," she said. "What did you do, after all? You kept your promise not to touch me."

"But Forbes saw me return you, unchaperoned,

to the house. It is disaster if not instantly retrieved by the announcement of our engagement."

She blinked rapidly, absorbing that. "No," she said.

"No, I did not compromise you? You are an innocent and do not know the *ton*. I have lived in it for years now and know every in and out. You must take my word for it, my dear. We must be engaged." He reached a hand out to draw her to her feet—and instantly jerked it back, a number of deep scratches down its back. He glared at the cat glaring at him. "You . . . !"

Matty hid a smile by leaning over the huge old tomcat and hugging him. "You would protect me?" she murmured. "I appreciate the thought, Ugly, but I fear it would be better for the both of us if you do not attempt such a thing again." The cat turned its head, ran a rough tongue across her chin, and then, with dignity, stepped from her lap to the floor. He moved regally toward the door, stepping around Rutherford—and turned to sink his claws, for just long enough to make the man jump—into Rutherford's calf.

Rutherford swung around, ready to kick the cat halfway across the room, but the wise old animal, long experienced with the human male's reaction to pain, was already well out of range. "I'll drown that beast if I ever catch him!"

"But you would have done the same," murmured Matty so softly Rutherford was uncertain he'd heard her.

"The very same—or so you claimed," said Matty as she stood and, quickly, moved behind the chair, putting it between them. "Should I threaten to drown you?"

"You are quick to come to that mangy animal's

defense," he growled, wiping blood from the back of his hand and hoping there would be no stains on the leg of his trousers.

"Ugly knew I was concerned, worried, and came to my defense as a result. Can you claim you were worried about me?"

He hesitated.

She smiled a cold smile. "No. You merely saw something you wanted, saw a way of getting it, and attempted to have your way with no thought to what anyone else might wish."

"I admit to selfish urges," he said stiffly. "But neither could I bear the thought of you in the magistrate's noisome cell awaiting the next assizes. I did have your interests at heart and you would not have found me ungenerous."

"Ah." Matty shook her head, her disapproval obvious.

"What? You did not know what I had in my mind for you?" He looked chagrined that he had, very nearly in so many words, admitted it. "I thought, from what you said, that you did."

"I suspected. I did not know."

He cleared his throat. "Well, it makes no odds. However it came about, you must wed me."

"No."

"Why do you continue to deny the obvious?" he asked, his irritation growing that when he had steeled himself to make the supreme sacrifice, she was not suitably appreciative.

"I will not wed you. You would make an abominable husband. Particularly when—" Matty found she was too embarrassed to suggest he would tire of her. "—when you will resent the fact you were forced into marriage."

"We have, I tell you, no choice."

"We do."

"We do *not*."

"*Do*."

She shook her head and he stood, arms akimbo, glaring. And then Matty did a very stupid thing. She turned her back on him.

Chapter Fourteen

"Where do you suppose she is now?" asked Miss Abby of Charles.

"Very likely she is in her favorite place. I will check the library."

Charles opened the door with no particular care, but it was unnecessary that he do so. The room's occupants would not have heard if he'd slammed it against the wall. Miss Seldon stood bound in Rutherford's arms. Charles, his heart leaden, backed up. He had begun to pull the door closed when he realized she was pounding on Morton's shoulders. He frowned. Rutherford ducked his head to nibble on her ear and she pushed at him.

"No. Do stop at once. This is nonsense. Stop." Her voice broke. "Oh, please do stop."

Charles was across the room in a handful of strides, his hand on Rutherford's shoulder, swinging him around and swinging a very good left hook up under his chin. Rutherford leaned back and fell with a thud to the floor.

"Miss Seldon! Are you all right?"

Matty had retreated to the wall against which she leaned, her hands covering the lower part of her face. She stared, wide-eyed, from the man on the floor to Charles and back again. "Thank you," she breathed. "It is totally inadequate to what I feel, but thank you." And then she straightened and glared down at Rutherford, who was groaning and turning his jaw from side to side. "I would have done it myself if only I'd been able."

"Miss Abby is looking for you," said Charles gently. "Why do you not go to her while I have a few, er, words with Morton here?"

"I think," she said reluctantly, "I should inform you that I had turned down a proposal of marriage before he attempted to use, hmm, other means to convince me to say yes."

"I see. Then I shall change the words I had in mind to other equally strong words, but *still* of a nature which need not concern you."

She nodded. "I was worried you might feel you had to call him out. I do not believe that necessary under the circumstances."

Charles smiled and gave her a gentle push toward the door. "You go along now. I will join the two of you soon. Miss Abby's little office. You know."

Rutherford, in the meantime, was rising to his feet. He had heard the last exchange and was rather bemused by it. The little Seldon, instead of running from both his importuning ways and from the violence Charles had risen to, had stayed to see that the fight did not escalate to something dangerous.

"You might," growled Rutherford, "at least admit you could not have done that if I had, er . . . well . . ."

"If you had not been preoccupied with, hmm, other things?" asked Charles politely. "Very likely that is true. On the other hand, I found myself so very angry that it is possible I might have achieved the same result even if I had remembered to be so gentlemanly as to give you warning of my intentions."

Rutherford rubbed his jaw and once again moved it from side to side. "You've a very effective left hook there. Have you done much boxing?"

"A little." It was a pastime Charles had once indulged to a much greater degree than in recent years, but there was no sense in getting into a discussion about his wilder youth. "I have a great deal of difficulty believing you actually proposed honorable marriage, Ruthie. I know you too well."

"Well I did," growled Rutherford. He pursed his lips and looked into some unseeable distance. "Had to."

Charles stiffened. "You compromised her."

"Unruffle your feathers! In the sense I tried to run off with her. She convinced me not to, but upon returning her, Forbes saw us. No chaperon. Had to offer amends."

"She turned you down. When she did, I would have thought you'd have felt nothing but relief to be well out of it and gone your way."

Rutherford frowned. Once again his lips tightened. Finally he seemed to collapse into himself, rather than to relax. He shook his head. "I don't know what got into me. I couldn't leave it. Something kept forcing me to insist."

"Perhaps," said Charles politely, "you have fallen in love with her."

Rutherford's eyes widened and his skin paled. "Nonsense. Utter nonsense. *Love?* No. Ridiculous."

Charles tipped his head, questioningly.

"Saw what love could do to a person," said Rutherford reluctantly. "Swore it would never happen to me. *Never.*"

"Your mother?"

Rutherford turned away, nodded once, stalked

to the window, and stared out it. "Suppose I'd better pack and be on my way. Meant to be in Brighton long ago. Only stayed on because . . ." He paused, uncertain why he'd stayed.

"Because, according to our Abby, you are a perverse creature and could not allow the vicar to think he'd chased you off. When he told you you must go, you immediately determined to stay—or so she says. And then you discovered another reason to stay, did you not?"

"I'm not proud of it," growled Rutherford. "I made a mistake." He swung around. "Charles, believe me, I was convinced she was the sweetest little schemer who ever lived. I thought I'd save Abby from whatever machinations the chit had in mind and when that runner showed up and Abby didn't tell me why—well, I assumed it was because she wasn't quite so naive as I'd thought and had put the man to discovering what he could of Miss Seldon so they could make a case against her."

"Not very flattering to either Miss Seldon or to Miss Abby."

Rutherford's mouth pursed still again. He did not like admitting he was wrong. He did not like feeling he'd been *put* in the wrong. But both were true and he had to swallow it. He nodded. "I'll be gone before an hour is out. Say all that is proper to Abby, will you?"

Charles watched Rutherford stalk from the library and admitted to himself that he was not unpleased to have a rival for Miss Seldon's affections absent himself from the house. With both Steven, whom no one had ever taken seriously as a suitor for Miss Seldon's hand, and Rutherford, who might not have been suing for her hand, but might nevertheless have turned her head and convinced her to throw her bonnet over the windmill—well, with both of them gone, perhaps he himself had a better chance of winning her. He hoped so.

He spent a good twenty minutes plotting out a strategy that would convince Miss Seldon he was the only man for her.

Chapter Fifteen

Miss Seldon spent a good half hour in despair, wondering how she had allowed herself to fall so deeply in love with Charles North that he would ever be the only man for her heart. Alone in her room where she went after leaving the men, she sat in her window lecturing herself on the proper behavior for a lovelorn young woman. Most of all, she must not embarrass Charles—

Mr. North, I must remember to call him Mr. North, even in my thoughts!

But her thoughts returned to the point. She must not embarrass him by allowing him to see how she felt about him. Convinced, finally, that she had herself well in hand, she went to find Miss Abby. And stood at the top of the stairs poised to run, when she heard Rutherford Morton's voice.

"I have been here far longer than I intended and I must go," he said in languid tones to Miss Abby, who stood near him, looking a trifle perplexed.

"Without saying good-bye to me? If I had not come into the hall just now, you would have left without even trying to see me? Ruthie, it isn't like

you. You are careless of the proprieties, but never
to the point of insult!"

He drew in a deep breath and let it out through
his nose, his mouth compressed.

"Ah. I see." She stared up at him. "You have
put your chances to the touch and been turned
down."

Even from the top of the stairs, Matty saw his
ears redden.

"There is no getting around you, is there, Abby?
Perhaps that is why I meant to steal away like a
thief in the night."

"Because you were unable to steal away *as* a thief
in the night?" she said, her gruff voice stern and
firm.

He cursed softly. "Abby, you are a witch."

"No, just very much aware of who and what a
person is. You amuse me, Rutherford, but if you
had managed to steal away with our Miss Seldon,
I believe I would have become very angry."

"Why do you think she'd not have gone willingly?" he asked with just a touch of his old arrogance.

"Why? Because I know her as well as I know you.
She'd not have done it unless you lied to her and
she believed you meant to wed her. But you are
not the sort to lie about such things. You would
have taken her off believing you could change her
mind."

"I will admit that I truly thought she would be
grateful." He looked at his nails and then at Abby.
"Perhaps if you had not been so secretive I would
have understood long ago that you believed her
tale. As it was, I convinced myself your runner was
investigating her with the intention of laying
charges against her."

"Convinced yourself," said Abby, pouncing on
the critical comment. She chuckled ruefully. "As

usual, you've disarmed me with your candor. And yes, I agree that I must take a trifle bit of blame for the whole but Miss Seldon's business was not yours. I would not discuss it with you for that reason."

"Charles tells me you sent Bitsy off to check if her story was true. You might at least have told me that."

She frowned. "Had you not yet arrived when I did that? I cannot recall. In any case, it is water over the dam or under the mill wheel. Rutherford, I will, eventually, welcome you back under my roof, but I believe I do not wish to see you for some months."

He nodded. "A punishment, my dear Abby, that will pierce me to the heart," he said in languid tones. "You, as you know, are the only one of my relatives I not only like but enjoy being near." He bowed, turned, and walked from the hall into the sunlight. In only moments Matty heard the clatter of his horses over the cobbled area near the house.

"You may come down now, Matty," said Miss Abby.

Matty gasped. "You truly are a witch! How else did you know I was here?"

Miss Abernathy chuckled. "Easily, my dear. I caught a glimpse of your skirts when I looked up into Rutherford's face when he still stood on the stairs."

Matty joined her hostess in the hall. "He is not bad by his own lights."

"I am glad you are mature enough to understand that, because I do not wish to ever lose your companionship and I will not, totally, give up Rutherford's. He amuses me when he is not angering me."

"He is your relative. Of course he must remain in your regard, Miss Abby." Matty frowned slightly.

"From something he said, I think he needs you. Probably far more than you need him."

Miss Abernathy nodded. "I was unaware of just exactly how deeply he held me in regard until he made that offhand comment about his relatives." Her lips compressed. "Ruthie, I have discovered, is never more serious than when he is pretending he doesn't care." She hooked her arm through Matty's and drew her off toward her study. "Did he really propose?"

Matty colored up. "He did."

"And you told him no. I almost wish you had not. You'd have been good for him, I think. You've a strongly moral nature and, although fun-loving, a serious side as well. You might, I think, have managed, over time, to cut through that cynicism he wears like a shield."

"*Like* a shield?"

Miss Abernathy missed a step. "Now why have I never seen that. No. Not *like* a shield. It *is* a shield, is it not? My wise little Matty!"

Miss Abernathy opened the door to the study and, as Matty was about to enter ahead of her hostess, she caught a glimpse of the man seated in one of the straight-backed chairs against the far wall, and stopped, turned, tried to push back around Miss Abernathy, and into the hall.

"Here, my dear, he will not hurt you!"

"Miss Seldon," said Charles from inside the room, "your cousin is under restraint. We merely await your presence to determine what to do with him."

Pelling's frown deepened. "Can't prove a thing."

"That there is something to prove is in itself proof of a sort," said Miss Abernathy sternly.

She put an arm around Matty's waist and gently urged her into the study. Charles came to her and led her to a chair as far from Pelling's as was possible in the smallish room.

"This is the man, is it not?" asked Miss Abernathy, just to make certain of it.

"Yes," said Matty, her voice unhappy. "Is he truly my cousin?"

"Yes," said Charles, "but you need not feel guilty for disliking him. You are not alone in that. His own father disowned him, so you need have no qualms at all in feeling he is not an admirable man."

"How did you . . . ?" Pelling clamped his mouth shut.

"How did we discover that? Because one of our first steps was to send someone to your father to see if, by chance, there was a Miss Seldon in residence and that our Miss Seldon just happened to look like the real Miss Seldon. There was not, of course, and our agent discovered all sorts of interesting things about you, Pelling. I doubt you will ever be welcome in the region again. No one has forgotten what evil you did while a mere boy and living there. The man you've become would be still less liked."

"Bah. Dowdy country matrons. Stupid farmers. Not a one of them worth a thought."

"Including, of course, your own family."

"Them most of all," spat Pelling, leaning forward against his bonds.

"Frankly, I am rather amazed you merely put your cousin on a coach."

"That I didn't ravage her?" Pelling grimaced. "Got better uses for females—assuming they know the game."

Charles glanced toward Matty, who looked as if she were curious, toward Miss Abby, who had stiffened, and then toward Ned, who had sat quietly in his corner, making himself small but busily writing down all that was said. He grimaced, but did not raise his head.

"I think we will speak of other things," said Charles. He waited patiently for Pelling's evil laughter to stop. "Yes, of other things. Such as cheating green boys of their patrimony. Who, besides Steven, have you in your power?"

Pelling turned as best he could, settled his gaze on the globes sitting in the corner, and said nothing. He continued to say nothing no matter what Charles asked or said. This went on for some time. Finally Matty squirmed in her chair and Charles looked her way. "You've a question, Miss Seldon?"

"Perhaps if he will admit to nothing else he will tell me what he did with my mother's jewelry. It was all I had of hers."

Pelling turned a curious look her way and looked back at the globes as if fascinated by them.

"Please? I know you cannot understand *why* it is important to me although you realize it is. Knowing that sort of thing, even when you do not understand it, is necessary if you are to do your evil and get away with it. Have you hidden them away somewhere, hoping to bribe me with their return if only I will not lay charges against you?"

Pelling turned a surprised look her way. "How'd you guess?"

"You are very obvious in many ways," she said in a simple fashion that outraged their captive and, at long last, made him lose his temper.

"Obvious? Obvious! Little cat. Stupid little cat. Of course I've put them away safe. So. Will you?"

"Will I promise to let you go if you return them?" Matty turned an exceedingly sad look down toward the floor. Her shoulders slumped and she felt a tear run down her cheek. "I cannot. If you are released you will go on behaving badly toward the innocent. I must give up hope of my few possessions because I've a duty toward humanity. My mother would want it that way."

Pelling stared at her. "You'd give up your own interests for others you don't even know? Why?"

"If you do not understand it, then there is no way any man can explain it to you. I pity you."

He cast her a baffled look. "Pity . . . Me?"

"You. Miss Abby, may I go? Is there something else I must do here or, if there is, may I do it later?"

"Yes, dear, you may go for now—"

Matty stood for a moment looking at her cousin as if memorizing his features. Then she nodded and left the room.

"—Charles, follow her. I think I know what she would do, but you had best go with her."

Charles caught up with Matty as she went out the side door nearest Miss Abernathy's study. "Wait up unless it is important that you be alone," he called.

"Hmm? Oh, Charles—Mr. North, I mean."

"Will you tell me your intentions?" he asked.

"I mean to have the dogcart harnessed up so that I can go into the village for a brief time."

"You would go to the church," said Charles, looking down at her.

"I must," she said simply. "It is what my father would wish of me."

"You will pray for that evil man's soul."

"Yes."

Charles, thinking it was unlikely to do a bit of good, nodded. "I will drive you and wait for you. Come."

A little while later Matty was leaving the church when Reverend Baxter rounded the corner on his way to the front gate.

"Why, Miss Matty, you have come to visit me?" He beamed.

Matty shook her head. "I had need of the church,

Vicar. The peace and quiet and the secure feeling
one has there."

His smile faded. "You are in trouble? You have
had bad news? Come," he said, taking her arm in
a firm grip, "I will help you."

Matty dug in her heels. "It is nothing with which
you may help," she said firmly. "Charles is waiting
to return me to Abernathy Hall. Please," she said
when he did not release her, "you are hurting
me."

Instantly he let her go, an appalled look in his
face. "Oh, I'd not hurt you for anything, Miss Seldon. Not for anything. Perhaps the thought I
might be of service to you made me insensitive
to . . . to . . ."

"To how tightly you held me." Matty held out
her hand in a positive fashion. "I must go now.
Good day to you."

"I will walk you to your carriage," he said, ignoring her hand. When they arrived, he frowned. "An
open carriage on such a hot and humid day?" he
asked Charles, disapproving.

"Now, Reverend," said Charles, smiling, "you
surely do not mean to say I should have brought
her in a closed carriage! Just the two of us. That
would never do."

Spots of color touched the vicar's sharp cheekbones. "No, no. Never." He sighed, looking at the
Abernathy gig. He had thought to ask for a seat
back to the hall with them, but there wasn't room
for three. He sighed again, thinking of Miss Abernathy's very good afternoon refreshments, but it
was not to be. Finally, he took Miss Seldon's hand
in his, squeezed it gently while looking soulfully
into her eyes, and then, when she insisted they
must depart, more hindered than helped her into
the gig.

She had been deeply embarrassed by that last

look. It occurred to her that perhaps the good vicar was falling in love with her. Vicar Baxter? "Nonsense," she said softly.

"What is nonsense?"

"Hmm? Oh—" Embarrassment returned. "—merely a thought that crossed my mind. Not at all sensible and I haven't a notion why such a thing occurred to me. Will you," she said, changing the subject, "tell me exactly what will happen to my cousin?"

Charles did so in more detail than she cared to know.

"Well," she said when he finished, "perhaps I should write Baron Pelling. Surely, even if he has disinherited Ervine, he will wish to know."

"It will be attended to. You need not concern yourself."

After a moment, she asked, "Has the baron been informed of my situation?"

"Both he and your mother's sister, whom we recently discovered, either already know or will soon receive word of your presence here with Miss Abernathy."

"I have an aunt?" Matty turned sideways, staring at Charles.

He nodded. "Yes. Did your mother never once speak of her own family?"

Matty frowned. "I may have one recollection, but it is vague. I suspect I was not supposed to hear. It was during her last illness and she was talking to my father. Something about apprising someone of her death. Or *not*, perhaps? But I was so unhappy that she knew she was dying that the name did not register and I never thought to ask."

"You knew?"

"That she was dying? It was obvious to those of us who cared for her, but so often the sufferer is unaware until very near their time to depart this

world. It is better so for those who fear death."
She frowned. "Perhaps that is it? My mother did
not fear it?"

"Perhaps that is it," he said gently.

They remained silent the rest of the way home.
Charles was unable to pull right up to the door
because a rather large old-fashioned carriage
blocked the way. A boy stood near it throwing rocks
at Miss Abby's cats.

"Stop that," called Matty, starting toward him
the instant her feet were on the ground. "You bad
boy! Don't you dare . . ." She put her hand to her
forehead, brought it down, and stared at the blood,
looked at the suddenly fearful boy, and, gently,
slowly, sunk to the ground.

Charles had returned to the gig after helping
her down, and was reaching to untie his reins pre-
paratory to removing it to the stables when he saw
her fall. He was out of the carriage and at her side
instantly. Once he was certain she was only partially
insensible, he raced after the fleeing lad, who was
too fat to run quickly, caught him, and dragged
him back.

Matty stirred, moaned.

"At least you will not hang," said Charles, giving
the boy a shake. "You did not murder her."

"Didn't mean to hurt her," whined the boy.

"Didn't you? Oh, but you did. Otherwise you'd
not have thrown that stone at her."

"She startled me. Wouldn't have done it if I'd
time for thought," wheedled the boy.

"Perhaps that is half your trouble," said Charles
giving him another shake. "You never think. Never
think how what you do will hurt others. You are
the boy who ran off with that village woman's dinner, are you not?"

"Who told you that? She did!" The boy kicked
out at Matty, who was starting to sit up. Luckily he

was not so near as to hit her with his heavy-soled shoe, but it was one more action in the scales weighing heavily against him.

Matty found her pocket handkerchief and pressed it against the wound, stopping the blood oozing from her temple and running down her cheek, where a little had dripped onto the collar of her gown. She stared at the boy. "You," she said softly. "You are the lad. The one Vicar Baxter was certain had learned his lesson. But you did not, did you?"

"Lesson? Lesson? I am the magistrate's son. No one teaches me lessons," said the boy, his nose in the air.

Matty stared at him and he squirmed, digging his toe into the sod. She nodded. "Charles, you are looking very worried, but truly I am not badly hurt. On the other hand, this lad is. He is wounded inside where it does not show. I think you should show him another man who is scarred inside and what happens if you do not heal inner wounds properly, but allow them to grow and get worse until you have finally done something for which you may be required to pay with your very life." She got to her feet, wobbled a trifle, but shook her head gently at Charles. "You go along, show Pelling to the lad, and explain what is to come to him. I will have Bitsy see to my head and then, I think," she finished a trifle more weakly than she liked, "I will lay down for a bit."

They walked in through the entrance with Charles holding Matty's arm while, at the same time, he did not release the magistrate's son. Forbes was horrified at the sight of Miss Seldon's blood. He actually lost his equanimity to the degree he called, loudly, for help. His voice brought every-one pouring into the hall who was near it. Everyone, that is, but Pelling, who was roped to his chair and could not escape.

"My dear," exclaimed Miss Abernathy, "what has happened? A carriage accident?"

"What happened," said Charles sternly, "is that we caught this thatch-gallows throwing rocks at your cats, Miss Abby, and Matty, soft-hearted woman that she is, could not bear to see it. She ran toward him, calling for him to stop. He turned and threw a rock at *her*. It hit her. In fact, for a moment, she was knocked unconscious, and as you see, she is still bleeding."

The boy had stilled and seemed to shrink somewhere in the middle of that tirade. Now Charles glanced at him, then across the hall to where a strange gentleman stood, puffed up and red in the face, his small eyes glaring at the boy. Charles sighed. He doubted very much that this man, obviously the boy's father, had any notion how to go about changing a bully into a decent sort of boy.

Meanwhile, Miss Abernathy was leading Miss Seldon toward the stairs. "Can you climb them, my dear? Should I have Charles carry you? Oh, and do you wish to lay charges against that horrid boy as well as against Mr. Pelling?" She, too, had caught a glimpse of the father's face but was more worried about her charge and had only a moment in which to give the man a hint of what lay ahead for the boy if the lad did not change his ways. It was her belief that even if Miss Seldon did not lay charges, someone in the not-too-distant future would do so for one reason or another.

"No?" she asked when Matty shook her head. "Then let us go up. Charles," she called over her shoulder, "you will know what to do about that awful Mr. Pelling. Miss Seldon and I are, as you see, occupied quite enough with this new contretemps!"

No one moved. Finally, once the women disappeared, the magistrate glared around the hall. "Well?" he sputtered. "Have you nothing to do with yourselves but stare at your betters?"

Those servants, who had responded to Forbes's cry for aid, effaced themselves. Except for Forbes. "Mr. North? Have you orders for me?"

"Not at the moment. Ned, take the boy. He runs if he gets the opportunity, so do not release him."

"Here now!" blustered the magistrate.

Charles turned a hard cold stare his way. "Here, now *what?*"

"Well! Well!"

"Yes? But it is *not* well."

Again the magistrate glared at his son. "You just wait till I get you home. You wait. Embarrassing me this way!"

"Embarrassment? That is all you feel?" asked Charles softly.

"Hmm? What? Oh. That female creature. Probably deserved it."

Ned put his hand around the lad's dirty neck and watched Charles stalk toward the magistrate. He hid a grin to see the older man cringe and begin to look very small despite his large girth. "Miss Seldon is not merely a female creature," he said softly. "Nor did she deserve to suffer such a wound at the hands of your ungovernable son. You, sir, are to blame for your son's behavior. I believe I will recommend that Miss Seldon bring suit against *you*, demanding recompense for the scar, which will surely result. It is after all, *you* who allowed the boy to grow into such an undisciplined, unfeeling brat that he not only steals from those in need, but wounds the innocent when she objects to his vicious behavior toward her hostess's pet."

The magistrate's eyes bulged. "Steal? Steal? My son! You accuse my boy of thievery?"

"There were witnesses. More than one. Shall I bring those others forward? Not Miss Seldon. At least, not until she feels more the thing, but those who observed the boy's attempt to take a poor woman's dinner?"

"I thought I came here to take a villain in charge. Why must I listen to slander concerning my son? Damned if I will. Won't." The magistrate headed toward where Ned still held the boy, tightening his grip whenever the lad moved a muscle. "You. We're going home."

"I believe not," said Charles, his voice icy.

"Believe what you will."

"You've a duty to the county. Or are you resigning your position rather than fulfill it? Will you put your son in prison as well as the man we've captured?"

"My son . . ." The man blanched, turning gray. He turned. "You didn't mean that . . . did you?"

Charles's mouth twitched in irritation. The man whined just like his boy. "*Miss Seldon* is unlikely to lay charges against the boy, but it makes no odds. Someone will do so before he is much older," said Charles, pretending indifference.

If anything, the magistrate turned an even more sickly color. It had finally reached him that his boy was not exactly an ornament on the family tree. Unfortunately, he was the only possible ornament, the only child, the only son, and the man was suddenly a very unhappy man indeed. "Let me get the villain I came for and I'll be on my way." He cast a baffled look toward the boy, shook his head, and followed Charles to where Pelling, sweating profusely because he'd no notion what was going on and, besides, was not at all happy about what he saw as his future.

Ned accompanied them to see that Pelling did not escape and Charles followed in the gig, knowing there was paperwork that must be done before the incident with Pelling could be forgotten. He was pleased that the next assizes would not be held for some time. Pelling would have a great deal of time in the magistrate's small and dirty cell awaiting his trial and could, if he would, use it to think about his sins.

He was on his way home before he remembered that tomorrow they were to go to Lady Portentmere's entertainment. He sighed. The magistrate would undoubtedly be a guest as well. He hoped the situation would not deteriorate into a social contretemps.

Once back at Abernathy Hall, after he had asked Abby how Matty was, he described the scene with the magistrate, which, unfortunately, had taken place where far too many servants had heard the whole.

"The tale of his lordship's embarrassment will be all about the county before nightfall," he finished.

"Good."

"What?"

"No one likes that boy. Very nearly everyone can tell a tale about him. But no one has had the nerve, before you, to tell the magistrate exactly what is thought of his son. The *magistrate,* you see?"

"Such nonsense."

"Of course. And yet I am as guilty as the next. Our Matty tried very hard to shame the vicar into doing his duty by the boy and telling the father of the theft, but the vicar flubbed it, soothing his conscience by making assumptions that were unwarranted."

"That the boy, seeing him in conversation with the father, would walk warily?"

"Yes."

"I will trust you that Miss Seldon goes on all right since I assume you would have called in the

doctor if you felt her in danger, but tell me again
. . . how is she? Truly?"

"She will be up and around tomorrow. I suggested she might prefer me to send our regrets to
Lady Portentmere, but she thinks it the better part
of valor if she shows her face and gives Lord Whitsome no opportunity to suggest she lied and is,
therefore, afraid of him."

Charles sighed a gusty sigh. "Fiddle."

"Music?" asked Abby, her eyes twinkling. "Yes,
I am certain Lady P. will have a fiddle or two . . . ?"

"No. Not that. I had hoped, you see, for an
excuse to avoid this particular party and the need
to make my bows to Miss Tenton."

Abby stared for half a moment and then burst
out laughing. "Charles! You are running scared!"

"I will," he said, very much on his dignity,
"depend on you and Miss Seldon to keep me safe."

A knock at the study door startled them. "Yes,"
called Miss Abernathy.

"A guest has arrived," said Forbes, his features
and body in the haughty pose that indicated he
did not approve.

"Company?"

"A Baron *Pelling*, Miss Abernathy." His brows
arched high, since he knew that was the name of
the villain only recently taken away. "I have put
him in the smaller salon."

Abby and Charles stared at each other.

"Well . . ." began Charles.

"I must . . ." began Abby.

"He asked after Miss Seldon . . . ? Not about that
thatch-ga . . . er, *man* of the same name?" added
Forbes, admitting he was confused.

"Ah yes. Our Miss Seldon," said Abby. "I fear
Baron Pelling will think we have not taken very
good care of his cousin. Well, come along, Charles.

You must support me. Ah! I do not wish to lose our Miss Seldon!'' Abby came very near to wailing.

Forbes cleared his throat.

"Yes, Forbes?"

"The baron has not come about his son?" he asked.

"Oh, he knows nothing about that. Yet." Abby sighed. "Another problem. Charles, when did life become so full of problems?"

Chapter Sixteen

Baron Pelling was a rather short, rotund little man, his hair receding and a permanently worried expression screwing up his face. "My cousin?" he asked, looking beyond his hostess when she and Charles entered the salon. "You are certain she is my cousin? Where is she? Why is she not here? Why was I not informed by . . . ?"

Charles strode forward. "Baron Pelling. Charles North." The baron, startled from his flow of words, blinked, took Charles's offered hand, and perfunctorily shook it. "And this is Miss Abigail Abernathy, who has taken Miss Seldon in and sheltered her. A delightful young woman, Baron," said Charles, smiling.

"Yes, of course. Delightful. How could it be otherwise? And . . . Oh. Yes. Miss Abernathy!" He more bobbed than bowed. "I must see her. I must do my duty by her if she is indeed Reverend Seldon's daughter. Nice old gentleman. Didn't know him well, of course. Sorry to hear he stuck his spoon in the wall, but that is the way of nature, is it not?" He sighed, the ridges marring his forehead deepening. "Oh well. Always room for one more," he muttered. "Somehow. Somewhere. Perhaps Jane and Susan can share their bed . . . Hmmm?" he asked, and then looked as if he'd been startled from what was obviously a soliloquy not truly meant for their ears.

"I asked if yours is a large household," repeated Abby, a frown very nearly the equal to the baron's creasing her brow.

"Hmm? Large? Not the house. Not so very large."

"But full, perhaps, to the rafters?"

"Hmm? Hmm? Full? To the rafters?" He heaved a huge sigh. "Large family, you see. Generous wife. Woman gave me proof after proof of her affection," he added, looking sorrowful.

Charles very nearly choked in his attempt to smother a laugh. He wanted to ask if the baron had not had part in the production of those *proofs*, but, unfortunately, it was not the sort of question one dared ask. At least, not in a lady's salon.

"And all at home?" asked Abby, attempting to infuse sympathy into her tone.

"All. Well. Most." The baron looked everywhere but at the two facing him. And, it seemed, he'd lost his ability to rattle on apace.

Charles cleared his throat. "As to that, perhaps you refer to the son you have, we hear, disinherited and told never to darken your door again?"

The baron turned bright red and puffed up like an adder. "Who told you that?" he asked, each word a distinct and separate thing.

"We have met Ervine. He is at this moment . . ."

"Don't want to hear," interrupted the harassed man. "Don't want to see him. Don't want to know anything about him. Don't want . . ."

"You must listen," interrupted Miss Abby sternly. "You son is in our local magistrate's cell awai—"

"Ha! Always said he'd come to a bad end!" He

drew in a deep breath. "That's enough. Now about Miss Seldon, you just . . ."

"But it is about Miss Seldon," said Abby, once again interrupting and this time allowing exasperation to show. "He stole her inheritance and did his best to send her to ruin. I hired a runner to track him down and that was accomplished just today. The magistrate has your Ervine in charge."

"Not *my* Ervine!" Then the baron's eyes bulged. "Miss Seldon is ruined? Oh dear. What am I to do? Cannot take her home to my innocent girls, now can I? Oh dearie me. What to do!" He ran his hand over thinning hair. "If it isn't one thing then it is another." Then he brightened. "But if she is ruined, then there is nothing to do. Such women take care of themselves." He beamed.

"You misunderstood, Baron," said Charles a trifle dangerously. "Your son did his best to ruin her, but she was lucky to meet new friends who took her in and protected her. She is *not* ruined. Not as you mean the word."

"Oh." His smiled faded and that sad look returned. "Then Jane and Susy . . ."

"Baron," said Miss Abby sternly, "I am glad to see you wish to do your duty by our Miss Seldon, but I fear it would be a true burden on you to do so. I believe she would do far better remaining here with me. If she will not stay as my guest, I will hire her as a companion and secretary," she finished sternly.

"Not stay as a guest? But why would she not?" He looked around the salon, envy in his eyes. "Very nice house, Miss Abernathy. Light duties, I am certain. Yes, it sounds an excellent solution . . ." He continued in much the same strain for some moments, obviously doing his best to convince himself he would not do the wrong thing by taking this opportunity to avoid adding another mouth to his already overfull table. "She will like staying with you," he concluded with only a faint hint of a question in his tone.

Just then the door opened and Miss Seldon, looking a trifle wan and with a sticking plaster adorning her temple, entered. "I have been informed that Baron Pelling is here," she said in her softest voice.

Charles went to her side and led her to a chair. "You should not have risen from your couch," he scolded. "You have suffered."

"Here now," said the baron, once again looking very much like a bantam fighting cock. "Here, what is this? What has happened to my Miss Seldon? What have you done to her? What are you planning to do with her? How can you sound as if you wish her company and then I see she has been beaten and battered and *what is this?*" He glared.

"Baron? You refer to this?" asked Matty, touching her forehead and then holding out her hand to him. "A very naughty boy threw a rock at me. Miss Abernathy has been nothing but kind to me from the day we met. You must not think otherwise."

"Miss Abernathy has invited you to remain here with her."

Matty blinked, glanced toward Abby, and back to her relative. "She is very kind," she said, not quite knowing what else to say.

"Happy to take you home with me. *Expected* to take you home with me. Thing is . . . well . . ." He looked flustered.

"The thing is, Matty," said Miss Abernathy, "that the thought of losing your company has me blue-deviled—as the saying is. I very much wish you will stay with me. If not as my guest," she repeated for Matty's benefit, "then as my companion."

"You've no need for a companion," objected Matty.

"Do I not? I had not thought so, but that was before I met you, my dear child. Will you not stay with me?" she asked wistfully.

Matty sighed, glanced at the baron, who was a relative and, in some sense, had a responsibility for her—even if he demanded all sorts of work from her to pay for her keep. That was normal. The poor relative in the house did that sort of thing. But to remain with Miss Abby? What was there she could do for Miss Abby? Was that not charity?

"Jane and Susy will share their room with you," said the baron.

His frown once again deepened and a still more worried look in his pale blue eyes made Matty wonder if Jane and Susy had agreed to that. "I know nothing of your household, Baron. Would it be a great deal of trouble adding the responsibility for me to your other obligations?"

The truth was in his gaze, although he blustered and insisted and went on at length that Reverend Seldon's daughter was, of course, always welcome.

Matty looked at Abby, who, tentatively, held out her hand to her. She looked beyond Abby to Charles, who, knowing he would pursue his suit wherever she might be, wore no expression at all. Matty drew in a deep breath. The right thing to do was to go with her cousin and make herself useful to him. If it was a large family, as he implied, then perhaps she could tutor the young boys, be governess to the young girls, and help chaperon the elder girls. Or peel potatoes in the kitchen if that was what was asked of her! That was what she must do.

She spoke and, having made a rational decision, was appalled at the words coming from her mouth. "Thank you very much, Baron. I am blessed that you would take me in, pauper that I am. But I think

I will accept Miss Abernathy's offer of work." She swallowed, thought quickly, and added, "And if I find she does not *need* me, but is offering me charity, I will accept still another bit of charity from her and ask her to find me work where I *am* needed. I am young and perfectly healthy. There is no reason at all I must be a burden on your pocket or, for that matter on Miss Abby's. And now, if you will forgive me, I think I must return to my bed."

Charles came to her and offered his arm. He took her from the room, where she insisted that one of the footmen should help her upstairs where her maid awaited her. "I hope I have done the correct thing," she said, unsure why she'd changed her mind.

"I am certain you have. Miss Abby was unhappy at the thought of losing your company, you know."

"Was she?" His words eased her conscience. "She is wonderful, is she not?"

"She is. Now you rest. She says you mean to attend Lady Portentmere's party. If you must go, then you must regain that of which you bragged to the baron." When she frowned he smiled. "Your health, my dear. Off with you." He watched her ascend the stairs and then returned to the salon. When the baron, after taking tea and eating well from a substantial meal Forbes spread over a side table, said he must leave, Charles went with him to the stables where his old carriage and the horses had been rested and baited.

Charles cleared his throat, somewhat embarrassed. "Since Miss Seldon's father is dead," he said, "I presume it is you, as her nearest male relative, who should be asked."

"Asked? Asked?" questioned the baron, blinking.

"If there are any objections to my suit for her hand in marriage," explained Charles.

"Marriage? You? But you are Baron Richfield's son!"

"So?"

"You can do far better for yourself, surely, than a penniless spinster of uncertain age!"

"No I can't. I mean, I have no desire to do other than take Miss Seldon to wife. You have not had an opportunity to know her, sir. She was not at her best today, thanks to that shagbag of a boy."

"Actually threw a rock at her?"

"She had merely objected to him throwing rocks at Miss Abernathy's pets," said Charles, dryly.

"Despicable behavior." The baron sighed. "Just the sort of thing Ervine used to do." He sighed again. Deeply. "I suppose I should stop and see the boy."

"*Not* a boy, sir. A man and not a nice man. I first made his acquaintance when he choused a young friend of mine out of a great deal of money by sharping practices. He also made life difficult for another acquaintance by organizing a scene in which the man appeared to compromise a supposedly decent woman. Ervine blackmailed him—not, in this case for money, but making him do things he didn't wish to do."

"A thoroughly bad lot. Have to admit it. Didn't," insisted Pelling, "get it from my family. Wife's family," he added as an afterthought.

"Occasionally there is no explaining a bad apple in an eminently respectable family. There are, you know, ancient titles who are forced to admit to the occasional black sheep within their ranks."

The baron looked much struck by this and straightened his shoulders. "Very true. Very true. Well, well, since I am here I will stop and see the boy. Nothing I can do for him," he added quickly. "He's made his bed. But I'll stop and see him if you'll give my driver directions." He nodded his head firmly.

Charles waved him off after only another fifteen minutes and was glad it was no longer. Perhaps the voluble man had such a large family he could get no word of his own in edgewise and so talked nonstop once out where he might be heard. Or perhaps the flow of words was merely the nervous habit of a man who had too much responsibility and too few resources. Whatever the case, Charles was glad to see the last of him.

One might have thought that life could settle into the sort of placid routine one expected of a country visit, but Charles had the suspicion they had not yet seen the end of complications raised by Miss Seldon's arrival on the scene. There was, after all, still Lady Southend, her aunt. Assuming the aunt was at all interested in a niece who was the daughter of a sister who had been thrown from the family for marrying a simple country vicar.

There was also the problem of Miss Tenton, and Lady Portentmere's machinations to find a husband for her spinster niece. Violet Tenton was not a bad woman. She was not even so very much a shrew. Nor were her features out of the way ugly. Not pretty, but definitely not ugly. She even had a bit of a dowry. Not a great deal, but she was not penniless as were most women still unwed at her age.

It occurred to Charles to wonder why she was *not* married. Had she had an unhappy affaire of the heart in her youth? Unreciprocated love, perhaps? Or had her hand been asked for only by men she could not esteem, let alone love? Or was she one of those women who simply faded into the background at society dos, unnoticed and unhappy that she was never once asked?

Whatever the case might be, Charles did not feel the pity necessary to seeing if he could help her to a marriage she could tolerate. And he certainly wasn't about to find *himself* walking up the aisle with her. It occurred to him that Miss Seldon could help him avoid that possibility, but before he went to her to request her aid, he hunted down Miss Abby, wishing to ascertain that what he intended would damage no one, especially Miss Seldon.

Miss Abernathy's eyes narrowed as he explained his simple plan. "I mean to appear to be pursuing Miss Seldon to the exclusion of any other woman, assuming she'll not be harmed in any way by my behavior."

"You could do better," she suggested.

"Better?"

"You could announce your engagement so that there was no mistaking the matter."

Charles felt his ears heat. In fact, they warmed to the point he had to restrain himself from rubbing them. "If I was certain Miss Seldon would have me, I would definitely ask her."

Miss Abby tipped her head. "And why would she not?"

"I don't know. I only know that on those occasions I have attempted to put our friendship on a less formal basis, she has rebuffed me."

"I am sure she holds you in affection," said Miss Abby thoughtfully.

"She does not dislike me. I agree with that. But she holds me at arm's length to such a degree I fear to put my luck to the touch."

"Let me speak to her," said Abby, her voice even deeper than usual in her concern that there might be an impediment to her plot to wed her protégée to her young friend.

"You will not . . . not . . ."

Miss Abernathy grinned. "Not make of you a laughingstock?"

"Not that. I wouldn't mind her laughing. I don't want her despising me!"

"Because you fear Lady P.'s plots?"

He shrugged.

She nodded. "You've reason, I fear, to fear them. The plots, I mean, not our Matty's laughter. Yes, I will speak with her and we will form a plan to keep you safe. She need do no more than accept your attentions so that all will believe you too interested in her to possibly be interested in Violet. Yes, that is what we will do."

She sent Charles off to take exercise on one of her riding horses. "Go up on the Downs. Blow the clouds from your mind and think up ways of impressing our Matty with your sincerity." She paused. "Charles, could that be it? That she believes you merely flirting with her?"

He looked appalled. "I hope not. What I feel is well beyond a mere divertissement."

"I will see if I can discover. Tactfully, of course," she added when he cast her a look of concern.

"I will be eternally grateful, Miss Abby," he said, and kissed her on both cheeks before leaving for his ride.

Miss Abernathy went up to her room. "Are you here?" she asked softly. He was. She talked to him for a very long time, held in the comfort of his arms. Finally she sighed. "It is so difficult. One cannot merely ask another if they have fallen in love with still a third party," she said a trifle irascibly. She listened, sighed again, and nodded. "Very well. I will arrange that she protects Charles, but will not probe into her feelings for him. Time will give us the answer to that problem, will it not?"

Miss Abernathy rang for Bitsy and when the maid

arrived sent her to find Miss Seldon and ask that she attend Miss Abernathy in her suite's sitting room. "And," she added as Bitsy opened the door, "ask Forbes to bring up a snack. Tea and . . . oh I do not know. Cook will decide."

"You wanted to see me?" asked Matty, tying her robe more firmly about her narrow waist. "As you see, I am not attired to attend you, but Bitsy insisted I must come at once. She said I looked fine . . . ?" The frown drawing together Matty's brows indicated she did not believe it.

Abigail waved toward a chair across the table from where she sat with tea and a particularly luscious-looking portion of pineapple on her plate. "Pour yourself some tea and choose some fruit. It is what Cook sent up. I would not have thought of fruit at this time of day, but it is very good."

"Is this why you asked me to come?" asked Matty once she had placed her own portion before her. "I know I sent my lunch back down to the kitchen, but I was brought such a huge breakfast I could not eat. I must apologize to Cook if she was so bothered she asked you to see I had . . . No?" she asked when Abby shook her head. "Then . . . ?"

"It is something quite ridiculous, Matty. Charles and I desperately need your help."

"But of course," said Matty, her brows rising. "Anything I can do . . ."

"Do not say yes until you have heard. In fact, my dear," scolded Miss Abernathy, *"never* say yes before you know what it is to which you are agreeing."

"You are my friends," said Matty quietly. "You have done so much for me. I cannot believe there is anything within my power that I would not do for either of you."

Abigail smiled broadly. "It is very like you, my child, and an admirable thought, but still—" She sobered. "—I urge you, even with friends, to be more cautious!" She sipped her tea, looking at Matty, who looked steadily back. She set down the cup and drew in a breath. "Have you heard me complain about Lady P.'s attempts to marry off her niece, Violet Tenton?"

"Did you not tell me Miss Tenton is . . ." Matty paused, her eyes widening. "Oh, no, her ladyship *would* not. Not Char—Mr. North!"

"I fear it. I also believe you can help put a spoke in her ladyship's plans. You do wish to help?"

"Yes. No one should be forced to wed where they do not wish it."

Miss Abernathy tucked that bit of wisdom in the back of her mind, wondering if Matty referred to herself and Charles, and if so, which she thought might be forced. Herself? But there was the fact that the chit had very nearly slipped and used Charles's Christian name, which a young unmarried woman as highly principled and well-trained as Miss Seldon would not do. Then Charles?

More problems, she thought, frowning as she stirred her tea.

"What is it you would have me do?" asked Matty.

"I would like it very much if you would be accepting of Charles's attentions this evening. If he is preoccupied with wooing you, he'll have no time for any machinations Lady P. may have in mind."

"I am to sit in his pocket, you would say?"

"Yes. And whenever her ladyship or Violet approaches, take him off elsewhere."

Matty swallowed. "Take him . . . ?"

"Or rather, allow him to take you, I mean. Matty, I am really concerned. Lady P. has become desperate. She will do anything to see Violet married."

"To anyone?"

"To anyone, but Charles, of course, would be an excellent party, if she could catch him."

Lady Abernathy was quick enough to see something inside Matty close away at that. She seemed to have . . . dimmed? The life drained from her? Abby was uncertain exactly what it was, but her lively happy guest, she thought, was, quite suddenly, unhappy.

"I will do whatever I can to aid Mr. North," said Matty in a rather colorless voice. "If you'll excuse me, my maid means to help me wash my hair and it is so long it takes forever to dry. Unless there is something else, I must return to my room."

"Run along, my dear. You will find your maid has a new gown for you. It is a gift and I want no nonsense about my not giving gifts where I wish to give them. I think you will like it. The mode may not be quite up to the knocker, since I've not been to Town recently and haven't seen the very latest styles, but I believe my modiste will not have done too badly by you. No, not a word. I want to give it to you!"

Matty curtsied, nodded, and then came to give Miss Abby a hug. "You are such a dear lady," she murmured. "Thank you."

When the door closed behind Matty, Abby asked, "Well? What did you think?" If there was a response, no one but Abby heard it.

Lady Southend, formerly Miss Susan Broadman and the dowager Lady Mercer-Bowman, arrived at Miss Abernathy's front door not over half an hour later. When Abby arrived at the salon door she saw a haughty woman near her own age. Her ladyship was dressed in the height of fashion, her travel gown and pelisse an odd shade of red that was not puce, but was equally hard to define. The stranger turned slightly, giving Abby a better view of her profile. Abby chuckled softly.

"Well, Sukey," she said, entering the room with a firm step, "still wearing colors which do not suit you, are you not?"

"Still . . . !" A high-nosed stare was turned on Abby. Suddenly the double chin was lowered, the mouth opened, and the nose, very nearly, twitched. "But it cannot possibly be!"

"Why? Because everyone was told I am dead? As you see, it was an exaggeration."

"But I know I read a notice of Lord Emery's death."

A sober Abby nodded. "Yes. I was in the house when it caught fire. He rescued me, Sukey, and another," she said softly, "but died in his attempt to reach all."

Lady Southend looked bewildered. "Then why . . . ?"

"Because, as the saying goes, I had made my bed and I could lie in it. It has, as you see, been a very soft bed," said Abby mischievously, gesturing to the house around them.

"But you do not even call yourself by your own name!"

"I took this one when he died. Sukey, I loved my Lord Emery very very much indeed. At first I could not bring myself to return to my parents' home, disgraced, and later, when everyone might have forgotten, might have forgiven . . . well, I did not wish to. I get along very well indeed. As you see."

"But not to let even your closest friends know!"

"My father loved me, but he loved society's opinion more. He made me promise to raise no waves and it was he who told the world I had died in that fire. As I said, at first I'd no desire to contradict him. And when I might have . . . well, there were other reasons why I wished to remain here and in obscurity." She thought of the tête-à-têtes she enjoyed in her boudoir and smiled slightly.

"A new name. A new home. A stranger to everything, everyone about you?"

Abby grinned. "But, Sukey, of course! You know I was always the most dramatic of chits. How could I not enjoy playing the role of local mystery lady? I still do!" She sobered. "But you've been offered no refreshment—" She stopped in midsentence. "Ah, Forbes. I should have trusted you to do the correct thing, should I not?"

He cast her a look that said, as though he'd spoken the words, that, indeed, she should. He then returned to overseeing that the light repast he'd considered proper was laid out. When the maid and footman left the room, he cast one last look around, and followed them, his tread stately.

"Now, my old friend, do nibble on something while I tell you the story of your poor niece."

"That is the first thing you may tell me. How can this *be* my niece when my sister and her child died at the child's birth?"

"And when was that?" asked Abby.

Lady Southend told her.

"Ah. But then your father was very nearly as rigid as was mine, was he not?"

Her ladyship straightened, sitting tall and stern. "You cannot mean he lied to us."

"Can I not? I'm afraid he must have. Your sister did not die until Matty was twelve."

Lady Southend stilled. Then tears rolled down her cheeks unimpeded and unheeded. "All those years . . ."

"She married against your father's will, did she not? And he was not pleased?"

Lady Southend sighed.

"From all Matty tells me, they were a very happy family."

"As my first marriage was not," said Lady Southend softly, "although I was a dutiful daughter and married where I was told to marry." She brightened. "But then, widowed, I met Southend. That *has* been happy!"

Abby held out her hand. After a moment's hesitation, her old friend placed hers within it. The two sat quietly, holding hands, and thinking of the past.

But then Abby decided they had had enough of unhappy memories and cleared her throat. Squeezing Lady Southend's hand, she released her, reached for the pot, and poured tea for the two of them. "Well. The bad in our life is over and done. We've the future to think about. And you've a niece you will wish to know but, Sukey, you must not interfere in my plans," she said, warningly. "Frankly, when Forbes came to tell me a Lady Southend had arrived, I was angry. My plans have not yet come to fruition, you see."

"No I do not see. But, Mary—"

When Abby shook her head, Lady Southend sighed.

"—Abigail, then—"

Abby suggested Abby.

"—*Abby.*" Her ladyship glared but Abby merely smiled an innocent questioning smile. Lady Southend shook her head. "You do not change. Not one whit! But, *Abby,* it will not do. Since she *is* my niece, I wish to take her to London. I want to present her, find her a husband, and *not* one like I was forced to endure."

"What would you think of Charles North?" asked Abby.

"North? Baron Richfield's second son?" demanded Lady Southend, her voice sharp.

"The same."

Her ladyship's eyes narrowed. "I don't know . . ."

"Then let me tell you. He is a wonderful man and will make her a delightful husband. I believe she is in love with him and he with her." Abby frowned. "I cannot determine why she holds him at arm's length, but have added a bit to the plot in the hopes it will bring her to her senses."

"Plot? Plot! Ma—*Abby*. I *will* remember," she said when Abby gave her a warning look. "But, *Abby*, I recall your plots and they always led to disaster. Why, just look at your own troubles!"

"I've no troubles, Sukey. I am, whether you believe me or not, perfectly happy here at Abernathy Hall. I've property and a more than adequate income, thanks to my beloved's forethought. He provided for me exactly as if we had been married, you see. I have friends and acquaintances in the neighborhood, so I do not lack a social life, and my family, now that my father is dead, has not totally turned its back on me." She smiled at the thought of Rutherford and Steven's visits. "Besides, I was never as enamored of society as were you. I do very well here in obscurity with visits from the oddities I've collected over the years and my reputation as an eccentric—if not worse than eccentric—suits me."

"But . . ."

Abby laughed and then, when the door opened, turned. "Ah, Charles! You are acquainted with Lady Southend, are you not? She has come about our Matty."

"Everyone who is anyone at all knows Lady Southend," said Charles smoothly and came forward to greet her ladyship properly. "Are you surprised to discover you've a delightful niece, my lady?"

"Since I have yet to set eyes on the chit, I've yet

to acknowledge I have a niece," she said, in keeping with her reputation as a cross-grained old lady.

"Nonsense," said Abby, laughing. "You'd not be here if you did not believe my letter. Admit it."

Her ladyship sighed. "Oh very well, I will admit anything you ask, but I have been patient and polite for quite long enough. Far longer than is normal with me. Would it be too much to ask that I meet my niece?"

Abby compressed her lips. "Well . . . yes."

"What?"

"She suffered an accident yesterday but insists on attending Lady Portentmere's ball this evening."

"That sort is she?" asked Lady Southend a trifle sourly.

"Not what you think," said Abby, severely. "Our local magistrate's son threw a rock at her, hitting her temple. She is likely to have a scar. The magistrate will attempt to make everyone believe it was Miss Seldon's fault rather than the lad's. She fears that if she does not appear tonight she will be felt to have admitted it."

"Hmm. I see. Yes, she must attend, must she not? So?"

"So she is resting. I am determined she will not leave her room until we are ready to depart."

"Perhaps you could take Lady Southend up and allow them a bit of time together before her ladyship goes to her own room to rest from her journey and prepare for our evening jaunt. You *will* come with us, will you not, my lady?" asked Charles, smiling. "It will be just the thing to set Miss Seldon's feet on the proper social path if it is known you helped sponsor her to her very first *ton* party. Even if it is nothing more than a simple country do, having you with her will give her that extra polish Abby and I cannot possibly contrive."

Lady Southend looked much struck by Charles's

argument and nodded. "You are a very wise young man. We will do just that. By evening's end—why, our Matilda will be thought just the thing." She turned back to Abby, a faint frown marring her broad forehead. "But what I do not understand, quite, is how she came to be here. With you."

Abby poured more tea and settled back into her chair. "Do try those lemon tarts, which are my personal favorites, and a slice of that dark cake while I tell you the whole story . . ."

Chapter Seventeen

The Portentmere ball was well under way when Abby's party arrived. For the first few miles, Matty had chatted with her newfound aunt, telling more about her life before her mother died. Lady Southend could not seem to hear enough and Matty was glad to oblige . . . but as they neared their destination, she fell silent.

Abby filled in the silence and she and her old friend reminisced about old times. Under cover of their conversation, Charles touched Matty's clenched fist. "Do not worry so, Miss Seldon," he said softly. "We will all be at your side to see you enjoy the evening."

"It isn't that," she said equally softly. "I have always enjoyed parties and would expect to enjoy this one as well if . . ." Her voice trailed off.

"If?" he encouraged.

"If I did not fear I will fail you in your need."

"Ah. Dear Violet." He sighed. "It is not that she is a bad woman in any sense, but she does not show well at social occasions such as this. It has been beaten into her that she is a failure, in that she is not yet wed, and that she must, on every occasion where she is given an opportunity, do her best to attract and attach a male of the species."

"What are her interests?" asked Matty, curious.

"I don't know that I know." Charles frowned. "Or do I? I believe I have heard she is a doer of good works, active on several committees of that sort. I assume she likes ancient music. There is an organization of musicians that give concerts during the Season and I have seen her in attendance at them in preference to other more exciting entertainments. What else?"

As he searched his mind, Matty thought of Vicar Baxter. She wondered if Miss Tenton would feel him too much beneath her and decided that, even if Miss Tenton did not, Lady Portentmere would. She sighed. Softly.

Abby noticed. "Are you concerned about this evening?" she asked.

"Only that I will somehow fail Mr. North."

"What is this?" asked Lady Southend. "Fail him? In what possible way could *you* do such a thing?"

They turned into the estate drive and Abby quickly explained about Lady Portentmere and Miss Tenton. "I have asked Miss Seldon to put herself in the position of allowing Charles to appear to be courting her in the hopes Lady P. will realize it is useless to pursue him."

"Hmm."

"That sounds disapproving," said Charles.

"Disapproving? No, just disbelieving that Ma— *Abby* believes that anything will deter Lady Portentmere when she has her mind set on something."

Abby sighed. "Well then, what would you have us do?"

"Whisper in her ladyship's ear that Charles and my niece have just this evening come to an acceptable arrangement."

Matty felt her skin burn and was glad of the deep dusk that, perhaps, hid her blush from the others.

"An acceptable arrangement! Why, Sukey, just the thing. It says nothing and implies all. I will let you tell her ladyship."

"But how can we allow her to believe . . . ?" asked Matty, horrified at the thought of pretending what she most wished were in fact the truth. "And what do I *do*?"

"You, my dear, need only remain the demure miss you are and, if occasion requires it, appear a trifle smug!"

"But will it serve?" asked Charles. "Will not Miss Seldon be embarrassed if . . ."

He stopped, uncertain how to phrase what he would say. He could hardly suggest he wished to wed her and that she might turn him down, as he feared she would do, and if she did so, she'd feel all the embarrassment of a young woman whom others believed jilted.

The coach pulled up and, moments later, the door was opened and the steps put down. The footman's gloved hand helped Abby from the coach. Lady Southend followed after. Charles dropped to the ground and it was his hand that helped Matty leave the Abernathy coach. He had her take his arm and followed the older ladies into the house, his free hand covering hers and, when she trembled, squeezing it lightly. "We'll come through with colors flying," he whispered. "This is one war we will not lose!"

She laughed at his nonsense and that was Lady Portentmere's first look at the young woman Miss Abernathy had taken under her wing. Lady Portentmere was not pleased. She was still less pleased when Lady Southend whispered her news, first that Matty was her niece and, second that Charles and Matty had come to an acceptable agreement.

Lady Portentmere offered Matty two fingers that she withdrew before Matty could touch them and then, gushing, drew Charles to the side in order to introduce him to Miss Tenton. "... not, of course that you *need* an introduction," she finished coyly.

Charles, with natural grace, turned to Matty and drew her forward. "Yes, Lady Portentmere, but here is one who *is* in need of an introduction. Since I see you've more guests arriving I'll do the honors." Somehow, without seeming to do so, he excluded her ladyship from their small circle. "Miss Tenton, be pleased to greet Lady Southend's niece, Miss Matilda Seldon. She is a delightful addition to our circle," he finished, beaming down at Matty, who looked up at him with a warmth she would never have allowed herself to reveal under any other circumstances.

It occurred to Matty that there was an advantage to her support of Charles and their pretended interest in each other. She need not hide her feelings as she'd been doing. She could look at him as she had wanted, allow others to see her feelings— feelings Charles would assume were pretense.

Suddenly Matty felt free to enjoy herself that evening in still other ways. She was no longer at home and the vicar's daughter, so she need not watch her every word and deed!

She could, if she wished, even flirt a little. The thought brought roses to her cheeks.

Vicar Baxter arrived just then and, with more speed than politeness, greeted Lady Portentmere so that he could join their group. "Miss Seldon," he said, bowing awkwardly, "I pray I am in time to gain your first dance and the supper dance!"

Charles cleared his throat. "I beg to inform you, you are too late. Those dances are mine." Daringly, he added, "And the last."

The vicar turned to stare at Charles, his skin paling. He swallowed. Hard.

Charles gestured at Miss Tenton. "You know Lady Portentmere's niece, Miss Tenton, Vicar?"

He introduced them, and, ever polite where it was to his advantage, the vicar asked for two of Miss Tenton's dances and was given, not the first, but the second and the supper dance. Matty noticed that Miss Tenton studied the vicar with more interest than that with which she'd inspected Charles. *Was* it possible . . . ?

While Miss Tenton and the vicar spoke, Charles eased Matty away and on into the salons which had been thrown together for the occasion. The carpets had been lifted and the furniture either removed or arranged at the edge of the floor and a quartet of string players were clustered at the far end, bringing their instruments into tune.

Matty looked around with interest. Even stripped of much of its furnishings, she decided these rooms had a far more welcoming feel to them than Lady Wilmingham's had. And there, across the room, was that lady. Lady Wilmingham glared at her. When she caught Matty's eye and Matty nodded a greeting, she turned her shoulder in a perfect example of the cut direct.

Matty's mouth firmed and her chin rose just a trifle. Her ladyship was a coldhearted and not very intelligent woman and Matty decided she would not allow herself to be hurt by her ladyship's behavior.

Charles introduced her to several young bucks who had stationed themselves so that they could watch everyone arrive and accost those they wished to ask to dance. With Charles standing there, they were not behind times in asking Matty for dances— and later, each and every one, was very glad he had, finding her dancing a delight and her conversation light and merry without demanding of them any sort of flirtatious response. By the supper hour they had decreed her a very good sort of girl altogether.

Nothing happened to cause Charles and Matty the least worry until the musicians set aside their instruments for their supper break. But then, as the two left the salons for the dining room, Lady Portentmere managed to arrange things so that they were seated at a table with Miss Tenton and Vicar Baxter. Lady Portentmere suggested, coyly, that her Violet and Mr. North had so much in common, both of them knowing the London scene as they did, that they would not lack for conversation.

Matty, once the men went to choose their dinner, turned to Miss Tenton and said, "Charles told me you belong to committees involved in doing good works. What exactly do they do, Miss Tenton?" asked Matty.

"Do? Oh well, we mostly raise funds, you know. One committee aids an orphanage and another is to help young girls of a certain class learn a trade in an attempt to keep them from . . . er . . . another trade entirely?"

Matty nodded, not pretending she misunderstood. "Keeping young girls from that temptation is not such a problem at the village level, of course, where we all know each other, but I understand it is a dreadful problem in the cities. How many children are in the orphanage, Miss Tenton?"

The men joined them just then and Matty informed the vicar they were discussing the charity work in which Miss Tenton was involved.

The conversation was, from then on, dominated by Miss Tenton and Vicar Baxter who, early in his career, had been a mere curate in a church in one of the poorer districts of London. He had been horrified by the gin drinking and prostitution, the hungry, and those who would work if they could, but for whom there was no work.

He and Miss Tenton, as it turned out, indulged in a great deal of conversation on the subject, which allowed Charles to talk quietly with Miss Seldon about other things.

Lady Portentmere approached their table near the end of the meal, listened for a moment, and was appalled. Her protégée was *not* taking proper advantage of the situation. Not at all. Her eyes narrowed and, making up her mind, she was about to interfere when Lady Southend, seeing what was about to happen, came up to her and whispered in her ear.

"What?" asked Lady Portentmere.

"It is likely I am wrong, but I am almost certain some boys laced the punch. You'd best see to it or we will have all the young and innocent ladies feeling their oats and behaving in ways which will distress their families—and themselves as well, once tomorrow's headaches disappear and they realize what they have done!"

Lady Portentmere, recognizing the truth of that, went off at once to check the punch. By the time she was certain no improper additions had been made to it, that Lady Southend was, as she'd suggested, wrong in her suspicions, it was too late to interfere with the quartet enjoying supper, each, from her ladyship's point of view, enjoying it with quite the wrong partner.

The rooms grew overly warm as the evening progressed and the crowd of dancers enjoyed far too many fast-paced jigs and trots. Charles noted that Miss Seldon returned from her last dance more than a trifle heated and suggested they adjourn to the terrace beyond the windows.

When she hesitated, he added, "I have seen a

number of people go outside in order to cool themselves."

"Then I see nothing wrong with it," she said, frowning slightly. She had, she had realized much earlier, enjoyed Charles's company far too much that evening. She would, she feared, suffer for it in the ensuing weeks, months, and, very likely, years to come. But if she must suffer, then she should have as many memories as possible, should she not? The decision made, she accepted Charles's offer and, without a glance around to see who might be watching, allowed him to lift her over the low sill of an open window and onto the terrace.

They glanced both ways, noticed a group of older people off to one side, a younger pair half hidden in the shadows on the other and, without speaking, walked straight ahead toward a low balustrade marking the edge of the paved area. Only a few steps from the house, Matty caught her toe against an unevenly placed flag and plunged forward. Charles caught her, drawing her up. . . .

"Outrageous," barked the vicar. "Hoyden," he said, pointing accusingly. "Jade."

Startled, Charles turned, Miss Seldon still in his grip. He opened his mouth to explain, but was himself castigated as a rake and roué before he could do so. Carefully setting Matty to one side, he turned to face the vicar, willing to explain, but given no opportunity.

"You are not the woman I thought you," said Mr. Baxter to Matty. There was anger and, contradictorily, a sad air to the man. "I had very nearly decided to honor you with a proposal of marriage, Miss Seldon, but my eyes are opened. I must inform you I am deeply disappointed. I was certain you were just the sort of modest woman to bring a proper dignity to the vicarage, to be a helpmeet in the difficult business of managing a parish, to grace my home and fill my nursery. But you have proven yourself a sly-boots, and not at all the prettily behaved woman I believed you. Miss Seldon," he finished, drawing himself up to his full height, which made him a scant half inch taller than herself, "I must inform you, you are no longer to expect a proposal of marriage from *me.*"

He turned on his heel and faced the house— only to be horrified by the small crowd that had gathered just inside the windows to listen to his tirade. He stuck his nose in the air and continued on, expecting the crowd to part so that he could stride on into the house.

It might have done so if Miss Tenton had not stepped into his path. She raised glistening eyes to his, and in a breathy voice said, "Oh, sir, how very terrible for you. Do come with me and tell me all about it. I am so sorry . . ." and much more of the same as she drew him away.

"If anyone is at all interested," said Charles, laconically, catching and holding eyes here and there among the group still facing them, "I merely caught Miss Seldon when she nearly fell. Lord Portentmere needs to repair his terrace." He pointed to the flagstone that had become raised from the general level of the others. "She could have hurt herself." He smiled at Matty. "Come, my dear, let us continue our walk—but more carefully, this time." He turned them so they could stroll along the terrace. Once away from listening ears, he laughed softly. "Were you aware the good vicar was courting you, Miss Seldon? I vow I'd seen no hint of it."

"I hadn't a notion."

"Will you be made unhappy by the loss of your clerical suitor?"

"Not at all," she said promptly. "He is a man of the church and I should say nothing against

him, but my father would have been appalled by
what I have seen of his behavior in this parish. I
feel very sorry for him."

"Because he hasn't a chance of winning you?"

"Because," said Matty softly, sadly, "he is a weak
man and will never be a truly happy man."

"There speaks your good heart. We have
become, you know, the object of scandal."

"Have we? Very likely." Matty drew in a deep
breath and continued. "There will be those among
the eavesdroppers who will be delighted to pass
on the story, giving it the worst possible twists and
turns. Very likely we will have been caught in an
amorous embrace—right there, directly in the
light that falls from the windows, uncaring that all
might see! People are truly credulous."

"Credulous? No, it has nothing to do with credu-
lity. They do not believe naively, are not so gull-
ible." His eyes on her moonlit hair, he spoke rather
absently. "What far too many are is malicious. They
wish to believe the worst. Miss Seldon, *would* you
do me the honor of marrying me?"

"Because you wish to save me from scandal? No.
I will not. Your family would be appalled that it
even crossed your mind to ask such a poor bargain
as myself, no matter what your reason."

"Even if the reason were that I have fallen deeply
in love with you? I think not."

"But you have not, so let us not speak of this
again." Matty spoke firmly. With great difficulty,
she contained her agitation, aware that if he per-
sisted she would break down. It must not be. He
must not sacrifice himself for such a ridiculous
reason. Ah! But if it *were* true! If only it were *true!*

"You do not dislike me, I think?" he asked after
a moment. It was, actually, half a statement and
only half a question.

"How could anyone dislike you?" she asked, startled from her thoughts.

"Then I will not despair and will persist. You see, I do love you and I do wish to wed you. I am sorry that I chose the wrong moment to propose. I suppose," he added thoughtfully, "I had it in my mind that perhaps the situation would suggest to you the advantage of saying yes before the scandal has time to grow beyond all reason. But," he added in such a mournful tone Matty knew he jested, "you are far too high-minded for your own good— or rather for *my* good—and I have failed in my object. Ah well. Shall we go in and add fuel to the rumors by dancing a third dance together?"

"No we will not. If this were a small impromptu dance, got up when there happened to be enough couples for a set or two, we could dance all we wished, but it is a ball, carefully planned, and invitations sent out ahead of time, so we must abide by society's rules."

"Fie upon society if it will permit me no more than two dances!"

She laughed. "Well enough for others to argue against the precepts of good behavior, but this is not for you, Mr. North. You are a barrister and must uphold *all* laws, both written and unwritten, and you are well aware of it."

Matty's experience of society was entirely that of a small village, but it was sufficient that it had taught her that she could do nothing to scotch the rumors which were even then running around the salons, dinner room, and the room set aside for card tables. Her best course was to pretend there was absolutely nothing wrong, that nothing had happened out of the way—which it had not, of course—and to go on as if she were unaware anyone was talking about her. To a surprisingly great degree she succeeded in convincing the right-minded, at least, and quite a few who would have preferred to have believed the worst, that there was no "worst" to believe.

In fact, when they finally entered their carriage for the journey home, Lady Southend complimented her. "You are wise beyond your years, my dear. How that awful man can have become a churchman I do not know. Saying all those terrible things when anyone with eyes in their head could see exactly what had happened. Were you," she asked, turning to Charles, "to let her fall? Of course not. And no one of any sense thinks otherwise— as I pointed out to several who did not see the accident. I am," she added, turning back to Matty and beaming, "excessively pleased with you."

"Hmm, er, thank you," said Matty, not quite knowing how to respond to her aunt's encomium.

The next day Charles found Miss Abernathy in her study where, having had a surfeit of her old friend for a time, she had gone to ground. Warily, Abby looked beyond him.

Charles grinned. "Her ladyship," he said, "is walking in the garden with Matty. Matty asked if her aunt would tell her about her mother, about their growing-up years, and I believe Lady Southend was excessively pleased by the request."

Abby relaxed. "Good. That will keep her occupied for some time and our Matty will appreciate her tales. Assuming, of course, that Sukey actually tells stories about her sister and not about herself."

"Lady Southend is, I believe, a rather lonely woman," said Charles, thoughtfully.

"That is because she holds herself so very much *up*. She would be appalled by some *I* call friends."

"Ned Bright, for instance?"

"Exactly. Where did he go after taking that awful

Pelling man to the magistrate? I expected him back for a long comfortable coze—and all he did was stop long enough to pick up his reward. I didn't even see him since Forbes gave it to him.''

Charles grinned a rather wicked grin. ''He didn't go far. He is putting up at the inn in the village. Perhaps you have been too busy to notice that Bitsy is away from home more often than not?''

Abby straightened. ''Is that going well, then?''

''I suspect you will be required to look for a new maid any day now. I believe that is Bitsy's real stumbling block. She does not wish to leave you when there is no one competent to replace her.''

''No one can possibly replace Bitsy. Ever. She has been with me since before I ran off with—'' She stopped. When she continued, she began a completely new thought. ''—so how is *your* wooing progressing?''

Charles sobered. He rose to his feet and began pacing the small room.

''Hmm. Like that, is it?''

''I don't understand it,'' he said swinging around to face Abby. ''I would swear I am not a mere coxcomb when I claim she loves me. I am certain of it, so I—''

''So am I.''

It was Charles's turn to change sentences in midutterance. ''—you are?''

''Yes. Charles, is it at all possible she is overly impressed by your status as the son of Baron Richfield?''

''Surely not. I am merely a second son. My brother will inherit and his sons after him.''

''Does she know your brother has a quiverful of boys to his name?''

''Perhaps not, but still, why would who I am deter her?''

''She is a modest girl. Perhaps excessively so. She

said something one day that makes me think that she once thought you a mere solicitor. Discovering you are a barrister as well as Richfield's son may have set you, in her eyes, so high above a penniless spinster, the daughter of a mere village cleric, that she dare not even think of wedding you."

"Surely this is nonsense. Matty is not only Southend's niece, but a most wonderfully sensible young woman and not at all stupid."

"And modest. Do not forget modesty. It can be a powerful motive when one is making decisions."

"Bah!"

"That," said Abby, "sounded very like your father. Your father as I remember him, that is. He was well on the road to becoming a prude and a prig, very well set in his ways, and only in his twenties at the time."

Charles replied absently, his mind on Matty. "My mother must have knocked that sort of nonsense out of him. He is nothing like that now." Suddenly he looked up. "You would say that *I* am becoming a prude and a prig!"

Abby laughed. "Well, Charles, if the shoe fits?" She chortled at his appalled expression. "I just thought perhaps I'd give you a hint." He looked still more revolted and she laughed again. "No, no, I merely tease you, Charles. Do you think I'd have you for friend if I thought you the least priggish or prudish?"

"You, Miss Abigail Abernathy, are a complete hand!"

She preened. "Well, one can only *try*, of course."

They chuckled, but Charles soon sobered. "It is all very well to tease me, Miss Abby, but what I need is advice. What am I to do?" He sat, leaning forward, his head bowed, his hands clasped and hanging loosely between his knees. "I actually asked her to wed me. Last night. She turned me down.''

"I suppose you'd been discussing the scandal the vicar made of you?''

"Were we? Perhaps. I only know how lovely she looked there in the moonlight, her hair up and that gown you gave her setting off her figure to perfection . . . I just opened my mouth and the words came out. And she turned me down.''

"I suppose you thought to mention the moonlight on her hair and how lovely she was?''

Charles straightened, a startled look in his eye. "No. I don't think I did.''

"Fool,'' said Abby affectionately. "She could only have thought you asked for her hand because you felt you had compromised her and wished to do the gentlemanly thing by her!''

"Oh . . .'' After a moment he added, "But I told her I loved her.''

"Which, given the situation, she assumed was meaningless?''

When he said no more, merely heaving a sigh, Abby smiled. She shook her head slightly and raised her eyes to the ceiling, looking blindly up toward her bedroom in the room above. She wondered if her dear friend was listening.

The young are, she thought, *so very shortsighted. Were we like that?* she asked silently. She thought about it. *No we were not. We very carefully discussed the advantages and the disadvantages and knew exactly what we did.*

"Miss Abby?''

"Hmm? Sorry. I was thinking of the past. You want to know what you can do about Matty.'' She tipped her head, thoughtfully staring at nothing at all. "Charles, you have been going the right way to work with her. I can see nothing to do but what you've been doing. Merely that time will convince

her you are serious about her and truly wish to
wed her."

"But why will she not believe that I love her?"

Abby pursed her lips. "If you had told her *before*
last night, she might have. Now? She may merely
think you Quixotic."

"That is what I feared," he muttered, morosely.

She chuckled. "Patience, Charles. She'll have
you in the end."

"I wish I could be certain of that," he said, still
more morosely.

While Charles talked with Miss Abernathy, Bitsy
leaned against a wall at the back of the village
inn and stared up into Ned's eyes. "Nothing has
changed," she said sadly. "My Miss Abby needs
me."

Ned, one hand against the rough stone against
which Bitsy leaned, bent over her. "Bitsy, lover,
has it never occurred to you that I need you? Maybe
more than Miss Abernathy needs you?"

Bitsy's eyes widened. "But . . ."

"Ah! You hadn't thought of that, had you?" His
eyes crinkled at the corners with humor, but there
was a wry shape to his mouth before he continued.
"One of these days, soon-like, I mean to retire.
I've a nice little bit put away for it and I thought
perhaps I'd buy me a neat little inn somewhere.
Maybe something like this one. Can't run an inn
proper-like," he said, his voice insinuating, "without you have a good woman at the host's back."

Bitsy's emotions roiled. The thought he might
retire was a very good thing. No one knew how
many nights she had nightmares in which some
villain objected to Ned's taking him to Bow Street
and did her love an injury. But that he might think
she would leave Miss Abby to run an inn with him?

Why that was outside of enough and then some. "Can't cook."

"Can you not?" He looked astounded for a moment and then shrugged. "My brother can."

"You mean your sister."

"No I don't. She can't cook neither. The modern woman," he said, only half jestingly, "is *not* up to snuff."

"I don't know about your sister, but I've worked as an abigail all my life and when I'd have learned to cook, I don't know and no one else does either."

He chuckled. "I will admit that I've no answer to that one. My sister, however, does not have an excuse. Bitsy," he said, changing the subject back to their future together, "my brother and I have long talked of going into the business together. I want you with us for more than that a good inn should have a mistress. I want you because I need you with me. I haven't pressed you—"

She snorted disbelief.

"—but now I'm not going to be running off all around the countryside, and will be settled in one place, and no danger involved, well, I feel it is only right you say yes."

Bitsy bit her lip. "Ned . . ."

"No, don't say it right now. I'll be here another week or so."

"But, Ned, can you afford it? Putting up here at an inn?" she asked anxiously.

He grinned. "Miss Abby just paid me and paid me well. Bitsy, lover, I know you'd be unhappy too far from our Miss Abby. Me too. I like the lady. But what I mean to say is that I'm spending my time when not with you looking for a proper inn right here in the region."

Bitsy's eyes widened once again. "Near Miss Abby?"

"As near as we can make it," he said and put a

hand to her cheek. She leaned into it. "Bitsy . . ." he whispered as he bent his head to hers.

While Bitsy and Ned talked at the back of the inn, Miss Violet Tenton, her maid discreetly in attendance, walked along the village street. Looking here and there and obviously paying no particular attention to where he strolled, the vicar approached. Violet, seeing an opportunity to advance her plan, a plan her aunt would dislike immensely, ducked her head a trifle and lifted her reticule, a bright blue bag almost entirely covered with large and obviously handmade daisies. She pretended she searched for something within it as she steered a course directly at the vicar.

"Oh!" she gasped and, wide-eyed, stared up into the vicar's startled face. "Oh dear, it is all my fault. I did not watch where I was walking."

She wondered if there was any possible way she could manage to trip so that his hands, now holding her shoulders, would be forced to clasp her to his manly breast. Her aunt might disapprove, but Vicar Baxter had proved himself just the man for whom she'd been searching for a very long time. Could she fall against him? Sadly, she decided she could not.

"My fault entirely," she repeated.

"No, no," said the vicar gallantly. "I was strolling along, not paying the least attention to anything at all, or we'd not have collided. May I say it is very pleasant running into you this way?"

For an instant Violet wondered if there was a double entendre hidden in his words but, reluctantly, was forced to decide the vicar meant exactly what he said. Unfortunately.

"I have hoped we'd meet again—" She spoke shyly and was astounded to discover she truly felt shy. "—ever since we met last night. I enjoyed our conversation. Very much."

This, surprisingly, was also the truth and not the pleasant sort of lie one spoke in London on such unexpected meetings. Men, in general, did not discuss serious subjects with young women but, after discussing London slums with her, the vicar had spoken of those among his flock who caused him concern and the difficulty of deciding what must be done. He had listened with patience when she spoke of her own charity work.

"I, too, have pleasant memories of our conversation," he said, interrupting her thoughts. It had indeed been pleasant after his humiliation at the hands of that jade, Miss Seldon. "Have you visited our church?" he asked, thinking of no other way of prolonging this interlude. "I will be happy to give you a tour. We have several bits of antiquity of which we need not be ashamed."

He offered his arm and Violet took it. She didn't even glance back to see if her maid followed. She didn't, for that matter, *think* of her maid and whether the middle-aged woman did or did not follow. Vicar Baxter beamed down at Miss Tenton. Violet smiled up at him. In perfect accord they wandered toward the church, speaking of this and that, and casting languishing glances toward each other as often as possible.

Meanwhile Lady Southend and Matty had enjoyed a stroll through Miss Abernathy's extensive gardens. Matty had shown her aunt all her favorite flowerbeds, especially those hidden in odd little nooks and crannies, until finally they came to a rockery through which ran a little stream. The water splashed over carefully placed stones, giving a cool moistness to the air, which was very welcome after their stroll, and the various mosses and ferns, sun-dappled beneath ancient willows, were gentle on eyes that had viewed and enjoyed a great deal of bright color in the various beds.

"Shall we sit here for a while?" asked Matty. She had heard a dozen tales of her mother's growing-up years and wished to contemplate what she had heard although she knew it would be impolite to do that until she was alone.

"A rest would be very welcome," said Lady Southend in her slightly pompous manner. "Yes, do let us sit. My dear," she continued as she settled herself on the seat Matty wiped off for her, "I have been thinking."

"Yes, Aunt Southend?"

"I have observed that you are reluctant to allow Charles North to approach you as he wishes to do, so," she continued before Matty could either agree or demur, "I thought perhaps it would be a good thing if you were to come home with me and we will present you to the *ton*. I think the little Season this fall would be an appropriate time."

"Present me . . ."

"Yes. I am aware you are a little long in the tooth and cannot expect too much in the way of a match, but I am certain we can, at the very least, find you a pleasant widower, perhaps someone who has been left with children for whom he needs a mother?" Lady Southend cast her niece a quick look and was pleased to notice how the chit's skin paled a trifle. "In fact, I happen to know a viscount who is nearly at his wit's end, wondering what to do with his large family. His wife died very nearly a year ago, so I am certain, if I approached him properly . . . no?" she asked when her niece made the tiniest movement of demurral.

"I'm listening," said Matty, her voice small.

"Well then. He is, as I said, a viscount and already

has a good-sized family. He'll not be the sort to importune you, my dear, if you catch my meaning. At least not often. He already has sons, you see, so need not concern himself with the succession. And, marrying him, you will have status and security.''

"Status and security? Status!" Matty sat up. "But, Aunt, a viscount? Surely this is nonsense. He'll not be interested in me. Why, I am no one at all and even if that were not a problem, I've no dowry. You should not jest about such things."

"The man I have in mind is a sensible sort and judges the worth of someone on the basis of character rather than who they are," said Lady Southend, her nose in the air. "You need not concern yourself. A dowry would be nice, but it is not necessary. No, the man I've in mind—" Again she cast her niece a quick look. "—has no need for money, but has a great need for a woman who will be more than a pretty face across the breakfast table."

"Aunt . . ."

"You need not thank me," said Lady Southend, interrupting. "And I believe I've rested quite enough. Besides—" Born a country woman, she automatically glanced toward the sky, determining the position of the sun. "—it is nearly time for luncheon. I have not, in the past, been one to eat in the middle of the day, but I find Ma—*Abby's*—cook produces such delightful dishes, I cannot resist."

"Ma—?"

"Never mind," said Lady Southend crossly. "I'm too old. That's what is wrong. Too old to be chopping and changing."

"I have heard there is a mystery about Miss Abby. Now I suspect that Abigail is not the name with which she was christened. I will say nothing. She is a good woman and if she has secrets, then she should be allowed to keep them."

Lady Southend bit her lip. "My child, the more I learn, the more I like you. It is no wonder that Charles wishes to make you his wife."

Matty turned eyes that were painfully wide open onto her aunt. "Please, Aunt, do not say such things. Mr. North felt he'd compromised me because of the way the vicar reacted when he saved me from that fall, but that is ridiculous, as I am sure we all agree."

"Do you really think that is why he asked you?"

"What else could it possibly be? No, do not answer," she said quickly when her aunt opened her mouth to reply. "I am not a proper wife for Charles North and I do not wish to be encouraged to think it might be otherwise." She rose and started down the path and then, realizing how rude that was, turned, apologized, claimed lack of appetite, and wished her aunt an enjoyable meal.

Lady Southend wanted to draw her back, wanted to argue, but she was, despite her arrogance, a wise woman and, in this particular case, decided she had better leave well enough alone.

For now.

Chapter Eighteen

Matty wandered off into a wilder portion of Miss Abby's grounds. The path meandered here and there around trees old before the Hanovers were offered the English throne. She came to a glade filled with huge rhododendrons, some of which still bloomed. Matty broke off a spray, gently touching the blossoms as she strolled. Then she tucked the stem into her belt and looked at her fingers. They wiggled in that way they had when she had something she needed to discuss and no one with whom she could discuss it.

"I suppose," she said, "I should find some pleasure in knowing I am not thought so very far beneath Charles—Mr. North!—so far below him as I had believed. I mean, if my aunt feels I could actually wed a viscount, then what is a mere mister? Even a mister who is a successful barrister?"

Her fingers wiggled in a rather agitated manner. Matty sighed.

"Yes, of course it is true that Charles is much more than a mere anything. He is also the son of an important peer. Charles is, in all ways, a nonpareil." This time she did not correct herself for using his name. There was a simple pleasure in it. "Charles . . ." she repeated softly.

She glanced down at her fingers, which were curling into fists. Her mouth compressed and tears moistened her eyes. She did not, however, allow them to fall, blinking rapidly and, seeing a low stone bench almost hidden by the bushes surrounding it, she seated herself on the only corner available for sitting.

"Yes, I know I am a fool, but who has such control of their heart they can determine with whom they fall in love?"

Her fingers expressed sympathy.

"Here now. No feeling sorry for yourself! Think instead of what a privilege it has been to know him. Think of whether you would wish to have never met him, to have *never* known him."

The fingers expressed horror at that thought.

"So you see, even though I must not even pretend that his proposal was anything more than a gentleman's effort to assure that I suffer no insult from those who would insist on misinterpreting what happened on Lady Portentmere's terrace, I can hold to myself the knowledge he did not despise me utterly. No one of any sense believed we had misbehaved."

The fingers wiggled.

"Oh well, I did say the sensible ones, did I not? We will not count the vicar." A tiny smile—a trifle sad, perhaps, but a smile—tipped her lips. "Besides, he thought he'd suffered a grievous disappointment."

The fingers continued to wiggle.

Matty frowned at them. Then she nodded. "We will not consider Lady Wilmingham's instant disapproval either. She, after all, must do her best to justify her original opinion of me."

The fingers stilled.

Matty's frown did not fade as she stared at them. "But the fact remains that I must be strong. I must not allow myself to believe that dear Charles has any other motive for pretending to find me attractive, interesting, and a proper mate. I must remember he is the most perfect gentleman I have ever met and not allow him to sacrifice himself . . ."

The fingers twisted and turned.

". . . not even if it is the thing I want more than anything else in all the world."

It was another hour before Matty felt she had talked herself into a proper sense of her world and her place in it.

". . . but," she told her fingers just before rising to return to the house, "I do not feel I can allow my aunt to find me a husband. Not just yet. Not until my emotions are better under control and I do not take a heavy heart with me into the sort of marriage of convenience she would arrange for me."

Abby, very nearly wishing all her frustrating company would take itself elsewhere, took herself up to bed after everyone but Forbes and one footman had gone to theirs. She entered her sitting room and looked around. And sighed. Then she went on into her bedroom, where she found Bitsy curled up on the chaise, a shawl thrown over her feet and legs.

"Poor dear," muttered Abby. "I wonder why she is here? She is never required to help me into bed . . ."

Her muttering roused Bitsy, who sat up and rubbed her eyes. "So. A bit late, aren't you?"

"Don't get sassy or I'll let you go without a character—" She stilled, a startled look in her eye. "—or is that," she said slowly, "what you want?"

"To be let go?" Bitsy stood up and rubbed her arms. She looked everywhere but at Miss Abernathy. "Well . . ."

"How soon?" asked Abby.

"What do you mean, how soon?" asked Bitsy, sharply, finally meeting Abby's eyes.

"When is the wedding?" asked Abby, grinning.

"I don't know what you mean," muttered Bitsy, again looking elsewhere, rather than at her mistress.

"Ha! Ned has finally convinced you. Oh, Bitsy, that is wonderful news."

"Just want to get rid of me," said the maid, pouting.

"You know it isn't that. You know it is that I believe in love." Abby glanced around the room and, finally, allowed her eyes to settle on the corner of the embroidered tester covering her huge bed. Unlike the tester over Matty's bed, this one was a mass of roses and Cupids and hearts and ribbons and all things romantic.

Bitsy flicked a quick glance up at nothing at all and her mouth compressed. "Yes. All the world well lost for love, but it isn't true, is it? One has responsibilities. One has conflicts. One has all sorts of reasons for dithering."

"But," said Abby softly, "you have *stopped* dithering, have you not?"

Bitsy sighed and her shoulders slumped. "Don't like leaving you."

"You think you are irreplaceable?"

Bitsy grinned a sudden wide grin. "Well, as to *that* . . ."

Abby interrupted. "*Difficult.* Not impossible." Then she walked nearer and took her maid into her embrace. "Ah, Bitsy, I admit I will miss you. You are one of the very few who knows my whole history. Perhaps the only one remaining who knows it all. You were a friend when we needed one, a companion when that became necessary. A rock on whom I have depended. But—'' She pushed Bitsy away and held her by the shoulders. ''—your work can be done by anyone and you will not be totally lost to me. You and Ned will visit.''

Bitsy grinned. ''Maybe more often than you think!''

''Hmm?'' Abby quirked a brow and tipped her head ever so slightly to the side.

''Ned and his brother are looking for an inn to buy. They are looking for one near here.''

Abby's eyes widened. ''But that is wonderful . . .'' Her voice trailed off as she recalled her maid's talents—and lack of others. ''Or is it?''

Bitsy, now that the difficult confession had been made was feeling more cheerful. ''Ned knows I can't cook. His brother *can*. Ned'll run the stables and I'll manage the inside work. Except for the kitchen. When I told him my savings, he was more than a trifle surprised at how much I can bring to our marriage. Until he thought about it. He says to give his thanks to *you*. You've been very generous over the years and your advice has made my little bit of savings increase far more than would have been the case without you.''

''You and Forbes have deserved every bit of advice I've ever been able to give you. So. Does that mean he and his brother will look for a larger inn than they'd thought of doing?''

''One they'd not thought possible, actually. That coaching inn over near Arundale—the one that has room for all the overflow of beasts from visitors to Arundale Castle—the owners have decided to sell and retire. Too much work, they say. And they've no one to leave it to, no sons or daughters. Rather sad really.'' Bitsy bit her lip.

"You are thinking you are too old to give Ned sons to whom he can pass on his holdings?"

Bitsy's mouth compressed, the lips very nearly disappearing. She looked sad.

"So adopt a likely lad or two or three."

Bitsy, startled, met Abby's steady gaze. "Hadn't thought of that."

"Suggest it to Ned and see what he thinks. And his brother, of course. He'd be part of it all, would he not?"

Bitsy plopped down on the chaise. "I don't know how you do it," she said, "but I no longer feel a traitor and feel, instead, quite excited about the future."

Abby laughed. "Yes, you and me as well. I'll come and be your very first guest, so save me the best guest room!"

"Yes, well, as to that, it'll be a bit before we get everything organized you know. I doubt it will all come straight for another handful of months. So—" Bitsy picked the brush up from Abby's dressing table. "—you just come over here and let me brush out your hair. You know how matted it gets under that silly wig you insist you will wear to your grave."

Abby, the feeling of exhaustion returning, meekly seated herself and allowed Bitsy to pamper her. She was too tired to insist she do it herself, and besides, Bitsy would feel less guilty if she was allowed to do for her. Abby did give one final glance to the top of the bedpost. And gave one very small sigh when she found it bare. She wanted a long, *long* talk with her lover and feared that, this evening at least, she'd not get it.

A little later, when she had assured Bitsy there was nothing more she wanted, she looked around, saw that she was alone, and, sighing deeply, went to bed. She had no sooner snuggled under the covers, however, than they were pulled away and wonderfully warm hands began kneading her back and shoulders.

"That feels perfect," she said and moaned softly when searching fingers found and relaxed certain tense muscles in her neck. "Oh yes," she murmured. "Dearest . . ."

"Shh."

"But . . ."

"When you are rested," murmured the beloved voice.

"Very well."

And very soon Abby drifted into a deep and restful sleep—to awaken to the very earliest sleepy cheeps of birds in the ivy beyond her window.

"Now?" she asked, returning, with fervor, the soft kiss that had awakened her. She pushed herself up against pillows that were, just then, pushed into position behind her. "I am finding the world a very complicated place."

"Tell me."

She snuggled against the shoulder and arm holding her. "I suppose I shouldn't exaggerate. We've got that villain Pelling boxed up. We've got Steven happy again. We've got Ruthie feeling just a bit of chagrin for behaving the fool—but, being Ruthie, I don't suppose he learned anything from it."

"No, you'll still have to deal with Ruthie, I think," said the deep rumbling voice beside her.

"Yes, that hasn't changed, but, right now, it is only Charles I need worry about. Especially now that Bitsy has finally admitted her Ned needs her more than I do." She lowered her voice. "Don't tell her, but I'll miss her sass." There was a warm, loving chuckle from her lover. "Yes, well, but I will. I must think up a very special wedding gift for them. Maybe three or four really good teams to add to their stables? That will give them a certain cachet right to begin with, will it not? At least with those who need posting horses."

"You have yet to get to the core of your problems, my eternal love."

She sighed and snuggled still nearer. "That Matty. How am I going to convince the dratted girl that Charles loves her to distraction? She is so modest it is very nearly *sinful.*"

"Perhaps you should let Charles convince her."

"Perhaps," agreed Abby, but doubtfully.

A door opened to Abby's sitting room. She glanced that way, glanced to her side, felt the softest of kisses . . . and was alone. She sighed. "Drat Forbes. He has trained my maids too well, I fear."

But when the young girl entered with her bucket and the ewer of fresh water, she discovered Abby with a book in her lap. Abby, usually sound asleep at this hour, motioned for the maid to go on with her work and looked back down at her book.

And discovered it was upside down.

Surreptitiously, she watched the maid. When the girl's back was turned, the book was turned. Abby actually began reading, became engrossed, and was more than a little surprised when, nearly two hours later, Bitsy entered to lay out her clothes for the day.

Abby rose and wandered to the window, accepting the robe Bitsy held for her without particularly noticing. She stared out over the neat rose beds in which several young gardeners were carefully digging dung in around the roots. An older gardener kept a close eye on them as he went from bush to bush, inspecting each carefully, snipping a twig here, there plucking leaves he put into a bag hanging from his waist, and shaking his head when he discovered greenfly infesting one of Abby's favorites.

As the gardener stalked off to find his own personal cure for greenfly, Charles approached from the opposite direction. His presence caught Abby's attention and she eyed him, wondering what he was up to. He, as had the head gardener, went from bush to bush, occasionally returning to one, shaking his head, and continuing down the row.

There was one bush he returned to several times but it was not until he had inspected the flowers on each and every bush that he went back, for the last time, and choosing carefully, cut one perfect rose. Rose in hand, he headed for the house.

Abby quickly opened her window. "Charles!"

"Yes, Abby? You have caught me, have you?"

"Stealing from my favorite rosebush? Yes, you are caught. Now tell me why you steal my rose!"

"A perfect rose for a perfect lady."

"Why, Charles," she said, pretending a coy expression that looked more a smirk.

His ears turned bright red. "Miss Abby, you know I think you perfection, but this is for another perfect lady."

"I'm glad you admit it and don't pretend. If you thought to have it placed on her morning tea tray, you are far too late."

"No. I will take it to where she should be finishing up the flowers." He waved the rose in the air, continued on toward the corner of the house, and disappeared.

Abby turned from the window.

"Did I hear you sigh?" asked Bitsy.

"Did I? Perhaps. I remember when I last received a rose from that very same bush."

"So—" Bitsy looked around the room a trifle fearfully. "—can I."

Something in the maid's tone caught Abby's attention and she chuckled. "You have never quite believed, have you?"

"No."

"Then how do you explain that identical rose in the middle of last winter when there were no roses?"

"I don't."

"Stubborn."

"Even if it were possible, how can you ... ?"

"But he is merely my own true love. How can I not?"

"But a ghost ... ?" Bitsy shrugged. Then she frowned ferociously. "It is all in your head," she scolded.

"Hmm. You would say I am mad, that I was driven mad by his death. Is that what you mean?"

Bitsy turned bright red. "No I would not, because there is no one saner than you in all of England. It is just ... I wish you'd not pretend ..."

"Bitsy, it is not pretense. We swore our love would hold true here and beyond the grave. My dearest one has merely found a way of holding to that vow. That is all. And you will never know the comfort he is to me."

"That I won't. That I surely won't. Now come here and let me get you dressed. I don't understand why you continue to wear that idiotic wig, either—"

"Because he likes it, of course."

"—but since you do, let us get your own hair brushed and pinned up properly and then I'll pour your water."

Abby looked toward the fireplace, where gently steaming ewers stood near a small fire and the hipbath awaited her. "Is it that time again? It seems I just had a bath."

"I know there are people who never bathe and others who want a bath so often the footmen rebel at carrying up the water. Both kinds are quite mad."

Abby laughed light chuckling laugh. "You sound very fierce, Bitsy."

"Well, I very much fear my Ned is nearer to the second sort. I have never once met him when he hasn't seemed clean and sweet-smelling to me. I think it is one of the things that drew me to him."

"Yes, cleanliness is said to be next to godliness. Therefore I will oblige you and bathe—even though it was only last week when you last had that tub brought in to clutter up my room!"

Abby would never tell a soul, but she disliked bathing. *Not* because she had any objection to the process—in fact, she rather liked it—but because she always feared her lover would be tempted by the necessary nakedness and *peek*. Bath time was the only time she worried about the possibility of his presence when she was unaware of it.

Loving was one thing, decently done in their bed and under the covers or, at the least, in the dark, but watching her bathe—that was something else altogether and quite indecent.

On the other side of the house Lady Southend was also awake and up. She, however, had been up and dressed for some time and sat at her window with her writing box on her lap penning a letter to her husband.

"... so, you see, Southend, she is quite as delightful as I'd hoped, but will not fulfill our desires in the other respect as I suggested in my last letter might be possible. We are too late."

Susan dipped her pen and then held it, rereading what she'd written concerning her niece. She sighed.

"She would have been so perfect, Freddy. Your son could not have helped but love her and would have changed his rackety ways. Almost I think of interfering, but these two are so very much in love. You would laugh to see them, Southend. Neither will accept the other's love is true. Charles pursues and Matilda retreats. It is almost a game—or would be if it were not so serious.

She thought again, decided she'd said enough, and set pen to paper on another topic.

"My dear, however silly it may be, I find I miss you dreadfully but I cannot return home. Not just yet. I must see that all ends well for the two of them. You will, I know, understand."

Her ladyship wrote a few more words concerning her husband's gout and her hopes that he was feeling more the thing and closed the missive, folding, sealing, and addressing it.

"Here, Miss Hoity-toity, come take this thing off my lap and put it away."

Her supercilious dresser, her nose well up in the air, came, picked up the lap desk as if it might bite her, and swept off with it.

"Very well done," said Lady Southend, with mock approval. "Worthy of the Queen. In fact, given our present Queen," she said with a touch of acid, "far better than she'd have done." She scowled. "I do not know why I put up with your airs and graces!"

"Because," said the maid in tone so genteel the words oozed from between her pursed lips, "there is no other who can possibly manage your completely unmanageable hair."

She tossed her head in the manner of a pert young girl, which made Susan chortle. "There is also the fact you make me laugh." Her ladyship had, however, had quite enough impertinence for the moment and turned to stare out the window. Almost instantly, she perked up. Matty was coming away from the rear wing of the house and coming toward her was Charles. Susan leaned forward, wishing she were nearer so she could hear.

The pantomime was almost as good however.

Matty looked up and saw him coming, stopped, looked as if she were thinking seriously of returning, *quickly*, to the house. Charles called to her. Faintly, Susan actually heard that . . .

Matty bit her lip. She had been doing her best to avoid Charles. He was too dangerous to her peace of mind. Why the man would not accept that she would not wed him merely to avoid scandal she did know know. If he did, then he would take himself off and perhaps she could begin forgetting him. A very long process, she feared that would be!

"Yes, Mr. North?"

"I have something for you," he said and brought his hand from behind his back. He extended the rose toward her. "I saw this and thought of you. I knew you must have it."

"One of Miss Abby's prize roses? Oh Cha—*Mr. North,* you really should not have done it. No one cuts Miss Abby's roses!"

"I did. What is more Abby knows I did. She saw me and she did not tell me to cease and desist. Is it a special bush to her?" he asked, changing the subject when he saw she was distressed.

"Yes. I think, if it could tell tales, it might explain part of the mystery about our Miss Abby."

Charles smiled. "Is there a mystery?"

"You know there is. The vicar thinks so. So, too, does Lady Wilmingham."

"Abby may be a trifle eccentric," said Charles, blandly, and then he lied. "I see no mystery."

"She knew my aunt when they were young and my aunt persists in . . . or at least, every so often when she forgets, and her tongue slips and she nearly calls Miss Abby by another name altogether. So you see, there *is* a mystery."

"Yes. Would you like to know?"

Matty bit her lip. "Would Miss Abby mind if I knew her story?" she asked after a moment's hesitation.

"So long as you tell no one who lives in the area, I don't think she'd mind. This is what she told me. When she was young, she fell deeply in love with the wrong man, a man married to a woman who was—well, she wasn't right in the head. *He* fell at least as much in love with our Abby. They ran away together and, from what my father told me, adding to the tale she gave me, they had several happy months. Maybe so much as a year. And then her lover rescued Abby from a fire and went back in to save an old couple along with their daughter from the burning building. He saved the daughter, but lost his life trying to save the girl's parents."

"How awful."

"The world," continued Charles, "does not forget scandal, so Abby has never tried to return to London. But it is also true that Abby has never forgotten her love. She is quite content here in her exile. It is just that she would not like it if any of her neighbors knew the tale."

"That poor child."

"Child? You are thinking of the daughter? But, Matty, that is Bitsy. And perhaps as much as a decade younger than Abby."

Somewhere during their conversation, the rose had changed hands and Charles had gently, his hand on her elbow, led Matty off for a walk in the shrubbery.

Charles had made up his mind to steal a kiss. He had checked a number of windows on each floor of the house and discovered that none of them gave a view of the interior paths of the shrubbery. He would have his kiss, and if she slapped his face, he had decided he would *not* apologize.

He kissed her. And she didn't slap him. So, as it turned out, he didn't have to. Apologize, that is.

"You shouldn't have," she said, breathlessly, knowing she could not have pushed him away for any reason whatsoever. She had wanted that kiss.

"No. I don't suppose I should have," he said, looking down at her well-kissed lips. "The trouble is I cannot seem to convince you with words, Matty, and I want to convince you we should wed. Will you marry me?" he asked wistfully.

She ducked her head. It was difficult, but she managed the one necessary word. "No."

He sighed. "Ah well, I will not despair. My mother always says I am the most stubborn of her children. I will stubbornly woo you until, merely to make me stop pestering you, you say yes. Stubbornness can be a good trait, I think."

"Charles . . ." Matty realized she used his name and turned on her heel, her neck bright red.

He touched it. "I give you permission to use my name whenever you like," he said softly. "I like it that you think of me that way. It gives me hope."

"Charles," she said firmly, "I think of you as my *friend*—"

"So I should hope. I want you as my friend, as well."

"—but that *must* be all." She didn't dare ask *as well as what?*

"Why?" he asked bluntly.

"Because you will wed a woman who will be good for you," she said, a faint frown between her brows. "Someone of whom your family approves. A woman who understands your world, who can fit smoothly into your life, and deal with the sort of people with whom you associate."

"Matty—"

The loud metallic clanging of a well-rung triangle sounded from the direction of the stables.

Charles's head jerked around and then back to Matty. "—I will explain what my life is like another time, my dear," he said, his words rushed. "Believe me, you will fit in quite nicely. But now I had better see what that is all about, had I not?"

He squeezed her upper arms, released her, and ran off between the bushes, disappearing in the direction of the stables.

Chapter Nineteen

Matty, curious about what sort of emergency had occurred that the bell calling all able-bodied men had been rung, hurried inside and up the stairs to a small sewing room that had windows looking toward the stables. Men and boys milled around, looking in all directions, trying to find the problem, and were finally called to order by Miss Abernathy's coachman. She couldn't hear what he said and frowned, watching him point here and there, and yet another way, sending a handful of men and boys off in each direction.

Finally, the only men remaining in the stable yard, Charles and the elderly coachie, conferred before Charles headed toward the house.

Matty hurried back downstairs, meeting him in the hall, where he was speaking with Forbes. "What is it?" she asked, standing on the bottom step, her hand on the newel post.

"Nothing about which you need concern yourself," said Forbes, his smile rather forced.

"I rather think it is," contradicted Charles. "I know you would save the women worry, Forbes, but they need to protect themselves. Pelling has escaped!''

Matty blinked. "Escaped . . .''

"Word just arrived from the magistrate—and frankly, I am not completely certain he sent the message. I think the young man, a groom, may have come on his own, worried about you, Miss Seldon, and about Miss Abby.''

"Oh dear. I hope he does not lose his place.''

"If he does, he will have one here,'' said Abby firmly.

Matty turned and looked up to where Abby stood on the landing.

"What has been done, Forbes?''

"Nothing. I only just had word,'' said the butler, bowing. "My first duty is to see the house is locked up.'' He turned and gave orders to the two footmen hovering nearby. "My next is to have all the maids and female staff go to the staff dining room and wait there. Then we will search the house and see that the fellow has not already gotten in!''

"Come,'' said Charles, holding out his hand to Matty, and looking up at Abby. "I'll take the two of you to your study, where you, Abby, may lock the door against all comers.'' He smiled, but his eyes remained sober.

"Is he truly dangerous, do you think?'' asked Abby, coming down the remaining steps and putting her arm around Matty's waist.

"According to the fellow who brought the word, he has been swearing vengeance on the two of you. The groom felt we should be warned, as we should, of course.'' Charles frowned. "Abby, has it occurred to you that your magistrate is as big a villain as any villain he ever has in charge?''

Abby chuckled. "Well, I cannot say it has not crossed my mind that he is rather unsuited to his duties, but I do not think I have ever gone quite so far as that."

"He should have sent someone here the instant he knew Pelling was missing."

"Yes."

"And he did not. Why?"

"He, like his son, is a great blustering bully, who would not care to be seen to be at fault, as he is with respect to his son. Matty made it necessary for him to see the boy in a bad light so he would dislike her and, perhaps, without thinking about it too much, rather hoped her cousin *did* do her an injury. Nothing too bad, of course, but enough to teach her the lesson he could not very well teach her himself. Ah," she said, her voice dry, "but I see we are too late."

Standing in the hall, waving a long-nosed pistol of ancient vintage, Pelling looked more than a trifle wild-eyed and very much more than a little dangerous.

"I wonder if he has noticed that if he uses that gun to shoot *one* of us, there are two others who will see he does nothing more to anyone ever," said Matty, her voice steady and her eyes never leaving her cousin's. "Put that pistol down. Now."

Pelling blinked and cast a rather dreamy look at the gun. "This old thing? No. I do not believe I will. I like it."

He actually caressed it as one might a cat or a velvet sleeve.

"Such a beauty it is," murmured Pelling, staring at it.

The three looked at each other and then back at Pelling.

"I found it in the magistrate's carriage, you see," he said, glancing up and then back at it, touching it, patting it, seemingly fascinated by it. . . .

He didn't notice the three had moved a step

nearer to him, Charles encouraging the women to step forward when he did. When he continued to touch the gun in that nearly obscene fashion, they moved again.

And still again.

Charles squeezed the women's waists, pressing downward, silently telling them they were not to move. He freed himself from them—and paused when Pelling looked up. But Pelling did not seem to see them. He stared up and beyond them, somewhere way off into a place that they could not see. Charles waited for him to look back down—and waited too long.

Before anyone could move to stop him, Pelling lifted the gun, put it in his mouth, and pulled the trigger. For half a moment the body stayed upright. Then, the knees buckling, it collapsed to the floor.

Matty loosed one sobbing breath and moved forward. "Poor boy," she said, staring down at him.

His face was undamaged, and, in death, began to smooth out, lines of dissipation fading, scowl marks lightening, his mouth losing its sneer. One began to see how young he was.

"I am still angry with him for what he tried to do to me, putting me on that coach as he did, but I am also sorry for him. I wonder what twisted sort of soul breeds the sort of creature he became?"

The sound of the shot brought servants running, Forbes only a few yards behind the much younger footmen. "Oh dear," said Forbes, glancing from the fallen man to the mess his death had made of the hall. "Oh dear," he repeated.

Matty knelt and touched her cousin's hand. "I wonder if you meant me to feel guilty," she murmured. "Was that your plan? I *am* sorry for you, but I cannot feel guilt when you were guilty of so much evil." She sighed and allowed Charles to pull her to her feet, but she looked back as he led her and Abby into Abby's study. "I cannot think what I should do," she muttered.

"You should do nothing," said Charles gently. "I will see to everything."

He glanced at Abby, who was white of face, but seemed to be holding up reasonably well. He raised a brow. She nodded. He left the room and quietly closed the door behind him. Abby went to Matty, put her arms around her, and patted her back. Matty leaned her forehead onto Abby's shoulder and, after a moment, began to cry.

"I know, my dear child. Such a waste. Such a terrible waste, that he became the sort he was." She continued muttering soothing words, patting Matty and allowing her to release the horror the experience had induced, the emotions clogging mind and body.

When she felt Matty had cried long enough, she reached for the young woman's shoulders, pushed her a little away, and said, "My dear, do ring the bell and order us a nice bite to eat. Cook will know *exactly* what to send up," she said and nodded. Firmly.

The funeral was quiet. Baron Pelling returned, looking more tired then ever, stood stoically and silently at the suicide's grave just beyond the hallowed ground of the churchyard. Nor did he say anything when the service ended. He merely returned to his carriage and his driver, who had never once looked anywhere but over his horses' heads, and drove off.

"What a strange man," said Abby, looking after him.

"A man very nearly at the end of his tether, I thought," said Charles, thoughtfully. "I wonder what the problem can be?"

"Too many girls and not enough money for dowries, would be my guess," said Abby, dryly. "At least in part." She stared hard at Charles.

Charles, his mouth set in a wry line, nodded. "Very well, Miss Abby. I will check and see if that's the problem."

"And if it is?" asked Matty, looking from one to the other.

"Never mind," said Abby, as Charles said, "Our Abby has the oddest notions when it comes to charity."

Matty's eyes widened and she stared at her blushing hostess. "You would give him money to help marry off his daughters?"

"No, she would give *them* money. She wouldn't trust him not to find ways he could justify using anything she gave him for some other purpose. Something necessary at the moment, but unhelpful as far as the young women are concerned. I'll write my man to get on with it," he said, shaking his head.

"You don't approve, but I remember how frightened I was when I finally understood I had nothing, no hope of anything, and faced a life of misery. That I was wrong, that I was blessed by my love's forethought, merely makes it more imperative that I do what I can to help other women who may face poverty and misery for no fault of their own."

"You would say—" A wicked grin flashed across Charles's face. "—that you were not at fault?"

Abby's head rose. "I did not say that. And I do not aid those that bring misery down on their own heads for no good reason." She cocked her head. "At least, not often . . . ?" She grinned her own grin, which was very nearly as wicked as Charles's.

"Then you came to my aid because . . . ?" Matty felt embarrassed.

"Because I saw a young woman in need, but—"

Abby nodded firmly. "—I would *not* have kept you around if I had not liked you. I would have established an annuity for you and placed you in rooms somewhere with a genteel lady companion. Perhaps Royal Tunbridge Wells since you came from near there?"

Matty experienced a mixture of chagrin and pleasure that made no sense to her. She had known she was the object of charity, so why did *knowing* it in another sense make any difference? Sensibly, she shrugged it off.

They returned to Abernathy Hall to discover a huge traveling coach of the latest design standing before the house and a large gentleman, softly swearing, allowing two footmen to help him from it.

Matty's eyes widened. "But it is Uncle Freddy!"

"Your *uncle*?" asked Abby, who did not recognize the gentleman.

"Yes. He isn't *really* my uncle, of course, but a friend of my father's who visited occasionally. They were at university together. Uncle Freddy," she called. He turned, saw her, and beamed. "Oh, Uncle Freddy, how wonderful to see you, but how did you know I was here?"

"Didn't. Knew my wife's niece was here. Now if it turns out *you* are my wife's niece, I'll—" He blinked rapidly several times and then grinned. "—well now, I don't know what I'll do." He sobered and, using a silver-topped cane, limped nearer. "My dear child, I read about your father's passing, but I was in the gout, you see. Then, when I could travel, I found you had disappeared. You haven't a notion how I've worried. Why did you not write me?"

It was Matty's turn to blink. "But, Uncle Freddy, how could I?"

"What do you mean, how could you?" he asked

a trifle testily. Now the first surprise was over, he was, as usual, feeling pangs of pain from his foot.

"You and Father never wrote. I only knew you as my wonderful pretend Uncle Freddy." Her mouth formed an O shape. "In fact," she said, after a moment, "I still don't know who you are!"

Charles, now that they were near to him, recognized him. He stepped forward. "Miss Seldon, allow me to introduce Lord Southend, Lady Southend's husband."

"But then—" They stared at each other. As one said "—I *am* your uncle," the other said, "—you *are* my uncle!"

"By marriage," said Abby, smiling and shaking her head. "The older I get the more I believe in miracles. Here are my footmen to help you into the house, my lord. If you will allow it, they will form a seat with their hands and arms and carry you. Do not allow pride to force you to endure more pain that is necessary," she added, shaking her finger at him, when she saw faint red spots appear on his cheekbones.

Some time later they were all seated around the breakfast table, enjoying one of Cook's special little refreshments, and explaining all the ins and outs of how Matty arrived at Abernathy Hall and how it had ended that morning beside a suicide's grave.

Lord Southend reached for his wife's hand. "It is quite wonderful that, in our old age, we have been given a delightful new daughter, Susan. We will take her home and pamper her and please her and make up for all the horror she has gone through."

"Yes, of course, dear, but you have traveled quite enough for a time, so I think you must come up to our suite and lie down for a bit. I've a few things to tell you and we will have a comfortable coze all by ourselves."

His lordship winked at Matty, excused himself to the others, and, having given in once, gave in again, and allowed himself to be carried up to their room.

Charles and Abby went off alone together, leaving Matty to wander into the salon, where she sat at the pianoforte, picking out a tune with one finger. A little later, Charles, looking a trifle glum, found her there and asked Matty if she would walk with him. After she collected her bonnet and a shawl against the wind, which was a trifle blustery that day, Matty went.

Charles trod at her side, silent, even, one might say, morose. Finally, Matty touched his arm, drawing his attention. "What is it?" she asked.

"Hmm? Oh I have been thinking that you were quite right to turn down my proposal," he said with only a trifling bitterness—but at the same time cast her a speculative look she didn't see.

"Whatever do you mean?"

"You will do far better than a mere barrister and second son. I hadn't realized it before, but of course Lady Southend will find an excellent match for you. Perhaps an earl, or at least the very least, an heir to an earldom. I am nowhere near good enough for you, my love."

Matty stopped. "What did you call me?"

He turned and stared at her white face. "What do you mean?"

"You . . . you said—" She blushed rosily. "—you said 'my love.' "

Her voice was so soft he barely heard it. He tipped his head frowning. "But, of course I did."

"There is no 'of course' about it. You proposed because you feared you'd compromised me. That isn't love."

"I did not."

"You did too."

Charles, about to descend into a nursery argument, drew in a deep breath. "Matty, I fell in love you with you almost as soon as I met you. How can you not know that?"

"Nonsense." But her eyes begged him to contradict her.

"How could I not? You are just the sort of woman for whom I've searched."

"But . . . but I'm just a vicar's daughter. I've no dowry."

"My dear Matty, what has that to do with anything?"

She gave him a look and he chuckled.

"Very well, dowries are the expected thing, but surely you know that would not weigh with me where my affections are involved—" He gave her back that disapproving look. "—or you *should* know. Besides, you are the niece of Lord and Lady Southend. Have you any notion who they are? And if that were not enough, your maternal grandfather, Sir Broadman, was a nabob and wealthy beyond belief." Something he hadn't known until Abby pointed it out to him.

"I don't believe my aunt mentioned that."

"It isn't the sort of thing one says, is it?" He raised his voice to a slight falsetto and said, "And of course, my dear, my father was wealthy beyond belief." He dropped to normal tones. "Now that I realize who you are, I remember my grandmother telling the story."

"Will you tell me?"

"Of course. Your mother was Broadman's eldest daughter. He had returned not many years previously from India, where he'd made a fortune and, when he looked about for a husband for your mother, he found an impoverished peer, an earl, I think, and made all the arrangements. The fact that your mother had fallen deeply in love with your father was irrelevant to him. Your mother ran away to her grandmother's and she and your father were married from that house, your great-grandmother giving them permission. Your grandfather was embarrassed she'd jilted the man he'd found for her and vengeful that he'd not be joining the highest in the land through his new son-by-marriage. He disinherited your mother and would not allow her name to be mentioned. And then he said she was dead in childbed, you with her. As we have discovered, your aunt, Lady Southend, believed him, and was astounded to learn you both survived and that you still live.''

''I wonder if my grandfather knew Miss Abby's father,'' mused Matty. ''He, too, must have been a nabob. At least, looking at the furnishings which came from India, I'd think he must have been.''

Charles chuckled. ''No, that was . . .'' His mouth snapped shut and cast her a sideways glance.

''Was?''

''Someone else.''

''Her love?''

''I told you that tale, did I not?''

''Yes. A sad story, I thought.''

''Abernathy is not her name, you know.''

''I think I told you that my aunt, every so often, starts to call her something else.''

''Yes.'' Then remembering Abby's directions and realizing he was off the path, he drew in a deep breath. ''Matty, we have gotten away from why I brought you out here. I must withdraw my offer of marriage.''

Once again Matty stopped short. ''But you . . . you said you loved me.''

''My dear—'' He walked on, his hands behind his back, not noticing that she had stopped. ''—I *do* love you and *because* I love you I must free you— not that you are bound in any way, of course, since you did not accept—but I do it so you may feel free to make a far better marriage than I can offer you."

Matty bit her lip. "Charles . . ."

He realized she wasn't at his side and turned, looked back the three or so yards to where she stood, her hands twisted together. "Yes?"

"Charles, will you marry me? Please?"

He blinked. "Will I . . ."

"I love you," she said in a small voice.

Charles whooped with joy and gave thanks for Abby's perspicacity, her insistence that if he insisted he was *not* good enough for *her,* then Matty would see that she *was* good enough for *him.* He drew her tightly into his arms in less time than it takes to tell it.

"When?" he asked, staring down into her bemused face.

"Soon?"

"Yes."

And that's all that was said for some time.

The wedding took place nearly three weeks later, but not in the local church as might have been expected.

Matty decided that she really could not bear to have Mr. Baxter officiate at her wedding, but with her father dead, she'd no notion at all what to do or where to go. Luckily, very soon after she and Charles agreed to wed, a young canon associated with Canterbury Cathedral arrived at Miss Abernathy's door. He'd been sent by the archbishop himself to discover exactly what had become of his wise old friend's daughter—Miss Abernathy's rather chatty letter raising more questions in his mind than it answered.

Vicar Seldon might never have risen above a

village priesthood, but it was not because the church had not tried to promote him. The archbishop, feeling remiss that he had not remembered earlier to see to Matty, was glad to be informed of the proposed marriage. He wrote her, asked that Matty and Charles come to Canterbury, so that he might officiate at her wedding. They were married in the Lady's Chapel with Charles's family and Matty's aunt and uncle, and all her new friends looking on.

Mr. Baxter, when he read about it in Lady Wilmingham's paper, was shocked to discover he had thought a woman about whom the archbishop felt highly was unworthy of himself. He instantly wondered how he could get back into Miss Seldon's—that is, Mrs. North's—good graces in time to prevent Miss Seldon ever mentioning his misjudgment to His Eminence.

So of course he asked Miss Tenton for advice, as had become his habit of late. Miss Tenton, pursuing her own ends, suggested that perhaps he himself should wed . . . ?

When he then asked her whom he should ask, she very nearly stamped her foot in frustration.

Lady Wilmingham, neither then nor later, mentioned that she'd met Matty under rather odd circumstances. It was something she wished to forget. After all, Miss Abernathy was, once again, proved correct and she herself proved wrong.

It was, felt her ladyship, beyond bearing.

Epilogue

Some years later, Charles recalled a dream he'd had before they were wed. In it he was walking around the decorative lake on his father's estate with Matty on his arm and several children running on ahead with a maid in pursuit.

And that was exactly what was happening. Almost exactly, anyway. He chuckled.

"What is it, my love?" asked Matty.

He told her of his dream.

"But we've only the one." She gestured toward where the nursery maid trailed after their daughter's unsteady footsteps.

"Only one, my dear?"

Matty, putting her hand over her stomach, blushed. She had not yet told her husband that their newest hope of a son and heir rested there and wondered how he had guessed.

"I love you," he whispered into her ear, and, turning off the path, led her to where they could be private and enjoy a quiet interlude, just the two of them.

Which they did.

Dear Reader,

I wonder if Miss Abby manages to reform her young cousin. Someone needs to take Rutherford in hand. I'll have to think about that. . . .

In AN INDEPENDENT LADY, due out in April 2003, our hero has a great need for a calm and peaceful marriage. His memories of his mother make him shudder and he will not live with arguments and controversy. This being so, he settles on a little mouse of a girl and, when the book opens, they are at the altar—where the mouse finally finds the courage to say she won't!

And disappears.

Our hero is distressed and, finally, resigned to wooing another in her place—but then he arrives at his aunt's and meets the heiress who lives nearby, who should be living with her but his sweet little mouse.

It requires a great deal of learning about others, most importantly the truth of his father's marriage to his mother, for him to overcome his notion of what makes a happy marriage. Luckily for both the mouse and himself, to say nothing of the heiress, he comes to his senses.

I hope you enjoy reading about Matthew and little Louisa Maria and Babs. I know I enjoyed writing about them.

Cheerfully,

Jeanne Savery

PS: I enjoy hearing from my readers. I can be reached by e-mail at JeanneSavery.Earthlink.net or by snail-mail at Jeanne Savery, P.O. Box 833, Greenacres, WA 99016.

BOOK YOUR PLACE ON OUR WEBSITE AND MAKE THE READING CONNECTION!

We've created a customized website just for our very special readers, where you can get the inside scoop on everything that's going on with Zebra, Pinnacle and Kensington books.

When you come online, you'll have the exciting opportunity to:

- View covers of upcoming books

- Read sample chapters

- Learn about our future publishing schedule (listed by publication month *and author*)

- Find out when your favorite authors will be visiting a city near you

- Search for and order backlist books from our online catalog

- Check out author bios and background information

- Send e-mail to your favorite authors

- Meet the Kensington staff online

- Join us in weekly chats with authors, readers and other guests

- Get writing guidelines

- AND MUCH MORE!

**Visit our website at
http://www.kensingtonbooks.com**